THINGS THEY NEVER SAID

An uplifting and emotional romance

LINDA MIDDLETON

Choc Lit

A JOFFE BOOKS COMPANY

Choc Lit
A Joffe Books company
www.choc-lit.com

This edition first published in Great Britain in 2023

Cover art by Berni Stevens Cover Design

ISBN: 978-1-78189-535-1

To my family, with love.
Firstly, to my parents, who have guided me steadfastly through
life, especially to my father who is no longer with us. I hope
I have made you both proud.
Secondly, to my husband and two sons, for all the support
you have given me while I have ignored you to find the time to write.
Finally, to Sue, Ali, Gail and Julia, my online writer friends.
I couldn't have written this novel without you.

ACKNOWLEDGEMENTS

I would like to thank the Choc Lit team for their support, encouragement and belief in me as a writer. I am so lucky to have you as my publisher.

Thank you to my wonderful editor whose keen eye for details helped to strengthen and shape this book. Thank you for your patience and your sound advice.

Thank you to the amazing Choc Lit family for their ongoing support. It means a lot to me.

Thank you also to my very talented book cover designer.

Thank you to the Tasting Panel who said "yes" to the manuscript and made publication possible: Shona Nicolson, Kate Avetoomyan, Jenny Mitchell, Janice Butler, Liana Vera Saez, Tracy Kean, Emily Smeby, Lynda Adcock, Gill Leivers, Julie Lilly, Lorna Baker, Fran Stevens, Honor Gilbert, Brigette Hughes, Aileen Marsden, Jo Osborne, Donna Morgan, Laura Sumner, Dimitra Evangelou, Bee Master, Janet Avery and Hilary Brown.

Thank you to everyone who has had faith that I could be a published author. It has been a long road, and without your support I may have well given up along the way.

CHAPTER ONE

'What's wrong with them?' Liz's heart sank as Emma, her waitress, carried the tray of half-eaten puddings back into the kitchen. It had been the same all evening with the guests picking at the food she had cooked for them. It wasn't just the apparent reflection on her cooking that appalled her, but also the waste.

'It's not the food,' Emma reassured her. The gooey centres of the perfectly cooked chocolate fondants slid down the plates as they scraped the remains into the bin. 'It's the guests.'

'What's wrong with the guests then?'

'All the women are models or wannabes. Allergic to food, I should imagine.' Emma grimaced. 'They probably haven't had a decent meal between them in weeks.' Liz winced as Emma's comment conjured up uncomfortable memories. 'The food was perfect. Stop beating yourself up.'

'Easy for you to say. It's my career on the line if I don't make this work.'

Liz had been thrilled when Tia McIntyre, a well-known interior designer, had asked her to cater for a dinner party in her luxurious Chelsea home. Tia lived the celebrity lifestyle, always being papped with the in-crowd and splashed across the glossies. Liz had only recently become a freelance private chef. Knowing that her business could live or die on word of mouth, she had hoped this would be her lucky break. *Not much chance of that after tonight, though*, she thought grimly.

'Shall I take the coffee in?' Emma asked.

'Please, and then you can go. I'll clean up here.'

'Don't mind if I do. My feet are killing me tonight.'

'I'm not surprised, you've worked really hard.' Liz was grateful to Emma, who was studying for a degree in hotel and catering management, but always tried to make herself available when Liz needed extra help.

She continued with her final clear-up until the door to the kitchen opened, and Tia clicked across the tiled floor in six-inch heels.

'Darling, dinner was divine.' Despite the lateness of the hour, her client's make-up was immaculate and her long, dark hair shimmied over her shoulders in glossy perfection. Liz knew her own face would be shiny from the heat of the kitchen and, feeling self-conscious, she brushed a strand of blonde hair, which had escaped her ponytail, away from her face.

'Did you enjoy it?' she asked, amazed that Tia hadn't come to complain.

'Absolutely! Especially the lamb. It simply melted in the mouth. And I could eat that fondant every day of the week, if only my figure would allow.' She patted her washboard stomach encased in crimson silk. 'Come with me and take a bow in the dining room.'

'I can't!' Her chef's whites, which at the beginning of the evening had been pristine, now bore the mark of her toil.

'Of course you can. Everyone's dying to meet you.' Tia placed her scarlet talons on Liz's sleeve. 'I won't take no for an answer.'

The noise of the dinner guests rose as they reached the dining room, but fizzled into silence as Tia presented Liz with a flourish.

'Darlings, let me introduce my new chef, Elizabeth Cartwright. Give her a round of applause.'

Liz felt her face burn as she smiled stiffly and glanced around the table littered with half-empty wine glasses. The women were intimidating with their flawless make-up and bodies. The men, equally glamorous.

Then her heart nearly stopped as she noticed the most handsome man of all.

Her stomach turned to liquid and her legs trembled so much she had to clench every muscle just to stay upright. It had been twelve years since she'd seen him last, but she'd recognise him anywhere; the square, determined chin, high cheekbones and chocolate-brown eyes which could make a person feel they were the centre of the universe if he chose. A winter suntan gave him a healthy glow against short, dark hair. Their eyes locked, and for one horrible moment, she thought he'd recognised her, but then he looked away; that he didn't appear to remember her was almost as embarrassing than if he had. She croaked a thank you and, before her legs gave way, escaped to the safety of the kitchen. She wanted to be as far away from Alexander Sinclaire as possible.

* * *

Alex watched intently as the young chef fled. It had been a long time since he'd seen anyone so shy. He glanced around the room, full of self-interested people. He'd thought them fun at first, had revelled in their lively company, but the novelty was wearing off. Now they made him feel almost as alone as he did in his empty apartment.

He was only here because of Tia, his business partner. She constantly nagged him to get out more; to enjoy himself. But joy was something he found difficult to capture these days. He watched as she worked the room, chatting to her guests. She was a formidable lady: beautiful and stylish, and with a sharp business brain. She'd been a lifesaver when he'd first come back to England, devastated at the turn his life had taken.

His gaze shifted towards another stunning brunette: his plus-one tonight. Nikki, a highly successful model, was seated next to him. They'd had an on-off relationship for a while now, but he was beginning to realise they had little in common. She'd started to become clingy, and he knew it was time to end their liaison. It was only fair when he didn't feel the same way. Besides, nobody could replace Kas. He shook his head and forced himself away from that train of thought. He was already far too melancholy tonight.

Nikki leaned in to him and gave him a peck on the cheek. 'Just popping to the little girl's room,' she announced, and he watched her walk away with a sigh of relief.

He drained his glass and decided he would leave soon. He wasn't in the mood to move to a club for the usual after-party. Tonight, his sterile apartment was where he wanted to be. The only redeeming feature of this evening had been the food, which had been worthy of a Michelin restaurant. And then Tia had brought her new chef into the room, stained by her hard work and devoid of all artifice. It was the girl's lack of make-up that had first caught his eye, so different from the perfection around the table. He liked that she presented her face to the world with honesty, and it was endearing the way she'd flushed as Tia had flung her into the fold. But it was her name which niggled him the most; a name he remembered from a long time ago. Surely it was a coincidence?

'Why such a cross face, darling?' Tia settled herself down in Nikki's vacated chair. 'Nikki said she couldn't get a word out of you.'

'Poor old Nikki.'

'Meow. So, come on, tell me what's bothering you.'

'Nothing. I'm just tired.'

'You work too hard,' she said, patting his arm.

'Takes one to know one,' he replied. 'I'm sorry, Tia. I'm just feeling jaded tonight.'

'You must be, darling, because when you're tired of my parties, you're tired of life.'

He laughed. 'Perhaps you're right.' Changing the subject, he asked, 'Tell me, where did you find your new chef?'

'One of my clients recommended her. She's quite something.'

'I think I might know her.' Apart from the name, there'd been something about her eyes — or perhaps it was that faint, shy smile — that had seemed familiar.

Tia shrugged. 'I know very little about her myself except that she used to live up north — Cheshire or somewhere. Can I get you anything before I join my other guests?'

Alex shook his head. 'No, it's okay. I might head off soon. Thanks for a lovely evening, though.'

'Pleasure's all mine.' She squeezed his arm and returned to mingling.

Cheshire, Cartwright. There could be no mistaking it then. Instead of leaving, Alex filled his glass up again.

Danny Cartwright, Elizabeth's brother, had been his friend at university. Alex had spent some of his holidays with their family in Cheshire as his own family lived in Dubai. Little Lizzie had been a dumpy girl, laughed at by the other boys because of her size and her obvious crush on him. But he'd always had a soft spot for her and thought of her as a younger sister. He'd enjoyed his holidays with them. It had been good to be part of such a noisy, loving family.

But then it had all gone horribly wrong . . .

* * *

Liz was packing the last of the boxes into her small white van when she felt a presence behind her.

'Can I help?' His deep voice, just as she remembered, gave her goosebumps.

She turned towards him. In the glow of the street lamp, his face was more planed than ever and, despite her better judgement, she felt an overwhelming urge to reach out and touch him. She steeled herself and turned back to her boxes.

'No, thank you. I'm nearly done.' She was pleased that her voice sounded normal, even though she was shaking inside.

'I'm sorry. I didn't recognise you upstairs.'

'Why would you?' An undercurrent of anger helped her not to betray her feelings. Whilst their past was so vivid to her, it seemed he barely remembered. She slammed the back door firmly shut.

'You've changed.'

'You don't know how much.' The words, full of resentment, slipped out before she could stop them. She had to get away. From this. From him. She moved towards the front of the van and pulled open the driver's door. 'I'm sorry. I need to get going.'

He stayed her with his hand and, despite herself, she enjoyed the warmth of his touch through her thin chef's jacket. She dared herself to look up at his face once more. He seemed puzzled at her reaction to him, but the flash of tenderness in his eyes rendered her speechless.

'I really enjoyed your food tonight.'

'Thank you.'

'I never expected to see you in London. You were always such a country girl.'

'I'm surprised you noticed.' She watched him flinch as she spat the words out, and felt a brief stab of satisfaction.

'Of course I noticed. Your family was important to me.'

'You've got a funny way of showing it. You weren't around when they needed you most, were you?'

He gasped. 'I didn't find out until it was too late. I—'

'I've got to go.' She shook her arm away from him, climbed into her van and drove off at speed, leaving him standing alone in the darkness.

CHAPTER TWO

Back at her flat, still shaking with anger, she opened the fridge and reached for a bottle of Sauvignon which was cooling in the door. It had been such a shock to see Alex after all these years, and although she'd always blamed him for what had happened, just one look at him had sent her insides squirming. For a long time, she'd tried to convince herself that her feelings for him had been a silly schoolgirl crush, but the electricity sparked by his touch earlier made her doubt that. She'd often wondered how she would react if she ever bumped into him again, hoping she'd be cool and aloof. Yet again, though, she was the bumbling schoolgirl of old, devoid of all social graces. How could she possibly still feel that way towards him after all that had happened?

She took the bottle and a glass into the living room and sank into her comfortable brown leather sofa. Her hand trembled as she poured herself the wine, and she willed herself to relax as she took a huge gulp. She would have to make sure she didn't bump into him again.

Her living room had always been her favourite place. With its high ceiling and large windows, during the day it was full of light. Books lined the walls, mostly cookery books, and she spent many happy hours in here poring over recipes.

It was her sanctuary, where for the first time in many years she'd felt safe. But now, after only seeing Alex once, she was suddenly vulnerable again.

She heard the front door open as her current flatmate, Jay, returned home from work and burst into the living room. Even after a full shift at La Emporium, the restaurant where he was a sous chef, he was bursting with energy. She didn't know where he got it from. His eyes crinkled into a smile when he saw her and, despite her mood, Liz was pleased to see him.

He plonked himself down on the opposite sofa. 'What's the matter? It's not like you to hit the bottle.'

She gave a half-hearted laugh. 'Bad day at the office.'

'Oh shit. Didn't it go well? And you had such high hopes.'

'No, not really,' she said, remembering the returned food followed by her encounter with Alex.

'Was it the chocolate fondant? I told you that would be risky in an unknown oven. The number of people I've seen bomb on *MasterChef* just because of a chocolate fondant. Personally, I wouldn't touch it with a bargepole.'

'Oh, you and your *MasterChef*! Honestly, Jay, I don't know why you don't just audition for the next series and put us all out of our misery. And for your information, my fondant was perfectly gooey in the centre.'

'Tested it yourself?' he asked.

'No, most of it came back on the plates.'

'Bummer. What did Tia say? Bet she wasn't happy.'

'Quite the opposite, which was odd. She even dragged me into the dining room so they could all heap praise on me. Praise which was about as fake as their tans.'

'That doesn't sound like such a disaster. Why are you drowning your sorrows?'

'It's a long story.'

'Well, it's not good to drink alone.' He smiled winningly at her and Liz grinned in return.

'I'll get you a glass then.'

'Thought you'd never ask. But first, I need a shower. Roberto's been cracking the whip as usual and we had a manic service tonight. I've been sweating like a . . . well, you don't want to know. Two minutes and I'm all yours.'

* * *

'So, come on, spill the beans,' Jay said, as he settled down on the sofa after his shower.

Although they'd been friends since they'd met at Roberto's restaurant two years ago, she'd never revealed much about her past to him. Or to anyone. Danny had always been her confidant in life, and the only other person she could show her true self to now was her older sister, Melissa — Melissa, who'd pulled her out of the mess she'd gotten herself into after Danny's death. Since her recovery, she'd been focused on developing her career. She'd even pushed her family away because she didn't want to be reminded of the past. It was hard work, though, constantly keeping a check on her feelings — and she *did* trust Jay, but she wasn't ready to open up to him just yet.

She shook her head. 'It's nothing. Just a blast from the past.'

'Oh dear.' Jay put his glass down. 'Old boyfriend?'

'No. I'm just being silly. It's not important. So, what about you? Any news on the Susie front?' she asked, changing the subject.

Immediately, his face crumpled and she wished she hadn't asked. 'She won't speak to me. Says she needs some space to decide if we have a future.' Jay had been staying at hers since his girlfriend, Susie, decided they needed a break; a decision that Liz knew had devastated him. Normally, he tried to put a brave face on it, but in moments like this, when they were alone in the flat together, or when he'd had too much to drink, he would share his feelings with her. Liz had never really liked Susie, who had always seemed strangely standoffish, but she'd tried her best with her for Jay's sake.

Personally, she thought he deserved better, but she knew he wasn't ready to let go yet.

'That doesn't sound good.'

'No, it doesn't.' Jay suddenly sprang up from the opposite sofa and sat next to her, putting a friendly arm around her shoulder. 'God, we're a right pair, aren't we? Tell you what, if we haven't got it together with Mr and Miss Right by the time we're both thirty-five, what do you say we marry each other?'

Liz laughed. 'That would never work, Jay. Two chefs, one kitchen? I don't think so.'

'We could always buy a house with two kitchens.'

'And take it in turns to cook?'

'Or just eat out? We'll probably both have our own restaurants by then, so we won't need to cook at home.'

'Oh, I wish.' Liz sighed. 'Do you think that will ever happen?' Her dream of owning her own restaurant seemed impossible at the moment.

'What? Us getting married?'

'No, silly, our own restaurants.'

'It could, if we believe in it enough.' Jay knocked back his wine and poured some more. 'We just need to blag ourselves a couple of millionaires to bankroll us. Don't suppose you spotted any at Tia's, did you?'

'No, just a load of wannabes and models,' she said, remembering Emma's description of them. As soon as the words were out of her mouth, she wanted to bite them back. Susie was also an aspiring model. '*She* wasn't there.'

He slumped back down on the sofa, deflated. 'Oh.'

'Do you know anyone called Alexander Sinclaire?' she asked, despite her better instincts.

'I've never met him, but I've heard of him. He works with Tia. He started out as an architect but now he buys properties and turns them into fancy apartments. Tia does all the interior design. Loaded, according to Susie. Hey, perhaps you could get him to invest in your dream?'

'I don't think so.' Her voice was sharper than she'd intended.

'Sorry, just a suggestion.' Jay held his hands up in surrender.

'No, *I'm* sorry. I didn't mean to snap.'

'I think he's a bit of a dark horse,' Jay continued. 'Not long back from Dubai. Something happened there, but I don't know what. He's been seeing Susie's friend Nikki for a while. She's a model too, but way more successful. Hey, is *he* the blast from the past?'

'No. Just a possible contact. Not important.'

'Oh, okay. Actually, I'm done in.' Jay got up from the sofa and stretched. 'I'm on shift in the morning. I'm going to hit the sack.'

'Yeah, me too,' Liz said, although she didn't think she'd get much sleep.

CHAPTER THREE

Alex unlocked the door to his apartment on the South Bank and quickly turned off the alarm. He sighed as he switched on the lights. Although his home was the height of luxury, and had been exquisitely decorated by Tia, it felt as though it had no soul. He thought longingly of the apartment he'd shared with Kas in Dubai, cluttered with her books and belongings, filled with the artwork she painted, often in various stages of progress. Unlike this place, that had been a proper home — but that was because of Kas, of course. He put on some music, hoping it would make him feel a little less lonely. Then he poured himself a large glass of whisky from a crystal decanter and stepped through the French windows to the balcony outside.

The apartment was perfectly situated between Waterloo and Westminster, and on the twelfth floor he had fantastic views of the River Thames. The neon blue circle that lit up the London Eye caught his gaze, followed by the familiar shapes of the Houses of Parliament and Big Ben. He loved the vibrancy of the city, with its mixture of old and new, and the river, like a huge artery providing the lifeblood to the centre.

But tonight, something was missing. Everything felt jaded, including his work; the buzz he used to get from buying a property, turning it into something new and beautiful, and selling it at a huge profit was elusive. He was going through the motions, not really living. As he stared at the magnificence of London's heart, all he could see was the anger on Liz's face as she accused him of not caring about her family following the death of her brother in a freak car accident. And then she'd left and, in shock, he'd stood and watched as she drove away. If only he could have followed her — but she'd left him in no doubt that she didn't want to rekindle their acquaintance.

He'd only found out about his friend's unexpected death the day before his funeral, and as he'd been living in Dubai, it had been too late to get a flight back to England in time to pay his respects. He'd written to Danny's parents though, expressing his sadness at the news, but he now felt guilty that he hadn't made any attempt to contact them since his return to the country.

He and Danny had met at university and formed an immediate bond, more like brothers than friends. Rather than enduring the long flight home every holiday, Alex was grateful that Danny always invited him to stay with his family. The Cartwrights had welcomed him with open arms onto their farm in Cheshire, which had almost become a second home. He shivered as he remembered his and Danny's last night at uni and the argument that had estranged them. He'd thought that Danny just needed some time to cool off and had gone round to see him the next morning, but his old friend had already packed up and left. The night of that argument was the last time he'd seen him.

Feeling the cold, Alex went back inside the apartment, shutting the door behind him. Walking over to the mantelpiece, he picked up the photograph of his wife, Kas. She was smiling into the lens; the most beautiful woman he'd ever met. Tall and willowy with long, glossy, dark hair and a Mediterranean complexion, she'd appeared feline and mysterious. But not to him. To him, she'd been open and loving. Alex brushed away a tear and put the photograph back on the shelf. Their life together had been so short-lived. Tonight, it seemed that death was all around him.

He drained his glass and went to bed, hoping sleep would obliterate his feelings of despair. He slept a little at first, but his dreams were haunted by images of both Danny and Kas — lives which had been taken far too soon. He woke in the early hours and watched as the digits on his bedside clock slowly moved forward, remembering again the fury on Liz's face. If he could find her, explain fully why he hadn't been at the funeral and what had happened since, then maybe she could find some peace. Maybe they both could.

Eventually, he threw back the covers, pulled his robe from the hook on his bedroom door, and padded through to his study. He switched on his laptop, needing something to do to while away the hours before he could take action. Then he did what he always did when he wanted to stop the memories: he buried himself in work.

* * *

Liz's head was thumping when she woke the next morning. She'd barely slept, her eyes were gritty and her body sluggish. She pulled on her joggers and a sweatshirt, put on her trainers and forced herself to go for a run.

The pounding of her feet on the empty pavements mirrored the pounding in her head, but she battled on towards Kennington Park. The day was a perfect testament to spring. Tiny shoots were unfurling on the trees and the borders were a riot of yellow daffodils. The sky was baby-blue and a hesitant sun promised a warm day ahead. It was the kind of morning that normally delighted her, but today she couldn't feel it. Instead, she concentrated on pushing her body to its limits so that she could find some focus.

Last night, the past had confronted her — but it was the future that counted. Since the beginning of her catering career, she'd been determined to become as successful as she could. She owed it to Danny. She'd worked hard at catering college and then come down to London to train in the best restaurants. It was difficult working in such a male-dominated environment, especially at La Emporium, where the deputy chef had seemed determined to make her life unbearable. Unable to cope with his constant bullying, she'd eventually left the restaurant and struck out on her own.

She knew she was a talented chef and had lots of personal recommendations, but building up her own business was proving to be more difficult than she'd imagined. Being recommended to work for Tia McIntyre had been a coup, but she couldn't rely on word of mouth alone. This afternoon, she'd concentrate on her marketing plan. If nothing else, it would help put all thoughts of Alexander Sinclaire out of her mind.

She arrived back at the flat, hot and sweaty. She'd really pushed herself, and her legs felt wobbly as she put her key in the door and let herself in. The living room smelt stale, and she opened a window to let in some fresh air. She decided she really had to sort out her cookery books, which were in a mess. The place could generally do with a good clean too.

Jay burst in, pulling a jumper over his head as he stumbled through the lounge. 'Oh my God, Liz, have you seen the time? Why didn't you wake me? Also . . . have you seen my trainers?'

'They're over here,' Liz said, picking them up from beside the sofa. 'Calm down, Jay – more haste, less speed.'

'Never mind haste, I need speed and plenty of it. You know what Roberto's like if anyone's late for their shift — he'll have my guts as the special of the day.'

Pulling his trainers on quickly, he grabbed his bag and raced out of the flat.

Liz bent down to pick up the empty wine bottle and their glasses from the night before, and spotted Jay's keys on the table. She raced after him, pulled open the front door to the flat, and then stepped back in surprise. 'Oh!' Standing before her was Alexander Sinclaire. 'What are you doing here?' she asked, barring the doorway. Her heart was racing as she glared at him. Again, he had caught her by surprise, but this was certainly not a nice surprise. Why was he here, in the space where she'd always felt so safe? She felt like she was being invaded.

'Your friend let me in through the main door.'

'He was late for work,' she said, and then stopped herself. She didn't need to explain herself to him. 'But I meant, what *are* you doing here? How did you know where I live?'

'Tia gave me one of your business cards. I implied I had some work for you. She thought she was doing you a favour.'

'Well, she had no right without speaking to me first. I want you to go. I have nothing to say to you.'

'Liz, please, I need to talk to you. Can I come in?'

'No!'

But he still didn't turn to leave. He was dressed casually in cream chinos and a black polo shirt which clung to his chest, and even as she steeled herself against him, a wave of attraction washed over her. *No, no, no! I can't feel like this.*

'I'm sorry I didn't make it to Danny's funeral. I was in Dubai and couldn't get back in time. I wrote to your parents, though.'

His words startled her. 'Did you? They never said.'

'I was really shocked to hear he'd died. I miss him.'

Her throat constricted at the thought of her brother and she blinked back the tears. 'Me too.'

'Please, can I come in? I just want to talk.'

She felt her body sag as she exhaled, her anger suddenly dissipating. He obviously wasn't going to go away, so she might as well get this over and done with — maybe then he would leave her alone. She led the way into her living room. Cringing at the mess, she gestured towards the sofa.

'Take a seat.' She didn't offer him a drink but sat down on the opposite sofa. 'So, what do you want to talk about?'

He was silent for a moment, as if choosing his words carefully. 'Last night, you seemed so angry. I suppose I can sort of understand, and it's made me realise that I could have done more to keep in contact, especially after coming back to England.'

16

She bristled at his words. 'You feel sorry for not keeping in touch. Is that all?'

'What else is there?'

She jumped up and went to stand by the window, as far away from him as possible.

'How about taking some responsibility for how he died?'

She heard him rise from the sofa and walk towards her. She turned to face him.

'What do you mean?' His forehead was creased in a frown. 'Danny died in a car accident. I wasn't even in the country. How could I be responsible?'

Liz almost gasped in shock at his reply. She had to get this man out of her flat. Out of her life.

'They said it was an accident, but it wasn't. I know how Danny felt. He did it on purpose. Because of you!'

Still that look of confusion on his face.

'Why because of me? We had an argument on the last night of university, but it wasn't anything that would have destroyed our friendship.'

'Friendship! Alex, he loved you!'

'And I loved him. We were like brothers.'

'No, Alex. He *loved* you.' She had to hand it to him, he was an excellent actor. 'Yes, that's right. Play the innocent. But my brother loved you and you rejected him. You made him feel his life wasn't worth living. So don't tell me you had nothing to do with his death.'

She watched as his eyes widened with incredulity before he returned to frowning again.

'How on earth could I have rejected him when I didn't even know how he felt about me?'

'He told me you rejected him, so you must have known!'

Liz remembered how depressed Danny had been all that summer and the night he had sobbed into her arms, distraught because he was in love with Alex but Alex didn't want to know. And then, when she had heard about his death, she had rushed to his bedroom, unable to believe she would never see him again, certain that she would find him there, and had found the note on his bed; a note that said he couldn't go on living like he was any longer.

'I didn't!' Alex threw his arms up in the air. 'We fell out because I was with Kas, and on that last night Kas and I announced our engagement.'

Liz was stunned. That certainly wasn't the way Danny had spoken about their falling out, and her brother wouldn't lie.

'That night, Danny ruined what should have been one of the happiest moments of my life,' Alex continued. 'He made no bones about the fact that we were rushing into things. That we were making a mistake.'

'And is Kas the woman you were with last night?' she asked, knowing full well that Jay had told her Alex was dating somebody called Nikki.

'No, we . . .' he faltered. 'We're not together anymore.'

'So, Danny was right then, wasn't he?' Alex had backed her into a corner and she felt the only thing she could do was to defend her brother. She watched as every muscle in Alex's body seemed to tense and she shrank back, suddenly afraid.

'No, he wasn't right. Kas and I were happily married'— he hesitated, and then in a voice that was thick with anger added—'until she died.'

CHAPTER FOUR

Liz slumped onto the sofa, her head in her hands as she heard the front door slam shut. *Oh God! What have I said?*

She'd never imagined Alex could be a widower. And what about Danny? He'd been heartbroken all summer over Alex. She tried to remember his exact words, but all she could remember was his utter despair about the man he'd been in love with. She'd been a naïve teenager back then. Could she have got the wrong end of the stick? It certainly seemed possible. She'd lashed out at Alex in anger and that was wrong. She raced to the door to catch him up, yanking it open. For the second time that day, she stepped back in surprise. In front of her, hand raised to knock, was her sister. Behind her were Liz's niece and nephew, Sophie and Ben.

'Mel! What are you doing here?' Liz repeated the very question she'd asked Alex. She rarely had visitors to her flat so today was beginning to feel surreal.

'Well, that's a friendly welcome, I don't think. Can we come in?'

'Of course,' Liz replied. She led them into her flat. There was no way of catching Alex now. 'Why didn't you let me know you were coming?'

Melissa shrugged. 'Spur-of-the-moment. Who was that good-looking man we passed on the way in? He looked familiar, but I can't think where from . . .'

'No idea,' Liz said, and to distract he sister's attention away from the subject of Alexander Sinclaire continued, 'Mel, you don't do things on the spur of the moment. What's wrong?'

Mel stopped at the entrance to the living room. 'Good lord, Liz, this room's a pigsty!' She moved inside, picking up the discarded cookery books and stacking them neatly on the coffee table. Liz bridled. Mel had always been a neat freak. It was one of the things that used to drive her mad when they were younger.

'Late night,' she said, picking the wine bottle and glasses up from the table. 'You haven't answered my question. What's the matter?'

'Nothing!' Melissa gestured towards the children and Liz nodded in understanding, although she didn't think that either of them would be listening. Sophie was on her phone, her thumbs darting over the keypad, and Ben's eyes didn't move from the screen of his iPad. Apart from a mumbled hello, neither child had paid any attention to her. Even though she was only twenty-nine, Liz felt suddenly old. As children, she, Mel and Danny used to make their own entertainment, usually roaming around on the farm, turning old sheds into dens; they hadn't been permanently plugged into electronic equipment.

'Do you want a coffee?' she asked, taking the glasses into the kitchen and herding Melissa in front of her. She closed the door. 'Come on then. Spill.'

'I'm glad to see your kitchen is a lot tidier than the living room.' The kitchen was immaculate. The chrome appliances gleamed and the white worktops were spotless and clear of clutter.

'Of course it is — and stop evading my question. What's the matter?'

'Nothing. Can't I come and visit my sister without the Spanish Inquisition?'

'Not when you're being so cagey.' Liz spooned two measures of coffee into a cafetiere and reached for the mugs.

Mel sighed and perched herself on a black leather and chrome stool beside the breakfast bar. 'Okay, you know me too well. Remember I said we'd booked to go to Crete for the Easter holidays?'

'Yes.'

'Simon never booked it. Said he was too busy to take time off from the surgery. What's worse is that he's been lying to me all this time.'

'Oh, that's not good,' Liz said, shocked at her brother-in-law's out-of-character behaviour.

'So, I thought, stuff you, we'll go away on our own. And here we are. Don't worry, we won't get in your way. The kids can stay in the spare room. I'll bunk down with you.'

'Okay . . . How long are you planning on staying?'

'A week, if that's alright with you? It is alright, isn't it?'

It wasn't ideal with Jay here, but she'd do anything for her sister. Mel had selflessly taken her into her home when she'd been ill, even though she was newly married, and had spent so much time helping her to recover. How could Liz possibly refuse?

'Of course it's alright. It might be a bit of a squeeze, though. I've got a lodger.'

Mel's eyes lit up. 'Who's that then?'

'Jay. He's a chef. He works at La Emporium.'

'Really?'

Liz pushed the plunger down into the cafetiere and poured the coffee. 'No, not "Really?" Jay's a friend. He split up with his long-term girlfriend and had nowhere else to go, so he's crashing here until they get back to together. Well, he's hoping they will, anyway.'

'I see. We could always stay at a hotel if it's inconvenient.' Mel was beginning to look uncertain. 'Oh God, Liz, I'm sorry. I didn't think. I was in such a rage with Simon that I just packed my bags and the first place I thought of was here.

'Don't be silly. I'll give Jay a ring later. I'm sure he won't mind crashing on the sofa for a few nights.'

'Thank you.' Mel looked relieved. 'I really do appreciate it and we can have some girly time together. Once the kids are asleep.'

Liz frowned. 'I've a few functions on. Mostly nights.'

'I'm sure we'll find the time.'

They drank their coffee in silence. Liz hoped Mel wouldn't be difficult this week. As much as she loved her sister, she was used to having everything her own way. Mel had married young. Simon, a successful country vet, had always provided for her, and over the years her sister had become used to buying whatever she wanted. Sometimes it irritated Liz — Mel just didn't know what it was like to fend for herself.

Mel and Simon had always seemed to be the perfect couple, so a rift between them worried her.

'Do you want to phone Simon to let him know you've arrived?' Liz asked. Mel looked away shiftily. 'He knows you're here, doesn't he?'

'Not exactly, no.'

'Meaning?'

'Meaning, let him stew. I bet he hasn't even noticed we've gone.' Mel blinked back tears and sniffed. 'Oh Liz, it's such a mess! I think Simon's having an affair.'

CHAPTER FIVE

Mel had burst out crying after her revelation, and Liz drew her into a hug. Over Mel's shoulder, Liz watched as the door opened and Sophie walked into the kitchen, stopping in surprise at the sight of her mother sobbing.

'What's the matter, Mum?'

Mel immediately scrubbed her tears away. 'Nothing. I'm just over-emotional at seeing your Auntie Liz. It's been such a long time.'

Sophie narrowed her eyes. 'I am nine, you know? You can tell me the truth. Has this got anything to do with Daddy?'

Mel managed a little chuckle at that one. 'I know how old you are. It's nothing to do with your dad. He's just busy at work.'

'Really?'

'Yes, really.'

'Come on, you must be hungry,' Liz said, diverting the conversation. 'Let's make something to eat.'

* * *

After lunch, Mel had taken the children out shopping. Typical of Mel, she'd spent a fortune, and not only on herself, Sophie and Ben. She had also brought back a beautiful dark green silk shift dress for Liz.

'Mel, this must have cost a bomb!' Liz exclaimed, examining the designer label. 'I can't possibly accept it.'

''Course you can. Call it rent.' And out of earshot of the children, she'd added, 'Bet it's less than Simon spends on his floozy, anyway.'

Liz couldn't get her head around Mel's suspicions that Simon was having an affair. He idolised Mel and was a wonderful dad too. She'd debated phoning him herself, but decided not to interfere.

During the afternoon, Liz had made some pizza bases, and Sophie and Ben happily added toppings to theirs before eating them hungrily.

'Mmm,' Ben enthused, as his pizza quickly disappeared. 'These are much better than shop-bought ones.'

Liz blushed with pride and Mel smiled at her. 'I've made a rod for my own back now. My cooking won't be good enough anymore.'

Later, once the children were safely tucked up in bed, and the two sisters were about to eat their own pizzas, Liz asked the question that had been playing on her mind all day. 'Are you *sure* he's cheating on you?'

'What else could it be?' Melissa asked incredulously. 'He's never at home, always claiming he's tired and we never make love anymore.'

'He could be busy. Is the practice doing well?'

'So he says, but I'm not convinced. He's so tight with money these days. The other week he even suggested I get a job.'

'Heaven forbid!' Liz replied, half joking. She couldn't imagine what Mel could do these days. She was so used to planning her time around the children and their leisure activities that Liz found it hard to see her sister knuckling down to a nine-to-five job.

'My thoughts exactly,' Mel said, not catching the note of sarcasm in Liz's voice. 'School hours, and all those holidays and inset days don't exactly fit with a job. I wouldn't have time.'

'What about working for Simon?' Liz suggested. 'You could do the admin. You did a business course at college, after all. That way you'd be able to keep an eye on him.'

Mel wrinkled her nose. 'I suppose so. I can't stand the women who work there, though. They really look down their noses at me. I'm just the wife, you know?'

'Yes, but you're their boss's wife and you can change things if you want to.' Liz sighed. 'Mel, I'm no expert on relationships, but I know that you and Simon have something special. If you have a problem, you need to talk about it. But first, tell him where you are.'

Mel took a slice of pizza and munched on it thoughtfully. 'I suppose you're right. I just wanted to make him sweat. These days, I feel like a single parent.'

'But if you're not at home and he *is* having an affair, all you're doing is giving him free rein, aren't you?'

Mel stopped chewing. 'I didn't think about that. Bloody hell, I've played right into his hands!' She dropped her pizza slice back onto the plate and scrabbled around in her handbag for her phone. As she scrolled down to her husband's number, she said, 'And he'd better be at home. Alone. Otherwise, he's had it!'

CHAPTER SIX

Alex was running late. He was due to meet Tia at Stephano's, a new restaurant in Chelsea, at eight. It was already ten to as he waited on the pavement outside his apartment for a taxi. He just hoped the traffic wouldn't be too bad. Tia wasn't a lady who liked to be kept waiting.

Finally, the taxi pulled up in front of him. Alex sank back into the seat. He didn't feel like going out; hadn't wanted company since his confrontation with Liz on Sunday. He was still astounded that she'd blamed him for her brother's death for so long.

When she'd told him that Danny had loved him, it had been such a shock that he'd dismissed it as impossible. But in the days since, he hadn't been able to get it out of his mind and had found himself searching his memories for evidence. All the time they'd spent together, and he hadn't even suspected. How could he have missed the signs? *But what signs?* Although Danny hadn't had a serious relationship at uni, he'd gone out with girls and he'd shown no indication that he preferred men. But then perhaps he was trying to keep it under wraps, or even convince himself that he wasn't gay? He wondered what Danny had told Liz to make her believe Alex had rejected him. His friend had always had a tendency to be overly dramatic, but he was never a liar. And why did she think the car crash was deliberate? Even their mother believed it was an accident, which she'd explained when she'd replied to his letter of condolence. Alex shook his head in frustration. He wished he hadn't left in such a hurry on Sunday; his knee jerk reaction to what Liz had said about Kas. He'd gone there to get answers, but now only had more questions. He shouldn't care what Liz thought of him, but he did. And that annoyed him more than anything.

The taxi pulled up outside the restaurant and Alex paid the driver. He was fifteen minutes late. Tia was already sitting at the bar drinking a glass of champagne when he got inside, her long, dark hair snaking down her back, her shapely legs crossed. She looked sensational, as usual. There had been times when their relationship could have gone further, but he'd always stopped himself. If he was going to have a relationship, it needed to be equal, and Tia was far too dominant for that. Besides, they worked well together and he didn't want to do anything to destroy their business relationship.

'Tia, I'm sorry I'm late,' he said when he reached her, leaning over to give her a kiss on the cheek.

'So you should be, darling.' She mock-pouted. 'I've been here alone with only the barman for company.' She smiled at the young, attractive barman who was now blushing furiously, and Alex laughed.

'Then I'm not sorry. You've kept yourself thoroughly entertained.' He ordered himself a gin and tonic and turned back to her. 'Although you might not be so happy when I tell you why I'm late.'

'The apartment block?'

'Yes. When the decorators started to strip the wallpaper, most of the plaster came away with it. Everywhere is going to need re-plastering.'

She sighed and took an elegant sip of her champagne. 'Don't tell me, that will put us over budget?'

'It's not going to come cheap so we'll have to do some cost cutting.'

'And by that, you mean the fixtures and fittings?'

'I'm afraid so.'

'Alex, darling, you know I don't enjoy skimping on the interior design. These are the things people see. As superficial as it may seem, it can make or break a sale.'

'I know, I do understand, but we don't have much choice. We have to make it look good at half the cost.'

'You mean, *I* will.'

He smiled. 'If anyone can do it, you can, Tia.'

She smiled back. 'Flatterer. Okay then. I'll see what I can do.'

The waiter arrived to take them to the table and Tia slipped down from her barstool.

'Ms McIntyre. How lovely to see you,' the waiter said as he greeted her. 'The restaurant looks good, don't you think?'

'It certainly does.' She turned to Alex. 'One of my projects.'

'You've done an amazing job.' Alex now noticed that it had Tia's stamp all over it; elegant, classy and very obvious that no expense had been spared. He was also surprised to see how busy the restaurant was for a Tuesday night.

'We're full every night,' the waiter continued. 'I think we're lucky. Or just very good.'

Tia laughed. 'I'm sure it's the latter, and I'm certainly looking forward to tasting your food.'

'We will not disappoint, I am sure,' he answered, pulling a chair out for Tia, and then placing the linen napkin across her legs. He handed them the menus and took their drinks order.

As Alex read the menu, his stomach growled in anticipation. He'd hardly stopped all day and certainly hadn't had a chance to eat properly. He looked up to tell Tia that he was spoilt for choice and was surprised to find her staring at him. 'What's up?' he asked.

'I was going to ask you that. You've been quiet this week and you look tired.'

'Just work,' he said, hoping she wouldn't ask any further questions.

'All work and no play makes Alex a dull boy,' she remarked. 'You should take some time out.'

'I'm fine.' He tried to change the subject. 'And you, my friend, look sensational as usual. I don't know how you do it with your work schedule.'

'It's all thanks to my masseuse. In fact, I think I'll book you in with her. She'll make you relax and no mistake.'

'I'll look forward to that,' he said with a mischievous grin as the waiter returned to take their order.

'It all looks so good.' Tia inspected the menu thoughtfully. 'But I'll have the mozzarella with roasted vegetables followed by the pork cheek.'

'And I'll have the scallops as a starter, and for the main'—Alex paused as he perused the menu again—'yes, I'll have the chargrilled lamb with spinach and borlotti beans.'

'Good choices, and wine?'

Alex flipped over the menu. 'Red?' He looked enquiringly at Tia, and when she nodded said, 'We'll have a bottle of the *Châteauneuf-du-Pape*, but not until the main. That alright with you, Tia?'

'Yes, I'm fine with champagne for now.'

'Very good,' the waiter said, leaving them alone again.

When their starters had been placed in front of them, Alex commented, 'I can't get over how busy it is in here tonight. The owner must be delighted.'

Tia speared mozzarella and courgette on her fork before she replied. 'That's exactly what I thought when I came in. It's all about the right venue and a talented chef.'

'I agree. I'll definitely come again, and I'd recommend it too.'

'I wouldn't be too hasty with your recommendations if I were you.' Tia chewed thoughtfully on her food. 'This is delicious.'

'And my scallops are cooked perfectly,' Alex agreed. 'So, why wouldn't you recommend this place then?'

'I was thinking on Saturday night, why do I have so many dinner parties?'

'That's easy,' he said, sitting back in his chair, 'Because you love having people around. If you had to spend a quiet night in by yourself watching the telly, you'd go mad.'

She nodded in agreement. 'Yes, but it's costing me a fortune.'

Alex ate the last scallop, chewing it slowly, relishing the flavour. 'You've always said you couldn't possibly spend all the money you inherited, let alone the money you've made for yourself.'

'That's not the point.' She paused as the waiter cleared their plates before continuing. 'I'm fed up with people free-loading off me all the time.'

Alex looked at her in surprise. Whilst it was something he'd noticed, he never thought he would hear the words coming from Tia's mouth. She thrived on being in control, and her dinner parties were always planned and orchestrated to perfection.

'Well . . . I'm tempted to agree with you,' he remarked. 'But what are you suggesting? Opening your own restaurant and getting everyone to put their hands in their pockets for a change?'

The waiter returned to their table, showed Alex the label of the red wine and poured a small amount into his glass. Alex took a sip and nodded at him. 'Perfect.'

They watched as the waiter filled Tia's glass before topping Alex's up. When he was a safe distance away from them, Tia leaned towards him and whispered, 'Why not? We could do it together.'

Alex laughed. 'Us? What do we know about catering apart from eating? I've lost count of the number of properties I've picked up on the cheap because a restaurant has just gone bust.'

'That's because people try to do it themselves. We wouldn't. Listen. You're the property expert, so finding the right property wouldn't be a problem. I'd design the interior, we'd get a managing chef and a top-notch *maître d'* to do the rest. With the number of contacts we have between us, we'd easily get the bums on the seats. It's win-win, and we'll both be in profit.'

Alex frowned. 'It's different, I'll say that, but in this financial climate? I'm not sure it's wise.'

'Alex, this restaurant opened up a month ago and look at it. I'm sure we could do better.'

'I recognise that tone. You've got the bit between your teeth. You're dead set on this, aren't you?'

'Of course I am.'

He took a sip of his wine. 'So go for it then. You don't need me to hold your hand.'

As if to contradict him, she placed her hand over his on the table. 'I don't need you, but I prefer to do things in a partnership. And we've worked so well together in the past.'

'That's different. That's selling on. This would be long-term.'

She pouted. 'Don't you want to be in a long-term partnership with me?'

'It's not that.' He hesitated. 'I'm not sure it's the right project for me.'

She shook her head. 'I disagree. It would be perfect, just what you need at the moment.'

'What do you mean?'

She stroked his hand with her finger. 'You said yourself you're feeling jaded. You need a new challenge.'

'Oh Tia, that's the last thing I need.' He sighed.

She took her hand away from his. 'At least think about it. Now, excuse me while I nip to the loo.'

As Alex waited for her to return, he mulled over their conversation. Perhaps she was right? Perhaps the buzz of a new project was just what he needed to get himself out of the doldrums? But then again, his present mood wasn't just a lacklustre attitude towards his business . . .

His thoughts drifted back to Liz, as they had done constantly since Sunday. There was just something about her. She was a complete contradiction. He remembered how shy she'd been when Tia introduced her at the dinner party; she could barely look anyone in the eye. He also remembered her as a teenager, when she used to follow him around the farm but couldn't string two words together in his presence. She'd shown no such fear when she'd confronted him about Danny on Sunday. Yes, she'd been angry, but she'd also seemed powerful. And how she had changed in looks too. Although he had only seen her in work or workout gear, she'd become stunningly attractive. In some ways, she reminded him of Kas. Although Kas was dark and Liz was blonde, it was the way she seemed oblivious to her good looks that made him think of his wife. It was coming up to the two-year anniversary of Kas' death, and although the pain of losing her was slightly easier to live with than it had been at first, he still carried a weight of grief which felt like it was constantly pressing on his lungs.

He looked up as Tia sashayed back across the restaurant, earning the admiring glances of fellow diners as she passed them. When she reached the table, she leaned over to him and stroked her thumb across his forehead.

'You've got that ugly worry frown on your face,' she said. 'Don't tell me nothing's the matter because I know something is.'

'I was just thinking about your proposition,' Alex lied, not wanting to confess his real thoughts.

She sighed. 'Well, it certainly doesn't meet with your approval if *that's* what you look like when you're thinking about it.'

They were interrupted by the waiter bringing their main course. Like the starter, both dishes were cooked to perfection and they were silent as they ate. Eventually, Alex spoke again. 'Perhaps it's not such a bad idea after all.' *At least it would stop me from wallowing in self-pity.*

Tia's fork paused halfway to her mouth. 'Really? But that's wonderful. I knew you'd come round.'

'Oh, no, not so fast. I'll think about it, but I'm not agreeing to it. We'll need to do some proper research first.'

'Of course,' Tia agreed.

'You'd need an excellent chef, though,' Alex continued. 'Someone who knows exactly what they're doing.'

'Actually, I was thinking of picking Liz's brains.'

'Liz?' Alex started at the mention of her name.

'Yes, you know, my chef? Did you get hold of her, by the way?'

He pushed the memory of Sunday away as he spoke. 'Yes, I did.'

When he didn't elaborate, Tia continued speaking. 'Did you want her to cater for a function? I do hope I'm on the guest list.'

'No, nothing like that. We have people in common, that's all.'

'Oh?' Tia's eye's sparkled with interest, and he knew he was going to have to distract her, and quickly. Once Tia caught the scent of intrigue, she wouldn't stop until she knew everything. And right now, he wasn't prepared to tell her anything.

'If you want this restaurant to be a success, I think you need to speak to someone with more experience.' The last thing he needed was be involved with Liz on a regular basis. 'How about Roberto? He's always banging on about new challenges.'

Tia leaned back and smiled. 'Yes, he might be just the man. I'll check when he's free and invite him round for dinner. Dinner for six it is.'

'Six?'

'Of course! We can't invite Roberto without inviting his wife. And Nikki — and a plus-one for me who can entertain her while we talk business.'

Alex grimaced. 'If you insist.'

'I do.' Tia smiled back.

CHAPTER SEVEN

Liz was having a bad day. In fact, she was having a terrible week. Although she loved Mel and her kids, it was difficult when they were living on top of each other in her tiny flat. Especially when she was trying to run a business. To make it even more crowded, after moving out for a few nights, Jay was back, sleeping on the sofa. The flat felt like a youth hostel. Mel had done her best, showing her children the sights, but it was chaos in the evenings and first thing in the morning. Liz couldn't wait until everyone sorted out their love lives and left her in peace.

She'd thought she'd cracked it on Sunday, when she'd convinced Mel to phone Simon. Certain that straightforward Simon wasn't having an affair, she'd expected their make-up to be swift. But their phone call had turned into a row about spending, and after slamming the phone down, Mel had declared, 'Well, if he thinks I'm going running back to him after the way he spoke to me, he's got another think coming.' And to annoy him even more, the next day she'd gone on another spending spree.

Liz sighed as she cleaned up in her client's kitchen. Today's meal hadn't been a resounding success. A soufflé had been a bad idea given her current state of mind. It had risen but wasn't as light and fluffy as she would have liked. The client seemed happy enough, but Liz knew it was below her usual standard. It wasn't just her living arrangements that were distracting her, though — since last Saturday, she'd been unable to stop thinking about Alexander Sinclaire.

He'd whirled up her emotions, which were still crashing around like angry wasps. For years she'd been steadfast in her hatred of him, but now she couldn't help wondering if she'd got it wrong. She knew she needed to apologise but wasn't sure how she could contact him. And she really didn't want to ask Tia.

She realised she should probably speak to Mel about Danny too, get her perspective on what had actually happened that summer. Finding the right time amidst the chaos was the problem, though. And, even though she was close to her sister, they had grieved for Danny in very different ways — Mel throwing herself into her relationship with Simon, and Liz going down a completely different route. A route that had ended up isolating her from their entire family – but no, she didn't want to think about that right at this moment.

Liz stacked away her utensils into the box she used to transport them and then packed them away in her van. Most of the time she enjoyed the varied challenges that private catering brought her, but she still missed the structure of working in a restaurant. But leaving La Emporium had felt like her only option at the time. She'd worked hard to impress the restaurant's owner and chef, Roberto, one of the top Michelin chefs in London. It was hard physical work, and Roberto expected absolute dedication. For a while, she thought she might succeed. Roberto noticeably made the time and effort to show her how to improve her skills, which didn't go unnoticed by his deputy chef, Louis. Louis, who believed a woman's place was in the home and nowhere near a professional kitchen.

He'd made Liz's life a misery, undermining her at every opportunity, bawling her out for the slightest mistake, even when it was someone else's. Gradually, she'd lost confidence in her abilities. Sometimes she wished she'd had the courage to stick it out, but as her anxiety levels had increased, her stomach had twisted into knots so that she found it difficult to eat. And that was what scared her most; falling back into her old ways, down the slope to the darkness she'd experienced after Danny's death. And so, to save herself, she'd left . . .

She started up the van, longing for a soak in a hot bath. That afternoon, though, Tia had asked her to call round after she finished to discuss a function, and it was a request she didn't dare refuse. She found the client side the hardest to deal with, especially when all she wanted to do was to cook.

When she arrived, she pressed the buzzer on Tia's intercom and pushed open the heavy, black door to the Georgian building. The thick pile of the hall carpet silenced her footsteps, but Tia called out to her.

'I'm in the living room. Come straight through.'

The living room was vast with a parquet floor, high ceilings and large windows on two sides. In the middle, nestling on an enormous white rug, were two equally white sofas. Tia was lounging on one, looking supremely comfortable yet stylish, in a pair of wide-legged trousers and a long, pale blue cotton shirt. As ever, her face and hair were immaculate. Liz wished she had even a tenth of Tia's poise and elegance.

'Do come and sit down,' Tia said, rising from her position on the sofa. 'You look done in.'

'Thanks.'

'Can I get you a drink? A bit of bubbly, perhaps?'

'No. I'm fine, thanks.'

'Are you sure? I'm having one and I hate drinking on my own.'

It looked like it was going to be a long evening, and Tia was right — she was shattered. 'Just a mineral water then, please. Sparkling, if you have it.'

'Of course.'

Liz waited impatiently while Tia fussed with ice cubes for her drink and popped the cork on a bottle of champagne for herself. She handed Liz her water and, after taking a sip of champagne, placed the flute carefully on the coffee table.

'So, what can I do for you?' Liz asked, wanting to get straight to the point.

'I'm planning a little *soirée* next week. I wondered if you could cater for me?'

'Of course. What date is it?'

'Next Thursday, actually. I know it's short notice, but I hope you're available.'

Liz reached for her diary, wondering why Tia couldn't have asked her on the phone rather than dragging her across London, and flicked through to the following week. The page was empty, as she had known it would be.

'That should be fine. How many people is it for?'

'Six. A rather select six. So I'll want top-of-the-range.'

'No problem. Did you have anything particular in mind?'

'Yes. One of my guests is a big fan of La Emporium.' Tia glanced at her watch and then continued. 'I want to impress him, so could you come up with something in a similar style? You used to work there, didn't you?'

'Yes, I did.'

The intercom buzzed, and again Tia looked at her watch. 'Oh damn, that'll be Alex. He's early. Do excuse me for a moment.'

Liz felt herself pale at the words and took a huge gulp of her drink, nearly choking on the bubbles. Alexander Sinclaire was the last person she wanted to see tonight. It wasn't the right time or place for an apology. As she heard their voices in the corridor, Liz struggled to find an excuse to make her escape.

But, suddenly, there he was, striding into the room behind Tia, wearing a crisp, dark, immaculately tailored suit, deep blue shirt and navy tie. He looked rich, confident and incredibly handsome, whereas she'd rushed over here straight from another job with no time to titivate. Why was it whenever she saw him, he looked perfect and she was unkempt?

'Liz.' He stopped in his tracks. 'What are you doing here?'

'I — er — I . . .' Liz hesitated.

'I was just speaking to Liz about a dinner party next week. I'm afraid we've run over a bit,' Tia interrupted.

Liz frowned. Hadn't Tia just said that Alex was early?

'Can I get you a drink, Alex?'

'No, thanks. I'm not stopping. I just came round to pick up the new costings.'

'Oh, don't be stuffy.' Tia took him by the arm and guided him towards the seat next to Liz. He sat down, holding his body, Liz noticed, as far away from her as he possibly could.

'I really need to get on,' Alex repeated.

'In that case, I'll get them for you.' Before either of them could speak, she swished out of the room.

'I'll get out of your way as soon as I can,' Liz said quietly.

'Don't bother on my account. Once I have the paperwork, I'll be off.' He strode across the room towards the window, his back to her.

She couldn't bear his hostility. 'I'm really sorry for what happened on Sunday. There's obviously been some misunderstanding. I'm especially sorry for what I said about your wife,' she blurted out.

Slowly, he turned to face her. He was rigid with tension and the anger in his eyes almost made her gasp.

'Thank you, for that at least. Do you still think your brother took his own life because of me?'

'You have to understand—'

'I understand perfectly,' he said, cutting her dead. 'I think we should agree to disagree and keep our distance. If we do bump into each other professionally, we need to be civil. Can you do that?'

Liz gasped at his condescending manner, but refused to rise to the bait. 'I don't need to be told how to be professional,' she said, turning at the sound of Tia's footsteps. 'I'm sorry, Tia, I really must go. I've booked you in for next week and I'll email you with some menu ideas so you can let me know what you think.'

'Of course, Liz, but—'

'Don't worry, I can see myself out.'

* * *

The room was silent as Liz marched towards the door, her head held high. Alex swallowed uncomfortably. He realised he'd overreacted, but she was the last person he'd expected to see tonight. Even though she'd obviously come straight from work, with her hair scraped back into a ponytail and very little make-up on, she was still incredibly attractive. He had hoped that the next time he saw her, they would be able to sit down calmly and help each other understand what had really gone on that summer. He suspected that Tia had set this up on purpose, and being backed into a corner, he'd bitten Liz's head off, even when she'd apologised. He wanted to kick himself. He'd never get the answers he needed now, and it was all his own fault.

'What was that all about?' Tia asked.

'Nothing,' Alex said, after hearing the front door close.

'It didn't look like nothing.'

'Tia, don't meddle. I don't know what you were trying to do tonight, but if you were trying to set me up, it won't work.'

Tia looked outraged but Alex could tell it was an act.

'Why would I do that, Alex? Especially when you're with Nikki.'

'I can see right through you. But please, concentrate on your own love life and leave mine out of it. Now, have you got those costings?'

'Here they are.' She handed him a black folder. 'Do you want a coffee?' She turned on her heel and strode towards the living room door.

'No, thanks,' he replied to her indignant back.

Alone in the living room, he flicked through the new designs. Once again, she'd worked her magic. They were almost as good as the original designs, but at half the cost. Every project they worked on was a success, both professionally and financially. He just wished she could keep the personal out of their relationship. Although she was content to be single, she had got it into her head that he needed to find a new love to replace Kas. It didn't matter how many times he told her that he just wasn't ready to fall in love again, she wouldn't listen and kept trying to set him up with people. He'd met Nikki through Tia, and although he'd enjoyed her company at the beginning, he was increasingly aware that it just wasn't working for him. Nikki phoned him constantly and he'd begun to make up excuses not to see her, but he'd have to speak to her soon. It wasn't fair to keep her hoping when he knew they had no future. He sighed, got up and went to find Tia.

She was making herself a strong coffee in her espresso machine. He leant against the kitchen door frame.

'I'm sorry,' he said. 'I didn't mean to upset you.'

'Well, you did,' she said, obviously still in a huff. 'I was only trying to help.'

'I don't need your help.'

She turned to face him. 'But I think you do, Alex. Don't forget, I know you and I'd be blind if I couldn't see how desperately unhappy you are at the moment.' She put her hand up as he tried to interrupt her. 'I know you'll never forget Kas, and a part of you will always love her and grieve for her, but now I feel you're ready to move on from the kind of superficial relationships you've been having recently.'

'Tia, I—'

'I said, don't interrupt. If you're ever going to be happy, you need to settle down. You were inquisitive about Liz on Saturday, then you asked me for her address, and there was definitely something shifty going on when I asked you about her earlier in the week. So, yes, I was meddling, but only because I wanted to help. It seems I misjudged the situation.'

Alex gave a half-hearted laugh. 'Oh Tia, you're right about that. In fact, you couldn't have got it more wrong.

There will never be anything between me and Liz, because she hates me.'

Tia frowned. 'They say there's a fine line—'

'Not in this case.' Alex shook his head. 'She thinks I killed her brother.'

CHAPTER EIGHT

Liz was still fuming by the time she got home. How dare he be so condescending? He'd made her feel like a child, yet again. Couldn't he see the woman she'd grown into? No, to him, she would clearly always be Danny Cartwright's little sister.

She remembered the first time he'd visited with Danny. He'd been charming, taking her mother's hand and telling her she didn't look old enough to have such grown-up children, and eyeing Mel's slender figure with unashamed approval. His eyes had merely flicked over her, no lingering there, but although he had only ever treated her as Danny's baby sister, she'd fallen completely and utterly in love with him.

She'd clutched her secret to herself throughout that long, hot summer, but still he hadn't noticed her, which made her want him all the more. During the autumn term, she'd dieted like mad, hoping that if he came back at Christmas, he'd see her transformation and realise that he couldn't live without her. But he didn't even notice. And then on Christmas Eve, when she'd been reading in her father's study, she'd heard him and some of the local boys laughing and joking as they waited for Danny to get ready before heading to the pub.

Her ears had grown hot when one of them had mentioned her name.

'She definitely fancies you.'

'Don't be daft. She's only a baby,' Alex had protested.

Laughter followed. 'Baby or not, she's got it bad for you. Look at the way she moons about you all the time.'

'Poor thing,' Alex had replied. 'But she's not my type.'

'You'd have to be mad to fancy her,' came the response. 'All that fat and blubber. *Yeuck*!'

'Don't be so cruel. You're no oil painting yourself, you know?'

She'd put her fingers in her ears after that, unable to bear hearing any more of what Alex really thought of her. Desperate not to give away her location, she was silent as tears rolled down her cheeks. It was only when they'd closed the front door behind them that she allowed herself to cry in earnest.

As Liz walked into the apartment, Jay was playing a noisy game with Ben and Sophie on the Xbox. Unable to face their noise, she turned towards the kitchen. As she stepped inside, she stopped in horror. Her kitchen was in complete chaos, with Mel in the middle humming happily as she made a lasagne. Every pan had been used and discarded in the process of her creativity. It was the last straw.

'Mel! What are you doing?'

'Oh! Hi, sis. I'm making a lasagne. What's wrong?'

'This bloody mess, that's what wrong.'

'Don't swear!'

Again, it reminded Liz of when they were younger. Mel had always been so bossy. She hadn't liked it then, and she certainly didn't like it now, especially in her own home.

'Have you spoken to Simon today?'

'No, why?' Mel looked up from spooning cheese sauce over the lasagne sheets. 'Want to get rid of us?'

'No, I want you and Simon to sort out your marriage. You belong together.'

Mel sighed. 'That's up to him.'

43

'No, Mel, it's up to you too. I'm going for a run.'

'You can't go at this time of night!' Mel protested.

'I can do what I like. I'm not a child.'

Liz strode into her bedroom and stripped off her clothes. Within minutes, she'd changed and headed back out of the door. She pounded down the pavements, trying to get rid of her frustration, but today running wasn't working for her. Eventually, she rested on a bench, and when she'd caught her breath, slipped out her phone from her running armband. She'd vowed she wouldn't interfere in her sister's marriage, but she'd had enough. To coin a phrase their mum had used a lot when they were growing up, "someone needed to bang their heads together".

Simon was reticent when he first picked up the phone. 'So, she's got you doing her dirty work for her now, has she?'

'Of course not! She doesn't even know I'm phoning. She'll go ballistic.'

'So, why are you?' She'd never heard him sound so hostile, but she wasn't going to let him put her off.

'What's going on, Simon?'

'I don't really think it's any of your business.'

'When my sister and your children are camping out in my flat, I think it's entirely my business.'

'Getting in your way, are they?'

No wonder Mel couldn't make any headway when Simon was being so snarky. She wondered if phoning him had been a mistake.

'That's not why I'm ringing you. I love you both and I can't stand to see you like this. Mel thinks you're having an affair.'

'Well, I'm not.' He paused, 'Frankly, Liz, the one good thing about this week is that at least I haven't had those accusations hurled at me twenty-four-seven.'

'Why does she think it then? She says you're never at home.'

He almost growled in frustration. 'Because one of us has to work to afford her spending habits.'

'Oh.' He had a point. She'd seen it first-hand this week. 'Is that all it is?'

'All? Come off it, Liz, you know what she's like. Mel doesn't want to keep up with the Joneses, she wants the Joneses to keep up with her.'

'So, tell her?'

Simon sighed. 'I've tried, God knows I have. But it doesn't sink in.' He paused. 'I shouldn't really be telling you this, but the practice is in trouble. I'm scared we might even go under.'

She gasped. 'Is it really that bad?'

'I'm afraid so.'

'Then you *have* to tell her, make her understand.' Liz thought about the amount of money Mel must have spent that week and cringed.

'She doesn't want to listen, and how can I speak to her properly when she's in London with you?'

Liz pondered for a moment. 'Look, if I put her on a train tomorrow morning, can you meet her? It is Good Friday, after all. I'll keep the kids here and bring them back on Sunday. Give you a bit of space to sort things out?'

'You'd do that?'

'Only if you promise to talk to her. Properly.'

He sighed. 'I will, if she'll listen.'

'Make her listen. I'll get her to phone you tonight. Just tell her you'll pick her up from the station.'

'If you think it'll work?' He still sounded hesitant. It felt strange being the one in control. Usually, it was Mel and Simon helping her out.

'It will if you want it to.'

'Then I'll wait for her call.'

Liz put her mobile away, did a few stretches, and ran back home. Getting Mel to agree would be her biggest problem, but she was determined her sister would be on that train.

When she got back to the apartment, it was quiet.

'Where is everyone?' she asked Mel, who was lying on the sofa reading a magazine.

45

'Sophie's having a soak in the bath, Ben's in bed and Jay's gone to work. Are you ready for some lasagne yet?'

'No, not yet.'

'Liz, you've got to eat! I hope you're not falling back into your old ways.'

'Of course I'm not.' It had always been this way. If ever she wasn't hungry, Mel assumed she was sliding back down the path of anorexia.

The dieting had increased after she'd heard the boys joking about her size, but had really kicked in after Danny's death. Rationing what she ate was her only means of having any control over her life. Even as the weight dropped off, all she could see was the chubby girl who'd been ridiculed. She wore layers of baggy clothes to cover up her weight loss, and for a long time no one noticed. Her parents were too lost in their grief for their son. They grieved in different ways; her mum was in constant pools of tears, barely able to get out of bed, and her dad worked all hours on the farm. Mel had just moved in with Simon. No one noticed what she was doing to herself.

Along with the diet, she'd taken up running, pushing herself to the extremes of her physical ability. Given her food restriction, it wasn't long until she'd pushed herself too far, collapsing outside Mel's house. She wondered afterwards if subconsciously she'd taken herself there on purpose; a cry for help to the only person she trusted? By then, her weight was so low she'd been admitted to hospital, where she began the long road to recovery. Mel was with her every step of the way, ready to pounce whenever she thought Liz might relapse. Which was more than could be said for either of her parents. At first, they had been full of contrition for not having noticed what was happening to her, but they were still too grief-stricken to give her the support she needed. Her mum had tried to help but didn't really understand how to, and her dad, being as old-fashioned as he was, even suggested that she should pull herself together and stop seeking attention all the time — something that she had never fully forgiven him for.

Bizarrely, while food had been her enemy for so long, it then became her saviour. Learning to eat healthily had inspired in her a desire to cook. And, as soon as she'd recovered enough to return to normal life, she'd enrolled on a cookery course and loved every minute. Mel had thought her mad at first, like a recovering alcoholic choosing to run a pub, but it had been the making of her — and now food was her biggest love. There was no way she was going to return to those dark days, whatever life might throw at her.

Liz saw the wary look on her sister's face and tried to allay her fears. 'I want to talk to you first, that's all. I want you to go home.'

'I'm outstaying my welcome, aren't I? Is that why you're in such a mood?'

'Of course not. I had a bad day, that's all.'

'How come?'

'Later. We're talking about you.' Liz sat down on the sofa next to her sister.

'I'll go home on Sunday, if that's okay with you?'

'No, it's not, actually.' She knew she was going to have to steamroller her sister into this. Mel just didn't get subtlety. 'I want you to go back tomorrow. Alone. I'll bring the kids back on Sunday. You need to sort this out with Simon properly, without Sophie and Ben around.'

Mel laughed. 'I'll have to find him first. He'll find some excuse to avoid me, even on a bank holiday.'

'I'm sure he's missing you as much as you're missing him.'

'I doubt that very much.'

Liz handed her the phone. 'Then why don't you find out?'

'What, now?'

'Yes, now.'

Mel shrugged. 'Okay then, but I bet he doesn't pick up.'

'Just try it,' Liz said and walked into the kitchen to give her some privacy. To her surprise, it was back to looking immaculate, and she immediately felt guilty for having a go at Mel earlier. The lasagne was still resting on the worktop and smelt delicious. It was nice having someone to cook for her, she decided, as she heaped some onto a plate and placed it in the microwave to warm up.

She opened the fridge and took out a bottle of wine. She had a feeling they were going to need it.

* * *

Later, as they stretched out on the sofa, Mel turned to her. 'Thanks, Lizzie.'

'What for?'

'For everything you've done for us this week. And for making me phone Simon tonight. You're right, we need to sort this out. One way or another.'

'You'll work it out. If any couple deserves to be together, then it's you two.'

'Thanks. But what about you? Is there a man in your life?'

'No.' An image of Alex popped up in Liz's head, but she pushed it away firmly. 'I'm concentrating on my career.'

'And that's going well, is it? You certainly seem busy.'

'It's going okay,' Liz said. 'Not brilliant, but okay.'

Mel took a sip of her wine. 'Do you remember I said I saw someone leaving here when I came in on Sunday and he looked familiar?' she asked.

'Vaguely.' Liz didn't like where the conversation was going.

'I know who he reminded me of.'

'Who?'

'Do you remember that friend of Danny's who used to come and stay with us in the holidays? His family lived in Dubai. Well, he looked a lot like him — older, of course. We all used to think you had a crush on him.'

'No, I didn't!'

Mel suddenly propped herself up on her elbow and stared at her. 'Don't give me that. You're blushing! You never could lie to me, Elizabeth Cartwright.'

Liz paused before answering. Mel was right. 'It's a long story,' she finally admitted.

Mel held out her glass. 'Top me up then. I'm all ears.'

So, Liz told her everything.

When she'd finished, Mel looked confused. 'But what I don't get is why you blame Alex? Danny's accident wasn't his fault.'

'I don't think it was an accident.'

'Of course it was. What else could it be?'

Liz looked away, unable to meet her sister's eye. As far as she was aware, she was the only one Danny had confided in that he was gay. And after his death, Liz hadn't wanted to add to anyone's grief, especially after finding the note which had convinced her that Danny had taken his own life. 'I think he did it on purpose.'

'Don't be daft. I know he was out of sorts, but he wasn't suicidal. He'd had a row with Dad that morning, so he was probably driving too fast, that's all.'

'How can you be so sure?' she asked.

'Because he'd had a letter that morning. He'd been offered a job in London and he was delighted. Then Dad came in, calling him an idle layabout because he didn't want to help him on the farm. Danny exploded and they had another massive row. Then Danny stormed off.'

Liz frowned. 'But that doesn't explain the note.'

'What note?'

Liz closed her eyes as she remembered. 'Mum and I were out shopping when the police came and told Dad. They'd gone by the time we got home so Dad had to break the news. I couldn't believe what he was saying. He said it so matter-of-factly.'

'He was in shock,' Mel said. 'And he was dreading telling Mum. I think he was just trying to keep things calm.'

'I'll never forget Mum's reaction. That howl! It was like a wounded animal. Sometimes I still hear it.'

'Me too. I'm sure I'd be the same if it was one of mine. I can't imagine anything worse.'

'I couldn't quite take it in. I didn't believe I'd never see him again. So, while you were both consoling Mum, I rushed to Danny's room. I had it in my head that he was hiding there. That none of it was really happening. There was a letter on the bed . . . It . . . it looked like he was saying goodbye. Like he'd left it there on purpose before he'd gone out.'

Mel frowned. 'There was no note when I went in there.'

'What do you mean?'

Mel paused before continuing. 'Dad blamed himself for the accident because of the argument they'd had. There were so many arguments between them that summer — do you remember?'

'Of course. It was like waiting for a volcano to erupt.'

'Dad used to talk to me, and so did Danny. I felt like I was piggy in the middle. Danny said some horrible things about Dad.'

'Dad was always on his case and Danny hated it,' Liz agreed.

'Did you know Danny kept a diary?'

Liz shook her head.

'He used it to vent his feelings, so I knew he would've written some pretty unpleasant things about Dad. Dad was upset enough, and I didn't want him to find it. So, before you got back, I made an excuse to go to the loo and grabbed it from his room. There must have been a loose page because when I read his diary later, I realised there was a part missing, as though it had been torn out. I tried to find it later, but it wasn't there. Have you still got the note?'

Liz nodded, put down her glass and made her way into her bedroom. She opened her wardrobe door and reached inside for a cardboard keepsake box she kept at the bottom. After Danny's death, she'd read the note constantly, but she hadn't felt the need to look at it for a long time and it took a bit of rummage to find it. She took it out, averting her eyes because she couldn't face reading the words again now. Not that she needed to. She could remember every single word. Back in the living room, she handed it to Mel, who read it in silence. After a few moments, Mel put the piece of paper down on the coffee table and looked at Liz with tears in her eyes.

'I'm so sorry. If I hadn't been in such a rush to hide the diary, I would have noticed. This is the missing page.'

Liz felt herself grow icy cold. 'So . . . it wasn't a suicide note?'

'No, just the ramblings of an angry young man.'

'But it looks like a letter.'

'It was. Or at least it was intended to be. The later entry says he was drunk when he wrote it. It was a letter to Alex. When Danny was sober the next morning, he realised he could never send it. But he was glad that he had written it because it gave him a sense of closure. From then on, he was determined to get on with his life — that was when he started applying for jobs.'

'Oh God.' Liz took a huge gulp of her wine. 'All these years, Dad has blamed himself, I've blamed Alex, and none of it was anyone's fault. Except maybe Danny's, who was probably driving erratically.'

'Exactly.'

Liz felt sick. 'Do you still have the diary?'

'Yes. Do you want to read it?'

'I think so.' Liz paused. 'I can't imagine it'll be easy, but I think the only way I can put this behind me is to know what was actually going on in his head.'

'It might help,' Mel agreed, and then sighed. 'I can't believe you thought he'd taken his own life. Why didn't you tell anyone? Why didn't you tell *me*?'

Liz shook her head. 'I couldn't. I couldn't tell anyone. It was just too much for me. I dealt with it the only way I knew how, and look how badly that ended.'

Mel hugged Liz to her. 'Oh, you poor love.'

'It's not just me though, is it? You lost your brother too but you didn't fall apart.'

'You were just a teenager,' Mel said, stroking her back. 'And besides, I had Simon. I don't think I would have got through it without him.'

'And you've still got him now,' Liz said. 'That's why you need to go home and sort it out.'

'I know.' Mel sighed again. 'I've been an idiot, burying my head in the sand.'

'Just like we all did then. Must be a family trait. When I look back, it seems that everything that went wrong with our family started with that crash.'

'I agree,' Mel said. 'Although it wasn't really that long ago, times are different now. If that had happened today, we'd all be in family therapy.'

Despite herself, Liz laughed. 'Can you imagine Dad talking to a therapist?'

Mel's mouth twitched. 'No, not really, although he has mellowed over the years.'

'Has he?'

'Yes, which you'd know if you bothered to come and see us more often.'

'It's difficult.' Liz took a deep breath. 'He was so critical of my illness . . . do you know he even told me I was just doing it for attention?'

'He told me.' Mel squeezed Liz's arm. 'It's something he deeply regrets.'

'Does he?' Liz was surprised.

'Yes, he does. Which is why when you bring the kids back on Sunday, you should go and talk to him. Take some of your own advice.'

'Maybe,' Liz said quietly, not sure if she was ready for that yet.

Mel continued speaking. 'He lost everything that summer, you know? Danny, you, and then Mum left.'

'I still can't believe she just walked out like that.'

'I know.' Mel nodded. 'Grief can bring people together but it seemed to drive them apart.'

'And you've never forgiven her for it, have you?'

'Nope,' Mel said resolutely. 'I could have forgiven her for splitting up with Dad. But she left us too, ran off with that bloke she met and went to live in Spain. And not even coming back for my wedding? I can't *ever* forgive her for that.'

'Most mums would be delighted that their daughter was marrying a vet, but she was so disapproving.'

'I don't think it was Simon she disapproved of. It was more the fact that we wanted to get married. She said we were too young and that I'd live to regret it, just like she did.'

'Harsh,' Liz agreed. 'But even so, missing your wedding.'

'She was probably too embarrassed. That first relationship didn't last long, and then she had a whole string of men before finally meeting creepy Carlos.'

'Ugh!' Liz grimaced. 'Don't remind me of him!'

Two years ago, Liz had gone to Spain in an attempt to reconcile with their mother, but it had been a difficult visit. Even the memory of it made her shudder with distaste. From the moment Liz arrived, Carlos had made her feel uncomfortable with his constant flirting and roving hands. She'd done her best to make sure she was never on her own with him, but one day she'd come back from the beach to find a bored Carlos alone in the apartment and in the mood for some entertainment. She'd fought him off and fled, not returning until much later when her mother had come back. By that time, Carlos had already spread his lies, which her mother believed. Liz had packed her bags and taken the next flight home. They hadn't spoken since. She'd told Mel a little of what had happened, but not all of it. She'd just been relieved that she had managed to fight him off before things had gone too far. Even so, she often wondered whether she should have reported him to the police — but then if her own mother didn't believe her, how would she have made the police understand in a foreign language?

'Have we got any more wine?' Mel asked, breaking Liz out of her troubled thoughts.

'Nope. And you've had enough. You've got a busy day tomorrow. You don't want to be dealing with it on a hangover. I'll make us some tea.'

When she came back into the living room, she found Mel staring into space. 'We should have done this years ago, you know?' she said thoughtfully.

'It has been cathartic,' Liz agreed. 'If exhausting.'

'You should come home more often.'

'I've been busy,' Liz said defensively.

'Yes. Busy avoiding us all.'

Liz sat down and sipped her tea. 'Yes, I know. I just wasn't ready to deal with it,' she admitted.

'But you are now?'

'Yes, I think so.' Finally knowing that Danny's death was an accident after all had changed everything for her. And to think that she could have found this relief years ago if only she'd been able to speak about it properly to Mel.

'Promise me you'll go and see Dad on Sunday? Talk to him properly?'

Liz nodded. 'Okay. As long as Ruth's not there.' Not long after their mother had left, their father had started seeing Ruth, a neighbour. They married quickly, and at the time it had felt like he was another one who had moved on from Danny's death while she was still suffering. They'd seemed so content together, it was almost as though the past had never happened, and although she felt bad about it now, she had resented their happiness and had behaved like the wicked step-daughter — something she now regretted.

'Ruth's a lovely woman. You just need to get to know her properly.'

'I know.' Liz sighed. 'And I will. In time. But I have to sort things out with Dad first. Just the two of us.'

CHAPTER NINE

'So kids, what do you want to do today?'

Ben and Sophie sat on either side of the breakfast bar as Liz cooked and served up fresh pancakes. Both children soon had smears of chocolate on their hands and faces as they piled liberal amounts of Nutella over each pancake. *Mel would have a fit*, Liz thought, also wondering if loading them up with sugar so early in the day might be a mistake. But then, as it was Easter Sunday tomorrow, an overload of chocolate was just getting them in training. She'd been out to buy both of them Easter eggs for the morning, and she was sure they'd get more when they arrived home.

Liz wondered how her sister and Simon were getting on. Mel had texted her to say she'd arrived safely yesterday, but there'd been nothing since. She could only assume things were pretty intense.

'No more sightseeing,' Sophie insisted.

'Or shopping,' Ben added between mouthfuls. 'Yum, these pancakes are great. Thanks, Auntie Liz, we'd never get these at home.'

'Yeah, we only get boring old cereal.'

Liz smiled, wracking her brains for how to entertain the children. She could always take them to the cinema or bowling. But that would only occupy a few hours. How would she entertain them for an entire day?

'Something smells good,' Jay said, giving a huge yawn as he walked into the kitchen.

'Pancakes,' Liz said. 'Want some?'

'Too right. As long as I can have chocolate spread.' He grinned at the kids. 'So, what's the plan for today then?' He pulled up a breakfast bar stool and squeezed himself in beside Ben.

'That's just what we were trying to decide. So far, we've got no sightseeing or shopping.' She paused, an idea coming to her. 'What about the zoo?'

Both children screwed up their faces.

'Nah. We've been to Chester Zoo loads of times,' Sophie said. 'It gets boring after a while.'

'Ouch, tough crowd,' Jay said, smiling at Liz as she put a pancake in front of him. 'I know! How about Chessington? I used to love going there.'

'What's at Chessington?' Ben asked, looking at Jay, his face animated. He'd clearly developed a bit of a hero crush on Jay during the week.

'It's a theme park.'

'What, you mean like Alton Towers?' Sophie asked, her face lighting up.

'Something like that,' Jay said. 'Probably not as big, though.'

'I'm not sure,' Liz said, wondering how she was going to cope with two children in an adventure park. 'I'm not even sure where it is.'

'But I am,' Jay said. 'And it's my day off, so I could come with you.'

'Would you?'

'It would be my pleasure,' Jay said as both children whooped in delight.

'In that case, we'd better finish these pancakes and get ourselves cleaned up,' Liz said.

* * *

56

They took the train from Waterloo to Chessington South, which Jay assured them wasn't too far away from the theme park.

'But how do we get there then?' asked Ben as they exited the station.

'We walk, of course,' Jay said.

'Walk?' Sophie looked horrified.

'Yes. That's what your legs were made for. The quicker we get there, the quicker we can get on the first ride.'

Both Ben and Sophie eagerly stepped in beside him as he walked. Bringing up the rear, Liz couldn't help but smile. She'd never seen Jay like this before. He seemed more like a big kid himself. Looking after two children on her own was completely out of her comfort zone, but with Jay alongside her, she had a feeling she was going to enjoy herself.

Liz stared up at the rides in awe when they arrived. As it was Easter weekend, it was crowded with long lines for each ride so she was glad she'd had the forethought to book online and buy fast-track tickets, otherwise they'd have spent most of the day queuing.

'What shall we go on first?' Jay asked.

'That,' Ben said, pointing to a massive stone crocodile. A tower rose from the reptile, and around the top was a huge round disc containing lots of screaming humans. Liz watched as the disc plunged suddenly downwards into the crocodile. Her mouth went dry and she felt slightly sick.

'I'm not sure,' she said, desperate for an excuse. She spotted the height restriction signs and added, 'that you'll be tall enough.'

'It says here that you have to be over 1.2 metres high,' Jay said, reading a brochure. 'Let's try, shall we?'

He led Ben over to the sign. He was just a fraction over the height restriction. Ben whooped with delight. 'Yeah, I can go on!'

Sophie looked nervously at Liz. 'I will if you will.'

'Okay then,' Liz said, not wanting to look more afraid than her niece. 'Let's go for it.'

Strapped to the ride as they inched towards the top of the tower, Liz regretted her decision. She'd never much liked heights. She closed her eyes, praying for it to be over soon.

'Are you okay, Auntie Liz?' Sophie whispered beside her. 'You've gone very pale.'

'Of course, I'm fine,' Liz tried to brazen it out as the ride began its sudden descent and knocked the air out of her lungs. It felt as though her stomach was lodged in her throat.

'Wow, that was brilliant!' Ben said once they'd come off the ride. Liz's legs were shaking so much she doubted their ability to keep her upright, but at least she'd survived.

'Let's go on a roller coaster next. What about Dragon's Fury?' Ben asked, reading Jay's brochure.

'Let's do it,' Liz said, enjoying seeing the delight on Ben's face, but also hoping there was a long walk to the next ride to give her a chance to recover.

* * *

'I think that's what you'd call a job well done,' Jay said, smiling at the sleeping children on the train home.

'Thanks to you,' Liz said. 'I couldn't have done it without you. They've had a great day.'

After Dragon's Fury, they'd gone on several more terrifying rides until Liz, in need of something gentler, had suggested Tiger Rock — a log flume which travelled alongside the tiger enclosure. Even that had its thrills and they'd all ended up getting soaked. But seeing the children's laughter had filled her with joy.

'Teamwork,' Jay said, interrupting her thoughts. 'I can't remember the last time I had so much fun.'

'Me neither,' Liz replied.

'Have you ever wondered what it would be like to have a family?'

'What, kids, you mean? No, not really.' She'd never imagined being responsible for the lives of children. She found it hard enough looking after herself.

'It's not just having kids though, is it? It's having some-one to share it with.'

'I know what you mean.'

'I'd like to have children of my own someday,' Jay said thoughtfully.

'You'd make a great dad.' Liz hoped her comment would be enough to put an end to this uncomfortable conversation. When she'd been recovering from her anorexia, she'd been told that she'd done so much damage to her body she might never be able to conceive, so it wasn't a subject she liked to dwell on.

Jay took her hand in his. 'And you'd make a wonderful mother. You have so much to give.'

'Do I?' She'd spent so long shutting herself off from people, his words made her wonder how he could see that in her. But maybe she could learn to give more of herself? Starting with her father, tomorrow.

CHAPTER TEN

The white stone cottage in the middle of the small village was just as she remembered it; a bold black door offset the white masonry walls, its porch decorated on either side with hanging baskets filled with vibrant spring flowers. The front garden, her father's pride and joy, had borders bursting with blooms of the new season, a tended lawn and stone path leading up to the front door. Liz took a deep breath and opened the gate. It was now or never.

Her knock echoed in her ears, but took a while to be answered.

'I'm sorry, I was out in the back,' the man said, opening the door.

Liz was stunned. Her dad looked so much older than she remembered, his face more lined, his sandy hair turned completely grey and balding on the top. He was wearing old gardening clothes; trousers baggy around the knees and the cuffs of his shirt were frayed.

'Hello, Dad.'

'Liz!' His face was a picture of shock, and he clutched onto the door frame as though he was trying to hold himself up. For a moment, he said nothing else, just stared and her, but eventually he smiled. 'Come in.'

The hallway was small but tidy. He led her through to a comfortable and cosy kitchen; too fussy for her liking, with flowered Austrian blinds and a dresser full of pottery, but homely.

'Would you like a cup of tea?'

'Please.'

'Sit down.'

She'd thought he might hug her, but no hug was forthcoming. Perhaps she shouldn't have been surprised as she hadn't seen him in over a year, and then only briefly. Did she even deserve to be hugged? Liz pulled out a wooden chair and sat down at the round pine table.

'Ruth not in?' she asked.

'No, her sister's not too good, so she's gone to look after her.'

'Oh. I hope she's okay.' She felt bad for Ruth, but part of her was relieved that she could speak to her dad alone.

Her father nodded but didn't reply, and she was glad he didn't immediately bring up the past and her reaction to Ruth coming into their lives.

'Shall we take these outside? It's such a nice day — a shame to waste it.'

Dutifully, she followed him into the garden. The long length of lawn was neat and green, and wouldn't have been out of place at the start of Wimbledon. The borders, like those in the front garden, were a riot of colour.

'Dad, this is amazing,'

He beamed with pride. 'All I ever wanted was a proper garden, but there was always too much to do on the farm. Now I'm retired, I can indulge myself.'

'It shows.' They sat down at the wooden garden table on the patio facing the lawn. Liz took a sip of tea as an awkward silence lingered. Eventually, her father broke it.

'So, to what do I owe the honour?'

'Dad!'

'Come off it, Liz. Your visits are few and far between.'

'I know,' she said, guilt engulfing her. 'I brought the kids back for Mel. They've been staying with me.'

'Yes, I heard.'

Liz thought his words seemed tinged with disapproval. 'Look, I'm sorry I haven't been to visit more often. I've been busy setting up my business. There never seems to be the time.'

He frowned. 'There's always time for family if you want to make it.'

'I can always leave if you don't want me here,' she said, standing up, feeling that their conversation was sliding into its old pattern.

'I never said that. Sit down.'

She lowered herself back into the chair and fiddled with the handle of her teacup.

'I'm glad you're here. We need to talk.'

'That's why I came.'

Silence descended again until her father said, 'You can't blame me any more than I blame myself, you know?'

She'd been about to come back with a smart retort, but managed to stop herself. 'I think we all blame ourselves in some way for what happened. But maybe we need to put the past behind us, remember the good things, not the bad,' she said instead.

Her father nodded, looking as surprised at her words as she was by saying them. She hadn't thought she'd be able to let it go so easily, but now she was here . . . it felt right. Perhaps it was that her father looked so much older — it made her feel she should cherish the time she had with him, not avoid it.

'Easier said than done, though. I've never been good with words. I've always been more of a doer,' he admitted.

'I know, but—'

'Let me get this off my chest,' he interrupted her. 'Just because I don't say things doesn't mean I don't feel them. It'll always be on my conscience that I wasn't there for Danny. Or you. I haven't been a very good father. In fact, the only one I seem to have got it right with is Mel. But I do love you.'

Liz felt a sob rising in her throat. 'I haven't been a great daughter either.'

'Come here.'

He wrapped her in his arms. He smelt like a mixture of sunshine and old tobacco, and instantly she was reminded of her childhood, when being wrapped in her father's arms had seemed to protect her from the world.

'Hey, hey don't cry.' He fumbled in his pocket and brought out his hanky.

'Sorry,' she said as she took it from him.

'No need to apologise. Shall I make some fresh tea?'

She nodded, glad of the chance to sit alone with her thoughts. When he came back and sat down, she asked, 'Are you happy, Dad?'

He nodded. 'Yes, I am. It's not been easy, what with everything. Ruth got me through the worst and I'm so glad to have her in my life. I know you thought I was moving on too quickly, but I couldn't have done it without her.'

'Then I'm glad for you,' Liz said, ashamed that she'd been so resentful. She'd been young and had jumped to conclusions, never stopping to see things from his point of view. This week was certainly making her face up to some painful realisations.

'What about you? Are you happy?' he asked.

It was a good question, and one she didn't really know the answer to. She'd spent so long fighting everything, she hadn't thought about happiness. She hadn't allowed herself to think of anything other than her ambition. It was only since she'd seen Alex again that she'd started to question her life.

'I'm doing okay,' she said eventually. 'The business is picking up.'

'That's good. And you're keeping well?'

'Yes.'

She noticed that he couldn't bring himself to talk about her anorexia directly. But then she wasn't good at talking about it either.

'You certainly look as though you are.'

'I have to work hard at it.'

'Yes, I suppose you do.' He paused as he took a sip of his tea. 'You know, I'll always regret what I said to you. I just didn't understand. But I've read a lot about the subject since . . .'

'Have you?'

He nodded. 'Yes, I needed to learn what you were going through, and you weren't here to tell me yourself. Perhaps, one day, you can tell me about it in your own words?'

She nodded. 'One day, yes.' She'd waited so long for this moment, for him to acknowledge her feelings. It was as though a weight had lifted. 'And in the meantime, I promise to visit more often.'

'Good.' He took her hand in his. 'Ruth would like to get to know you too.'

'Would she? I haven't been kind to her.'

'She understands. She's a very understanding woman.'

Liz heard a car pull up at the front of the house, then the sound of footsteps along the pathway to the side before Mel appeared at the gate.

'Hiya, you two.' She walked into the back garden. 'Sorry to drag you away, but I've come to give you a lift to the station. You'll miss your train if you don't hurry.'

'Of course.' Liz stood up but found she was reluctant to leave. There was so much left to be said, but perhaps it needed small steps. They'd built some bridges today, at least. 'I need to go now,' she said as she stooped to kiss her father on the cheek. 'But I'll sort something out so that I can come back for a proper visit soon.'

'I'd like that.'

'Me too.'

'I'll pick you up on the way back,' Mel called over her shoulder to their father. 'You are still coming to tea, aren't you?'

'Oh yes, I'll be coming to tea.'

* * *

'It looks as though it went well,' Mel commented as she drove to the station.

'It did. I suppose I should have done it a long time ago.' Her eyes started filling up again as she spoke so she changed the subject. 'So, how's it going with you?'

'Oh Liz, you wouldn't believe what a mess we're in.'

'That bad?'

'Yes.' Mel indicated to turn into the station car park, pulled into a space and turned off the engine. Then she looked at Liz. 'Simon wasn't having an affair at all. It's the practice that's in trouble. And I mean trouble! I honestly don't know why he let it go this far. I'm so angry with him for not telling me sooner. He says he kept hoping he could sort it out before he had to tell me, but it's too late for that now. It looks as though we might lose everything.' She burst into noisy sobs and Liz leaned over to give her a hug. When she was all cried out, Mel took a hanky out of her pocket and blew her nose.

'When you say "everything", what exactly do you mean?' Liz asked tentatively.

'He re-mortgaged the house and now he's struggling to make the repayments. No wonder he was always on at me to curb my spending.' Mel sighed. 'When I think about all the money I've frittered away, I feel so embarrassed. Half the stuff I've bought I've never even opened. So, the first thing I'm going to do is sell as much of it as I can on eBay. At least that way I'll feel like I'm doing my bit.'

Liz stared at her sister, genuinely shocked. Simon may have told her the trouble he was in, but he hadn't told her the extent of it. This was more than just Mel's spending habits. 'But is there anything else you can do?'

'I've already been into the office while no one was around. It's a real mess. Completely overstocked with medicines, so the ordering system is the first thing to tackle. We need to shop around to get the best deals. And there are bad debts too, which need to be called in. I'm going to be making a lot of difficult phone calls in the near future. But I'm determined to claw back whatever money we can to stop us from going bankrupt. I'm afraid we're going to have to make a couple of redundancies too, which I'm mortified about.'

'How are you going to fit all this in?' Liz asked, remembering their conversation earlier in the week, amazed at her sister's apparent transformation.

'I have no choice. We're going to sit the kids down and tell them a bit of what's happening. I wanted to give them everything, so they have all sorts of after-school activities going on. I'm hoping that, if we explain why we need to cut back, they'll pick their favourite things to do and let some of the others go. It's my fault because I've mollycoddled them, but we're a family in a crisis and we're going to have to get through it together.'

'I'm impressed. You seem to be handling this in the best way you can.'

'Lots of businesses are struggling. There's no shame in it. It's just the economy.'

Liz turned away so that her sister didn't see her smile. Mel had convinced herself that this could happen to the Jones too, and she was pleased that her sister hadn't had a complete personality transplant.

'Do you have to go back so soon?' Mel asked.

Liz nodded. She needed some time to herself to understand the conflicting emotions which were battering around in her head before she had to focus on work again. 'Afraid so.'

'I'm sure it'll be nice to have the flat to yourself again.'

'It's been wonderful spending time with you all,' Liz protested. 'But you have to admit, it *is* a small flat.'

Mel reached into the backseat and picked up a small book. 'Well, before you go, I thought you might like to have this.'

'Is this what I think it is?' Liz felt her mouth go dry.

'Danny's diary? Yes.'

Liz turned it over in her hands. 'Wow . . . I'm not sure if I'm brave enough to read this.'

'It's not an easy read,' Mel agreed. 'But take it with you anyway, and then you can decide what you want to do.'

'Yes, I will.' Liz placed it carefully in her handbag.

They hugged, said goodbye, and Liz got out of the car and walked towards the station. This week had been a real eye-opener, and one she already realised would change her life forever.

CHAPTER ELEVEN

All through the journey home, the diary seemed to burn a hole in her handbag. But she refused to be tempted to read it. She needed to be somewhere private when she plucked up the courage.

At home, she tidied up the living room and kitchen, then pulled off the sheets from the spare bed. Jay was working a late shift and wouldn't be back until much later so she'd have plenty of time to look at the diary, but she was procrastinating, putting off the moment when she'd read her brother's words. Eventually, she made herself a cup of tea, sat down in the living room and opened the book.

It's excruciating being with him every day, knowing how I feel about him. When he's close to me, when I can smell the scent of him, his citrus aftershave, it's all I can do not to reach out and touch him. I long to feel his strong arms around me, his lips on mine. Oh, it's just too much! But I know he'll never be mine. He would never love me, not like I want him to.

Liz sighed as she read the entry. She understood how her brother felt. Hadn't she felt the same so many years ago? She read on.

I know I should be concentrating on studying, or I'll mess up my finals and that will be three years down the drain, but I can't stop thinking about him. Yesterday, after too many vodkas in the student union, I nearly blurted out my feelings, but I stopped myself just in time. I'm afraid that if I told him I'd lose his friendship, and that's the last thing I want to do. Being around him might be excruciating but not having him in my life at all would be so much worse.

She read the next entry.

Tonight was the night of the May Ball. We'd all been looking forward to it for weeks and it was great to get dressed up. Alex already had a tux; as usual it was expensive and of the best quality, just like everything he wears. I didn't have one but he came with me to hire one. It was wonderful having some one-on-one time with him rather than being with him as part of a crowd. I'd really been looking forward to tonight, hoping we could have a laugh together but SHE put paid to that. Her name is Kas and she's been on the periphery of our crowd for ages, but Alex hadn't noticed her until tonight. Mind you, it was hard not to. She was wearing a red satin dress which pushed up her boobs, showed off her tiny waist and long legs. If I wasn't gay, I might have fancied her myself. I couldn't keep my eyes off them. I was so jealous. I feel like she just marched in and took him away from me. Which is mad because he was never mine in the first place. And never would be. I know deep down he would never have feelings for me, which is what hurts the most.

Liz put down the book and thought for a moment about her brother's words. It was so sad to see how unhappy he was, and tears pricked at her eyes at the thought that he never got the chance to live a full life and find a love that was returned. She took a sip of her tea, grimaced when she realised it had gone cold, and made a fresh mug before returning to read the next page.

I don't see him anymore. He and Kas are together all the time and he doesn't have the time of day for his old friends. I'm going to concentrate on studying from now on. Make the most of the time I have left here and get a decent degree.

And then:

They're engaged! Can you believe it? They've only been together for five minutes and already they're talking about spending the rest of their lives together. It will all end in tears, mark my words. I told him that too. He actually expected me to be happy for him. But how can I be when he's rushing into it? We ended up having a massive row and I stormed out. I doubt he'll ever speak to me again. Ah well, I was planning on leaving tomorrow anyway but I'm going to get an earlier train. My uni days are over and it's time to get on with the rest of my life . . .

So, Alex had been telling the truth? Every single word. She was so ashamed of what she'd said to him about Kas. She'd tried to apologise but somehow it didn't seem to be enough. She stifled a yawn and shut the diary. She wanted to read on and find out if Danny's entries would explain why he'd led her to believe that Alex had betrayed him, but it would have to wait. It had been an exhausting day, both physically and emotionally, and right now all she wanted to do was sleep.

* * *

Liz peeled and diced the shallots, blinking back the tears at the strength of the onions. Although she was only cooking for six, the menu was complicated, and as some of the dishes were Tia's suggestions, they weren't familiar to her. Tia had been fussing over the menu all week, changing her mind so frequently that Liz was almost pulling her hair out. She'd been dreading tonight as she was sure that Alex would be here, but she doubted there would be an opportunity for her to speak to him properly. She just hoped the atmosphere wouldn't be too awkward as she needed all her focus for her work.

She'd read the rest of Danny's diary on Monday morning. There were several entries about how miserable he felt being back at home, how he was still pining for Alex and how much their dad was getting on his nerves. There was an entry the day after he'd spoken to Liz about Alex, explaining how drunk he had been and maudlin; how he'd gone on about Alex betraying him. Now sober, he'd been ashamed at his outburst because none of it was Alex's fault. He'd written a goodbye note to Alex but then torn it out and put it in the back of his diary. He knew he would never send it, but by writing it he hoped it would give him closure so that he could get on with his life. Liz had breathed a sigh of relief when she'd read that, knowing, finally, she hadn't got it wrong or misinterpreted what Danny had told her. After that entry, Danny seemed to pull himself together. His results came through and he was pleased to receive a 2:1. There were more entries about job applications, and then about the job he desperately wanted in London — which he'd found out he'd got on the morning of his accident. Mel had been right — his death hadn't been suicide but a stupid, senseless accident, killing a young man who had everything to live for.

Liz took a deep breath and focused back on the dishes she was preparing. If only she could smooth things over with Alex, she might finally be able to put the past behind her. But for now, work must come first. She needed tonight to be a success.

She slid the shallots into a bowl, covered it in cling film and put it to one side. Then she started on the fresh egg pasta for the smoked mozzarella ravioli she was serving for the starter. It had always been one of Roberto's favourite dishes at La Emporium, and Tia had told her it was special to her guest too. It was a tricky dish and would take all her concentration.

Time passed quickly while she was cooking, and before she knew it the first of the guests were arriving. She moved the six glasses of lavender and blackberry mousse from the freezer into the fridge and glanced at the kitchen clock. She had half an hour before she needed to serve the starters. The tomato sauce for the ravioli only needed reheating. She just had to finish the basil cream for the starter, cook the ravioli and plate up. So far, today had gone without mishap. She only hoped she'd sealed the ravioli sufficiently so that it didn't come apart in the pan. She'd made a few extra just in case but wouldn't have time to make a fresh batch of pasta if it all went wrong.

Liz cleaned down her work surfaces and began to organise herself for the final push. This was the time she liked most; just before a function when everything had to come together and the adrenaline kicked in.

'How are we doing?' Tia asked twenty minutes later as Liz was gently heating the basil cream sauce. Beside it, a pan of water for the ravioli was bubbling nicely. She was hot and sweaty but bang on time.

'No problems.' She smiled at her client, who was looking spectacular in a skin-tight, navy-blue dress.

'Good. I'll get everyone a drink and settle them all at the table. Just need some more champers.' Tia opened the fridge door and pulled out a bottle.

When Tia had gone, Liz took the ravioli out of the fridge and offered a silent prayer as she gently lowered the pasta into the water. Slowly, they bobbed to the surface, and to her relief, didn't split open. Mentally uncrossing her fingers, she successfully cooked the rest of the pasta, covered it in the fresh tomato sauce and then drizzled the basil cream around the edges of the plates. Satisfied, she placed them on a tray and carefully took them through to the dining room.

She looked up as she entered the room and nearly dropped the tray. She'd been worried about how she'd react if Alex was at the table, and sure enough, there he was with the dark-haired beauty she had previously seen at Tia's sitting closely beside him. It wasn't Alex's presence that had startled her, though, but that of her old boss, Roberto, from

72

La Emporium. Why hadn't Tia warned her? How would he react to being served one of his own signature dishes? Would he think she'd stolen his recipe and was passing it off as her own? With trembling hands, she began to put the plates down in front of each guest.

'This looks good.' Roberto examined the pasta gently with his fork. 'A variation on one of my own themes, I think.'

Liz stopped in front of Alex's partner.

'Yes.' Tia saved her. 'I love that dish so much, I asked Liz to make it in your honour.'

Liz relaxed, but as she did the plate nearly slid from her hand.

'Hey, watch out!' Nikki exclaimed, just as Liz corrected the plate and put it down in front of her.

'Nikki!' Alex hissed. 'Shush.'

'Don't shush me. This dress cost a fortune and I don't want it ruined.'

'I'm sorry,' Liz said, her face flushed with embarrassment as she put the last plate down in front of Alex.

'Thank you.' He caught her eye and smiled.

The flush spread further as she turned to collect the now empty tray.

'Ah, don't go yet,' Roberto ordered, and Liz forced herself to stand awkwardly at the edge of the room. Roberto placed a second forkful of the dish in his mouth and considered it for a moment, frowning in concentration. 'It's similar, yes, but different. Tangier, I think. The basil cream seems stronger.'

'Too much basil?' Liz asked, unable to help herself.

Roberto shook his head. 'No, it's perfect.'

'Really?'

'Yes, although I hate to admit it. I didn't think this dish could be improved. What are you cooking for the main?'

'Roast cod with clams, bacon mash and shallot sauce.'

'Sounds interesting. And dessert?'

'Lavender mousse with blackberry sauce and a brandy snap toile.'

'Good.' He nodded. 'I'll look forward to both.'

Back in the kitchen, Liz nearly bubbled over with excitement, scarcely able to believe that a two-star Michelin chef had told her she'd improved one of his dishes. She couldn't let it go to her head, though. She still had a main course and a dessert to produce.

* * *

The evening had gone like a dream, Liz reflected, as she loaded up the dishwasher with the dessert plates. Although scary at first, Roberto enjoyed the main course and had congratulated her again on the dessert. Earlier, she'd wished that Tia had forewarned her about her guest, but thinking about it, it was probably better that she hadn't had time to panic. Tonight had drawn a line under her employment at La Emporium. She'd always respected Roberto and wanted him to think well of her. At least now he could judge her on her merits, if not on her personality. She wondered why he was here, though. She knew Tia dined often at La Emporium but hadn't realised they knew each other so well. Mind you, it was hardly surprising. Tia seemed to know everyone.

The only downside to the evening was having to see Alex with his uppity girlfriend, Nikki. She certainly looked like a top model; tall and skinny, with perfect features and glossy dark hair. In fact, she looked a bit like a younger, thinner version of Tia. Nikki might have the looks, but she wasn't a nice person. At least not to the hired help. Liz had forced a smile whenever she'd served her, but Nikki had only glared at her in response.

She pushed the thought of Alex and Nikki away. Work was her priority. Those few words of praise from Roberto had given her heaps of confidence. From now on, her business could only grow stronger.

* * *

Roberto leant back in his chair and smiled.

'Thank you, Tia. That was a wonderful meal.'

'I'm glad you enjoyed it. Liz and I worked together on the menu.'

'And you certainly have good taste,' Roberto remarked.

It irked Alex that Tia was taking most of the credit for Liz's talent. He'd enjoyed every mouthful, unlike Nikki, who'd picked and complained her way through the meal. *Nikki*. He drew in his breath as he thought about her. She'd barely left his side all night, and her high-handed manner towards Liz had aggravated him. He'd been relieved when, obviously briefed by Tia, Frazier, Tia's sometimes companion, had drawn Nikki and Roberto's wife to one side to admire Tia's latest art acquisition. At least they could talk business in private without her hanging on every word.

'Good taste, contacts and, of course, money. But that's just me. Alex has the property know how. I don't think the three of us could fail.'

At the mention of his name, Alex forced himself to concentrate on the immediate conversation.

'I admire your confidence,' Roberto said. 'And I have been giving careful consideration to your proposition. I'm not sure it's the right time for me to expand at the moment, though.' His mouth twitched as he said the words and he looked over at his wife. As though sensing his gaze, she turned, excused herself from the other two, and came over to him.

Roberto snaked his arm around her back and pulled her closer to him. 'I was about to tell our friends here our news.'

Without waiting for him to carry on, Maria interrupted excitedly. 'Roberto and I are expecting!'

'Oh . . . congratulations,' Tia said. 'When are you due?'

'The fifteenth of October,' Maria replied, beaming with pride.

Alex jolted at their conversation, suddenly remembering when he and Kas had made the same announcement. Despite the pain of the recollection, he followed Tia and congratulated them warmly.

'I see what you mean about the timing,' Tia said, the note of disappointment clear in her voice. 'I'm sorry. If I'd known, I wouldn't have asked you.'

'Well, I haven't said no yet. I've got some talented chefs coming through, chefs who might go elsewhere if I don't present them with a challenge. I want to take a step back from the kitchen, so this may be just the thing. The restaurant needs to open quickly, though. Preferably before the baby's born.'

'That shouldn't be a problem,' Tia said, the smile returning to her face.

'It depends on the property,' Alex interrupted, hoping Tia wasn't about to get too carried away. 'Especially if we need planning permission and extensive renovations.'

'Of course it does. Have you viewed any properties yet?' Roberto asked.

'A few, but so far nothing suitable.'

Roberto nodded. 'Come back to me when you have a definite timescale and we can talk again.'

'Over to you, Alex. The sooner the better.' Tia grinned at him.

'No pressure then? Thanks, Tia,' Alex said, and Tia and Roberto laughed.

Alex forced himself to join in with them, despite the fact that he felt anything but joyful as the memories of Kas and their unborn child flooded through him.

CHAPTER TWELVE

The music in Crystal's pounded through Alex's head as he watched Nikki gyrate on the dance floor, completely oblivious to her surroundings. He'd never been very good at dancing and needed to be in the right mood. Tonight was definitely not that night. The dull, repetitive beat was claustrophobic and he wished he could escape. But, of course, he couldn't abandon Nikki, however tempting that might be. He'd have preferred to have gone home after the meal at Tia's, but Nikki had insisted — and he hadn't wanted to be alone with her. But it had been a mistake to prolong the evening. He wished he hadn't let Tia steamroller him into inviting Nikki to dinner, and wished even more that he'd ended their relationship before now.

Alex sighed as he drained his glass. This evening had been a step too far, the final straw being in the taxi when she'd derided Roberto and Maria's announcement.

'Did you see the way they were grinning like imbeciles?' she'd scoffed. 'Don't they realise it's an end, not a beginning? They'll be tied to the child for the rest of their lives. Yuck! Not for me.'

And not for me either, Alex thought. He tried his best to be happy for other people when they had children, but he still had to work hard to overcome the memories it raked up. Amanda, a cousin of his who lived in London, had given birth three months ago to a beautiful baby boy. And while he adored Sebastian and was so happy for Amanda and her husband, he couldn't help feeling a stab of jealousy whenever he held the baby in his arms. Thinking she was helping him, Amanda had asked him to be godfather at a christening which was due to take place at the weekend. He had accepted, although he was partly dreading the day which he knew he would find painful. But being a godfather looked like the nearest he would get to having a child — for the time-being, at least. And he certainly wouldn't want to have a child with Nikki. He'd wondered how she could say that in front of him, knowing that he had lost his own child. But then he realised that she might not even know. He'd never confided in her about the things that mattered to him most, so unless someone else had told her, Nikki was more than likely completely unaware that he had lost a much-wanted baby.

He remembered coming home from a long day at work to the apartment he shared with Kas. Usually such an untidy person, he'd been surprised to find that she's cleaned up so that everything was spotless. There was a delicious smell coming from the kitchen. The table was set for dinner and she had even lit candles.

'What's all this for?' he asked, surprised at the uncharacteristic show of domesticity. He loved Kas to bits but she was no domestic goddess. In fact, it was usually him who cooked and kept on top of the household chores.

She wrapped her arms around him and kissed him passionately. 'Are you complaining?' she teased as she pulled away.

'Not at all. Especially when you greet me like that.'

She led him to the sofa and they sat down. 'I've decided that I need to be more of a responsible adult.'

'Why?' he asked. 'I like you the way you are.'

'Because,' she'd paused, 'we're going to have extra responsibilities from now on.'

'We are?'

'Yes.' She reached over to the table at the side of the sofa, picked something up and handed it to him.

His eyes widened in surprise when he realised it was a pregnancy test. 'You're not?'

She grinned. 'I am. Or rather *we* are. We're expecting a baby.'

He couldn't remember ever being as happy as he was at that moment. He'd wanted to wrap Kas in his arms and protect her and the growing baby inside her from the outside world.

And what a mess I made of that. Alex shook his head to clear the memory away. And now he was in another mess. *But not for much longer*, he decided. He put down his glass and walked over to the dance floor.

'Ah, you've come to dance,' Nikki cried, clutching hold of him.

He wriggled out of her grasp. 'No, Nik. Let's go.'

She pouted at him. 'But it's early yet. Too soon for bed unless, of course . . . naughty boy!' She giggled as she allowed herself to be propelled towards the exit.

They took a cab back to her apartment.

'Do you want a nightcap or are you too impatient?' Nikki whispered into his ear as they walked into the living room. She wound her arms around his neck and pushed her body close to his. Despite his determination to finish with her, Alex felt himself reacting. He took a step back.

'Neither, Nik. I'm sorry.'

'What?'

'Why don't we sit down?'

'I'd rather lie down,' she tried again, throwing her arms around his neck once more. As he pulled them away for the second time, she took a step back, her face full of hurt. 'You're dumping me, aren't you?'

'I'm sorry. It's just not working for me.'

'Why? What's the matter? Is there someone else?'

'No, there's no one else,' he said, thinking of Liz. But there was nothing between them and nothing to feel guilty about.

'Then what is it? Don't tell me you don't fancy me because I can't believe that.' She ran her hand down his leg, but he sidestepped away from her.

'Who could not fancy you?'

'Then what?'

'It's just not working. I'm sorry. I want to love you and I've tried to, but I don't. And you deserve better.'

'Oh, that old chestnut,' she scoffed. 'It's not you, it's me, when really it's the other way round.'

'It's not that at all. This is for the best. You'll see.' He turned to go, but she barred his escape.

'You should let me be the judge of what's best for me.'

He shook his head sadly. 'I'm only trying to be honest.' He turned his back on her, but she grabbed hold of his arm.

'No! Don't go.'

Her pain brought a lump to his throat, and as she clutched at him, he felt his arms close around her.

'I'm sorry, Nik. You're a beautiful girl and I never wanted to hurt you.' Gently, he eased himself away from her.

She stared at him, her hands hanging limply by her sides. She didn't move as he opened the front door, but just as he closed it behind him, he heard her say, 'Don't think this is over, Alex, because it's not.'

He turned and carried on walking.

CHAPTER THIRTEEN

Liz had been up for hours working on the food for a christening. Most of the preparation was done, but the cake was still causing her problems.

Cake decorating wasn't her forte, and if she'd had any sense, she'd have bought one in. When she'd taken the booking, though, she'd had a foolish notion that she should improve her skills and thought she'd have plenty of time to experiment. That was before Tia's time-consuming dinner party.

She'd baked the cake the day before, a gooey chocolate confection, and now she was trying to apply a chocolate frosting to its sides. The aim was "messy chic", but as Liz stepped back to assess her efforts, she had the awful feeling the only thing she'd created was "messy".

She put the palette knife down in disgust. She was running late with no more time to waste. Hopefully, when she added the decorations — presents made out of coloured moulding icing and a pale blue crib — it would look so much better. She'd have to attach them to the cake when she got to the venue and hope for the best.

The Sunday traffic was light, and when she pulled up outside the Victorian house in Maida Vale, she was pleased to find a nearby parking space. She quickly unloaded her van, and was soon taking everything in through the massive hallway to the kitchen.

Once inside, she took a quick peek into the dining room. As requested, they had placed the right number of chairs under the table. On the dresser, to the side of the room, was a selection of crockery, cutlery and glassware. She glanced at her watch, hoping that Emma, who she'd booked to help her today, wouldn't be long. She wanted to get the room set up so that she could concentrate on the food.

As she returned to the kitchen, her phone rang. Emma's croaky voice came through on the other end. 'Liz, I'm really sorry but I've got the lurgy. I can't come in today.'

'Couldn't you have let me know earlier?' Liz cried out in disappointment.

'I was hoping I'd be okay, but I woke up this morning feeling even worse than yesterday. I've been trying to find a replacement for you, but no joy.'

'Okay, well, thanks for trying, anyway,' she said more softly. 'I hope you're feeling better soon.'

'I'm *really* sorry. I do hate letting you down.'

'I know.' Emma was usually true to her word. She must be feeling really ill if she was calling in sick. She was just going to have to do this one on her own. 'You just concentrate on getting better,' she said before hanging up and hurriedly going to set up the table.

White linen, sparkling crystal and cutlery, and small vases of delicate cornflowers supplied by the florist that morning provided the perfect setting for the little boy's christening. Liz took a step back and admired her handiwork. She nodded to herself in approval and headed to the kitchen to start cooking. Time was running out.

* * *

Liz smoothed back her hair, which was slipping out of her ponytail, and washed her hands under the cold tap to cool herself down. She checked her watch. The guests should be arriving soon. Right on cue, she heard the front door open and the happy chatter of people in the hallway. She took a deep breath and went out to greet them.

'Ah Liz, you're here. Is everything alright? It smells wonderful, by the way.'

Liz smiled at her pretty client. Amanda was in her mid-thirties, the wife of a financier. She had short, curly, brown hair, smiling eyes and a kind of understated elegance, which she wore like a regal cloak. Liz had worked for her previously and always found her pleasant.

'Everything's fine,' she said. 'In fact, the starters will be ready in about thirty minutes. I thought that would give everyone time to have a drink first.'

'That's perfect.' She turned as the door opened. 'Ah, here comes the man himself.'

The baby, swathed in white silk, was carried through the door in the arms of his father. Amanda reached out to take him in her arms.

'Did the christening go okay?' Liz asked.

'Like a dream,' Amanda said, her eyes fixed on her child. 'Sebastian was perfect, didn't cry one bit.'

The front door banged open. 'Where do you want me to put the buggy?' a rich male voice asked. A rich male voice Liz instantly recognised. She looked up and stared straight into the eyes of Alexander Sinclaire. Her stomach lurched and her heart started to beat faster. *What is he doing here? That's all I need!* She tore her eyes away from him, made her excuses and hurried back into the kitchen. Safely inside the kitchen, she fetched the tray of tian of crab which she'd put in the fridge earlier to set. With the plates garnished, all she had to do now was to remove the ring moulds from the delicate white meat and avocado bases and position them on the individual plates. She just hoped they'd set properly and didn't collapse when they were out of the rings.

'Come on, Liz. You can do this,' she muttered to herself as she began to plate up.

'It's not a good sign, you know?'

'What?' She spun round to see Alex standing in the doorway with an empty champagne bottle in his hand.

'Talking to yourself.'

She stared at him, open-mouthed, unable to think of a suitable response. How did he always manage to wrong-foot her? The shy schoolgirl yet again.

'I just came to get some more fizz,' he continued when she didn't answer.

'It's in the fridge.' She turned back to her task, carefully placing another tian delicately on its plate.

'Are you okay? Is there anything I can do to help?'

Why was he always asking if he could help her? Did he think she was incapable?

'No, thanks. I can manage.' Her words were harsher than she'd intended, and as she looked up, she saw him purse his lips in annoyance.

'Of course you can,' he said and walked out of the kitchen.

She could have kicked herself. She wanted to make things better between them, not worse, but he'd caught her by surprise. Yet again. Why, after all these years, did he suddenly keep turning up everywhere she went? It was almost as if he was stalking her.

Liz returned to her task, made harder because her hands were now shaking. She must get a grip on herself. Any minute now, she'd have to go in there and serve the food. She didn't want any near misses with the guests' clothes like last week. She drizzled coriander oil around the edges of the plates and took the first batch into the dining room. Alex looked up as she entered, but she refused to meet his eye. Instead, she efficiently presented the plates of crab and retreated to collect the rest of the starters.

* * *

'This food is just gorgeous,' Amanda declared as she pushed a perfectly cooked flake of seabass onto her fork. Alex had to agree. Each time he'd eaten Liz's food, it had been exceptional. He was beginning to think he'd underestimated her when he'd thought she was inexperienced. The fact that she had single-handedly served up two courses to twelve people also proved she could work under pressure. The food had been delivered so efficiently, it was as though a team of people were working behind the scenes. She was clearly still angry with him, though. Her curt responses whenever he'd tried to start a conversation made that obvious. He just wished he could talk to her properly. He still had so many questions about Danny and what had happened to him. Normally, he didn't care what people thought of him — if they didn't like him, that was their problem — but with Liz, it was different.

Again, he remembered when he used to stay with Danny during the holidays. Liz had seemed like such a child to him then — someone he used to tease but forgot about easily, never someone he ever imagined he'd be attracted to. But he *was* attracted to her, and found himself a little more each time he saw her. It disturbed him how many times thoughts of her popped into his head when he wasn't with her.

Justin stood up to get some more wine, and Alex was instantly on his feet. 'Here, let me do that. You relax and enjoy yourself while Seb's asleep.'

'Thanks.' Justin handed Alex the empty bottle and sat back down. 'I knew there was a reason we asked you to be Sebastian's godfather.'

Alex smiled, glad to be doing something. The obvious love that Justin and Amanda had for each other and for their child was bittersweet to him. He and Amanda had grown up together in their early years, but drifted apart as teenagers. Like Tia, she'd been a rock to him since his return to London, and he genuinely enjoyed being in both her and Justin's company. He was glad that she had found someone she loved and who loved her, and he was so proud of the mother she had become. But today was stirring uncomfortable emotions in him. His own child would be a toddler by now, and he couldn't help wondering what he or she would have been like. His eyes welled at the thought, and he turned away. The last thing he wanted was to spoil this happy day.

'Won't be tick,' he managed to say in a voice that was little more than a croak.

He opened the kitchen door — and there she was in front of him again. The woman he had been unable to keep from his mind since that night at Tia's. She was so focused on her work, she didn't even see him. In front of her was an enormous chocolate cake, which she was carefully adding decorations to. She lifted something delicate in her hands, placed it carefully in the centre of the cake, and stood back, frowning to assess her work.

'It looks beautiful — a work of art.'

She jumped at his words and looked up at him, confused. 'Sorry, I didn't realise you were standing there. Again.'

'You were concentrating so hard; I didn't want to disturb you. Can I have a look?'

'Of course.' She nodded, and he saw a faint blush rise in her cheeks.

'Oh, I see. It's a baby in a crib,' he said, looking more closely. 'What's it made of?'

'Moulding icing.'

He stepped forward. 'It's exquisite,' he said, admiring the detail. 'Where did you get this from?'

'I made it,' she said hesitantly.

'You did?'

'Yes. I must admit, it was a bit of a challenge. I haven't done much confectionary work. It took me a few goes to get it right. But in the end, I think it's turned out okay.'

'It's more than okay, it's magnificent.'

'Thank you.'

He stood up and looked at her closely. 'Liz, I just wanted to say that I'm really sorry for the other night at Tia's. I wasn't expecting to see you there and it caught me on the hop.'

The colour rose even more in her cheeks, and Alex's heart did a little jitter in his chest. He loved the fact that she was so modest. A breath of fresh air.

'Actually, I'm sorry as well. It's been a shock for me too, seeing you after all these years.'

'Apology accepted.'

She looked away, seemingly unable to hold his gaze. 'Did you come in for some more wine?'

'Yes, Justin will wonder where I've got to. I'd better take it through.'

'Have you finished the main course?'

'More or less.'

'I'll clear the plates.'

'I'll take this in and give you a hand.'

It felt strange them being so polite with each other, strained even. 'There's no need, I can manage. And you're a guest.'

'I know you can manage, but I'd like to,' he replied pointedly. 'Amanda is used to me pitching in. She won't mind.'

'Thanks then,' she said as she went into the dining room.

* * *

Liz was glad that she didn't have much more to do other than clear the plates and deliver the cake to the guests. It had been nerve-wracking knowing Alex was in the next room, especially as Emma wasn't here to serve the food. But it had all worked out, and she just hoped the cake tasted as good as it looked.

Alex's apology had surprised her and she was more than a little pleased by it. Few people would have admitted that they'd spoken hastily, and it had taken him up in her estimation.

The last week had certainly changed her perspective. She hadn't realised it before, but she'd allowed the past to keep her in its grip, and although she'd fooled herself that she was striving towards her future, she'd still been holding herself back. *Not anymore.*

'I can stay and help you clear up,' Alex offered as Liz brought in the last of the plates.

'No, you mustn't,' she replied. 'I'm just about to take the cake in. You have to be there for that.'

'Yes, of course. But before I do, can I just ask . . . will you come out for a meal with me one night? It would be good to talk when you're not working.'

'What would Nikki say about that?' The words slipped out before she could stop them. What did Nikki have to do with anything? He'd obviously only want to talk about Danny.

'Nikki and I have split up.'

'Oh,' she said in surprise. 'That was sudden. You seemed so together on Thursday.'

He shook his head. 'It wasn't working. I ended it later that night.'

Liz couldn't believe how pleased she felt at his words. 'Well, in that case, yes. I'd like to have a chance to talk to you properly.'

'Are you free tomorrow night?'

'Um . . . okay.'

'Great. I'll pick you up at yours. Seven o'clock?'

'Yes, that's great,' she said, hoping she wasn't setting herself up for more heartache.

CHAPTER FOURTEEN

Liz spent Monday in nervous anticipation of the meal with Alex. Her first concern was what she would wear. She didn't have an extensive wardrobe, as most of the time she wore either chef's whites or casual clothes. Her suits were too formal and clothes she wore for clubbing entirely unsuitable for a dinner date.

Date. Was it really a date? Years ago, she'd have passed out with excitement if Alex had suggested they go out for a meal, but today she was filled with so many conflicting feelings. She kept telling herself that he just wanted to talk about her brother and tried to ignore the fact that he'd split up with his girlfriend.

Just as she was giving up all hope on the contents of her wardrobe, she remembered the dress Mel had bought her the week before. She hadn't even tried it on. She'd actually tried to take it back, but as she didn't have the card it had been bought with, the shop had refused. Liz slipped it off the hanger and held it out in front of her. It was perfect, even more so when she tried it on. The dark green satin clung to all the right places without being obvious, and she decided that it was the type of dress that could be worn anywhere. Liz smiled at herself in the mirror and silently thanked her sister. She would find some way to repay her for the gift; a way that didn't offend her.

The buzzer sounded as she was applying her lipstick, and nervously she answered it. Alex stood, fresh and handsome in a light blue linen shirt and navy chinos.

'Wow, you look fantastic,' he said as he eyed her dress. 'I knew you'd scrub up well.'

'Excuse me!' She feigned astonishment and then burst out laughing. 'Well, I suppose it's a change from my chef's whites.'

'You'd look good in anything,' he said. She blushed and looked away. 'I don't suppose you're ready, are you?' he asked, and the awkwardness was broken.

'Yes, of course. You said seven.'

'Yes, but . . .' He laughed.

'What?'

'It's just that a lot of women I know wouldn't take that literally. But I'm glad you did. Come on, I've got a taxi waiting downstairs.'

He instructed the driver to take them to Ristorante Angelo in Fitzrovia when they'd climbed into the taxi. Then he turned to her. 'Is that okay? Or is going to a restaurant a bit of a busman's holiday for you?'

'Not at all. I love eating out, but don't often get the chance. I've never been to that restaurant before. Italian, I presume?'

'Yes, and very good too.'

'Maybe it will give me inspiration for some new dishes.'

'I hope you won't be thinking about work all night.'

'No, of course not,' she said, then added, 'We have other things to talk about.'

A while later, the taxi stopped outside an ordinary looking Italian restaurant by the side of a busy road. Momentarily, she was disappointed. It certainly didn't look like the sort of upmarket place he'd take his model girlfriends. Inside, it looked like a traditional Italian, warm and cosy with delicious smells. If the food tasted as good as it smelt, then perhaps that's why he had chosen it.

'Ah, Mr Sinclaire. So nice to see you again.' A waiter greeted him at the door and smiled at them both. 'We have your favourite table downstairs,' he added as he led them down the stone staircase to the basement restaurant, where the atmosphere was completely different. She gasped as she took in the stone walls and arches, enormous chandeliers, and little nooks and crannies where secluded tables were set with white linen tablecloths, napkins, and shining glass and silverware. The whole place oozed romance and Liz was momentarily stunned.

'It's fabulous, isn't it?' Alex said quietly. 'Some restaurants these days are so noisy you can't hear each other talk.'

She nodded. That's what he wanted to do. Talk. 'It's lovely.'

'And the food is excellent. I wanted to bring you somewhere you'd be impressed by the food. Not an easy task.'

'Not having to cook it myself is impressive enough for me.'

The waiter led them to a table in one of the more secluded nooks. Alex pulled out the chair for her and she smiled at him as she sat down, although she felt her nerves rising.

He ordered wine while Liz concentrated on the menu, more to hide the fact that her conversational skills had deserted her. Everything on the menu looked wonderful, and she was spoilt for choice.

'Do you eat here a lot?' she asked. 'The waiter seemed pleased to see you.'

'I've eaten here a few times, yes.'

'Do you have any particular favourites on the menu?'

'The pear and blue cheese salad is great as a starter, and the roast poussin with wild mushrooms is delicious.'

'I haven't had poussin for a while and the starter sounds good too,' she said, shutting her menu.

He did the same, and the silence between them elongated.

'It's good to see you when you're not in work mode,' Alex said eventually.

'Or screaming abuse at you.'

'You had your reasons.'

'At the time, I thought they were very good reasons . . . but now I'm not so sure.' Her mouth was suddenly dry and she reached for a glass of water.

'Go on.'

'It's a long story.'

'We've got all night,' he said, smiling at her.

His smile made her feel like she was melting, and she took a deep breath to steady herself. After all these years of hating him, now she desperately wanted him to like her. It was an unusual feeling. When the waiter had taken their order and retreated, she plucked up the courage to say what was on her mind. 'First of all, I want to apologise again about what I said about your wife. I was out of order.'

He nodded. 'I think I backed you into a corner. And I could have reacted better. Storming out was childish. I do regret that.'

'Do you?' Her heart started to thump in her chest.

'Yes. Because it left so many unanswered questions.'

'Yes, of course,' she replied, disappointed. He was making it obvious that this dinner was all about Danny. She mustn't let her own feelings get carried away. The waiter arrived with the wine and they were silent as he poured it. When they were alone again, she carried on. 'When you left my apartment the other Sunday, did you notice anyone coming in?'

He frowned. 'Yes, a woman and two children.'

'That was my sister, Mel, and my niece and nephew.'

'Mel?' He looked at her in surprise. 'That was Mel and her kids?'

'Yes, Sophie and Ben. They're nine and six. She's a great mum.'

'She was always looking after stray animals on the farm.'

Liz smiled. 'She still does. Her husband's a vet, so there's plenty of opportunity to collect waifs and strays.'

'I'll bet. It would have been nice to catch up with her.'

'We weren't exactly at the point of offering friendly invitations.' Liz tried to make a joke out of it but he remained serious.

'No, I don't suppose we were.'

'Anyway, she stayed for a few days and we talked about Danny. Seeing you brought everything to the surface, and it turns out that we remember things very differently.' She paused and took a sip of her wine to ease the constriction in her throat. Her voice broke a little as she continued. 'I idolised Danny but Mel saw things more clearly. We've never been able to speak about it until now.'

'I thought you two were really close?'

'We used to be,' she admitted. 'But I have to confess that I've kept my distance in recent years.'

'Why?'

She sighed. She wasn't going to tell him the truth, that being with her family reminded her of her illness. Instead, she said, 'I suppose because I've found it all too painful.'

'That's such a shame.'

'Yes. But maybe things can be different now.'

The food arrived and Liz was grateful for the space it gave her, as she felt she was doing all the talking. The salad she'd ordered was delicious; the pear, walnuts and blue cheese an excellent combination.

When she put down her knife and fork, Alex was watching her. 'What actually happened, Liz?' he asked suddenly.

She took a deep breath and told him everything. When she'd finished, she added, 'I'm so sorry. Danny made it sound as though you knew how much he loved you and that you'd knocked him back rather cruelly. He was heartbroken, but then he always was a bit of a drama queen.'

When she'd come to the part in his diary about him writing the goodbye note, she'd re-read the note she'd shown Melissa. It was totally clear now that it wasn't a letter declaring his intentions to leave them all, although the way it was worded had made it easy to think that. It was a relief to know that it was just his way of moving on from unrequited love.

'I'd agree with you there,' Alex said, interrupting her thoughts. 'We had some real humdingers over the years.'

'Especially the night you announced your engagement?'

* * *

93

Alex took a sip of his wine before he answered her. He remembered so vividly that last night at university. 'I've been thinking about that since I bumped into you. I suppose I didn't really see what was going on under my nose. I was too in love.'

'With Kas?'

'Yes. We got together at the May Ball and we just clicked. From then on, there was no stopping us.'

He recalled how wonderful life seemed then. His entire future was ahead of him. He'd had big plans to move back to Dubai, and he had a good job lined up. When he'd first met Kas, he couldn't believe that she also came from Dubai. Like him, she'd been sent to boarding school in the UK and had wanted to stay in the country to do a degree in art, but she was more than happy to go back to her family so that they could be together. Life was perfect and he'd felt that nothing could go wrong. What a mistake that had been.

'I was so sure about Kas that we got engaged really quickly. Danny was furious. I thought it was because he felt we were moving too fast, but now I realise that wasn't the whole story. He never let on, though. Like I said, I had no idea how he felt about me.'

'Yes, I get that now.'

'We had a massive row that night and he stormed off. I decided to give him a chance to cool down, but when I went round the next morning, he'd gone. Packed up and left. I never saw him again.'

Liz leant forward, put her hand over his and he felt a frisson of excitement at her touch.

'I'm sorry,' she said. 'I really got the wrong end of the stick.'

'I can understand why. But I did hurt Danny, whether I meant to or not. When Kas and I got together, I never wanted to be apart from her. I neglected my friends and I wish I hadn't. I'll always feel guilty about that. At that age, you think you have all the time in the world. When Danny spoilt the announcement of our engagement, I was furious with him. I was even more furious when I found he'd done a disappearing act. But I never for one moment thought that we wouldn't have the time to re-build those bridges. If I'd known what would happen, I'd have tried harder.'

'It's easy to see with the benefit of hindsight. I'm sure we'd all have done things differently if we'd known what was about to happen,' she said softly.

He smiled, glad that they had sorted out their differences.

'What happened with Kas?' she asked. When he didn't reply, she added, 'Sorry. You don't have to tell me if it's too painful.'

He blinked back the tears which were already welling in his eyes. He wasn't going to fall apart in front of her.

'It's not something I find easy to talk about,' he said, but then rushed on before he lost his nerve. 'She died of sepsis. It was all very sudden. She'd cut her finger, and then she started to feel unwell. I didn't realise how serious that was. My head was full of a property I was trying to buy, but if I'd paid more attention . . .' He faltered. 'By the time I got to the hospital, it was too late.'

'Oh Alex . . . I'm so sorry!'

He was about to tell her that it wasn't just Kas he had lost that night, but by the look of shock on her face, he decided he'd said enough. 'No, I'm sorry. I didn't mean it to come out quite like that.'

'It's okay, I understand.' Her hand squeezed his.

'I suppose if anyone can understand, you can. You've been through a lot too.'

* * *

They sat in silence for a moment, each lost in their own thoughts. Liz had come here tonight prepared to make amends, but she hadn't anticipated the depth of feeling she was experiencing now. They'd both been through so much, but neither of them could speak fully about it. The waiter cleared their plates, and in an attempt to lighten the mood, she said, 'I'm glad we've had a chance to clear the air, but maybe we should talk about something else before we get too downhearted?'

'Yes, let's.' He smiled and she could see the relief wash over his face. 'Tell me a bit more about yourself. Do you live with someone? The guy who let me in last week?'

'Jay, yes. He's a fellow chef. He's just split up with his girlfriend, so he's staying with me until they either get back together again or he finds something more permanent. He's desperate to get back with her, though. I hope they work it out. Much as I love him, I prefer having the flat to myself.'

As she spoke, she couldn't help noticing Alex smile, which gave her a sudden feeling of exhilaration.

'So, what made you want to be a chef?' he asked. 'I thought you were dead set on doing an English degree?'

'I was . . . but it all went to pot after Danny died. I dropped out for a bit,' she said, evading the real reason.

'I can quite believe that.'

'I started to cook as a kind of therapy. It just grew from there.' The waiter brought them their main courses, and she began tucking in eagerly.

'What other restaurants have you worked at apart from La Emporium?'

Liz gave him a quick outline of her career to date and hoped he would be impressed. She realised that she wanted him to believe in her more than anything.

He nodded appreciatively. 'That's more than I thought. You're certainly very determined.'

'I am,' she agreed. 'I'm doing it for Danny.'

'I can see how that would drive you.'

They chatted non-stop during the meal, and after declining dessert but accepting coffee, Liz noticed that the restaurant was emptying. Despite the lateness of the hour, she found she didn't want the evening to end.

'Do you fancy going on somewhere?' Alex asked, as though reading her thoughts. 'Crystal's is usually good on a Monday night.'

Liz almost gasped in shock. Crystal's was one of the most exclusive nightclubs in Chelsea. It was members-only, and from what she'd heard, the fees were extortionate.

'That would be lovely,' she said, eventually finding her voice and hardly daring to believe her luck.

CHAPTER FIFTEEN

Outside Crystal's, a formidable brick building, Alex whisked Liz past the queue of night-clubbers and straight up to the front.

'Good evening, Mr Sinclaire,' the doorman said, ushering them through into the club. Inside, it was hot and noisy and the blue neon dance floor was already overflowing with gyrating bodies. Crystal's certainly lived up to its name — hanging from the ceiling were a myriad of crystal chandeliers.

'Is it always this busy on a Monday night?' Liz asked, incredulous.

'Most of the people who come here don't have to get up for work in the morning,' he replied. 'Every night is Saturday night to them.'

Alex led her towards a bar spanning the width of the room. Along the length of the bar were hundreds of bottles, lined up against the exposed brick wall.

'Do you fancy a cocktail?' he asked.

'Um, yes please. I'll have a mojito.'

'Why don't you grab a seat over there?' Alex suggested, as he motioned to the barman.

Liz walked over to a table and sat gingerly on the edge of one of the cream leather stools. Despite the novelty of coming here, she half wished they'd gone somewhere quieter where they could have continued their conversation. She looked towards the dance floor. The heavy beat of the music thrummed through her body but it didn't make her feel like dancing.

* * *

Alex waited impatiently while the barman mixed the cocktails. *Why didn't I just order a bottle of wine?* he thought as he glanced at Liz. It would have been much quicker. She was perched on a stool, looking uncomfortable. He was beginning to wish he'd taken her somewhere more intimate so that they could have carried on with their conversation. He was amazed at how much she'd revealed of her past, and how much she and her family had suffered after Danny's death. He still missed Danny, but through Liz, he felt closer to him. And although he hadn't been able to tell her everything, he could envisage a day when he could be completely open with her. Since losing Kas, he hadn't felt able to open up to people fully, not even with Tia, and certainly not with Nikki.

He'd brought Liz to Crystal's to impress her, but he suddenly realised how easy it would be to bump into Nikki here. Since walking out on her, she'd left numerous messages on both his mobile and email, each one becoming increasingly hysterical. She'd done this before when he'd tried to create some distance in the past and, like a fool, he'd always given in to her. This time it was different. This time it was definitely over. When he'd phoned her back, it was to make sure she realised that. He knew she had an important photo shoot in the morning and she never stayed out late before a shoot — it was one of her principles — so hopefully now she'd be tucked up safely in bed. He would only stay for one drink, he decided, and then take Liz home. He glanced back over at her. She looked beautiful sat alone at the table — a natural beauty. He paid the waiter and hurried back to her side.

They sipped their drinks in silence, watching the dancers on the floor, taking in the heavy beat of the music.

'Do you want to dance?' he asked after a while. It wasn't his kind of music, but he didn't want Liz to think that he was an old fuddy duddy.

'Okay then,' she said, putting her glass down and getting up from the table.

As they reached the crowded dance floor, miraculously the music changed to a slower beat. Alex took Liz in his arms and it felt as though she was melting into him. Their bodies fitted perfectly together as they swayed in time to the music, and when she looked up, he couldn't help lowering his lips towards her for a kiss.

* * *

Liz couldn't believe it when Alex pulled her body closer to his. His hands were hot through the thin fabric of her dress and she felt a sudden surge of longing for him. She'd tried to bury it in anger for so long, but now she realised it had never gone away. As she looked up and his lips brushed hers, she thought she might explode with happiness. Her surroundings faded out as she concentrated on the feeling of his mouth on hers. She felt alive and wanton, as though anything could happen between them. For years, she'd imagined what it would feel like to be kissed by him, but she'd never for one moment imagined it would make her feel so alive.

Eventually, he pulled away. 'I think we'd better sit down before I get carried away,' he whispered.

She excused herself to freshen up in the bathroom, brimming with joy as she glided across the floor.

The ladies' was as sumptuous as the rest of the nightclub, with huge marble basins, freshly laundered hand towels and a selection of hand creams. Liz contemplated her reflection in the mirror as she washed her hands. Her cheeks were pink and glowing, and she reached into her handbag for some powder to tone the flush down before applying some fresh lipstick.

'You ought to be careful whose boyfriends you mess with.'

Liz jumped at the voice behind her and smudged her lipstick. Carefully, she wiped it off and then turned to her accuser.

'I'm sorry?'

Behind her stood Nikki, encased in a sheath of black satin, her dark curls cascading around her shoulders like Medusa's snakes.

'Alex. You know, the man you were clinging to on the dance floor? He isn't up for grabs, especially not by someone like you.'

From her height, Nikki looked down on Liz, and Liz sensed her hackles rise like a cat's. This wasn't like at the dinner party, though — Liz didn't have to be polite this time.

'Well, I don't think Alex would agree with you. He told me you and he weren't together anymore.'

Nikki's face puckered into an ugly frown. 'Well, he would say that, wouldn't he? But he's lying, of course. We're practically engaged. We just have to keep it under wraps because of my career. Timing is key, you know?'

'I'm sure it is, although I never credited Alex with such good acting skills. He certainly doesn't behave like he's about to get engaged.'

'Oh, you're so smug, aren't you? But you'll soon have the smile wiped off your face. Alex may stray, but he always comes back to me in the end,' Nikki said, before flouncing out of the toilets.

Liz stood at the sink, trembling. If Nikki was telling the truth, then she'd seriously misjudged Alex. Could she have got him so wrong? She didn't think so, and she certainly wasn't going to take a stranger's word for it. She'd see what Alex had to say for himself. If he thought he could make a fool out of her, then he had better think again. Liz held her head high and marched out of the toilets towards their table.

Halfway there, she stopped in her tracks. Nikki was completely wrapped around Alex. There could be no doubt about their closeness; she wouldn't be able to prise them apart with a crowbar. Maybe she *had* got it wrong? But then he'd seemed so sincere this evening and she'd wanted to believe him. She realised now that she should have trusted her original instincts. She turned round and walked towards the door. Outside, she hailed a cab to take her home.

* * *

Liz seemed to be taking forever in the toilets. Alex had already finished his cocktail and was itching to leave. Perhaps she'd invite him in for coffee and they could continue talking. He didn't even mind if coffee meant just that, although after her kiss he'd have to work hard not to kiss her again. But he wanted to take things slowly with her; he sensed that was what she needed. As he looked towards the toilets, he froze. Heading straight towards him with a determined look on her face was Nikki.

'Alex darling, are you waiting for me? I'm so parched.' She picked up Liz's half empty glass and waved her long, elegant fingers at a passing waiter who scuttled towards her. 'Could you get rid of that for me, please? And bring me a glass of champagne?'

'Actually, Nikki . . .' He stood up, hoping that would prevent her from sitting down at the table.

'What have you been doing with yourself today? I've missed you.'

'Nikki, don't pretend that we're still together. I've made myself perfectly clear.'

'Oh, never mind about that. I'm sure you didn't mean it. You never do. Honestly, Alex, I don't know why you say these things to me. Is it just to keep me on my toes?'

She pressed herself against him so tightly that his stool almost tipped backwards. He flung his arms around her to stop himself from falling, but her lips clamped over his before he could stop her. As soon as he had regained his balance, he pushed her away.

'Just what the hell do you think you're doing?' However long Liz had spent in the loos, he hoped to God she didn't come out now. He had to get rid of Nikki and get rid of her fast. The waiter arrived with the requested glass.

'Thank you so much,' she gushed at him, giving him a heart-stopping smile which made him blush and sent him scuttling away again. She turned back to Alex. 'Now, darling, you haven't told me what you've been up to today.'

'Don't "darling" me, Nikki. Please go away. I'm here with a friend.'

'Really? That scraggy blonde cook I just met in the loos. I think you'll find she's gone, dear.'

'I don't believe you! Liz wouldn't just walk off.'

'Well, I just saw her leave. And I don't lie.'

Alex pushed past her and rushed towards the exit, just in time to see Liz climbing into a black cab which pulled straight into the traffic. In desperation, he grabbed his phone and rang her number. It went straight to voicemail.

'Liz, I don't know what you saw, but it's not what you think. Can you give me a ring when you get this message? We need to talk.' Alex sighed as he ended the call. If Liz had seen Nikki pouncing on him, he doubted she would call him back. He already knew she'd have more pride than that. *Bloody Nikki.* He wished he'd never got involved with her. Instead of going back inside, Alex turned on his heel and walked away from the club. He was going home. Alone. And the long walk would do him good.

CHAPTER SIXTEEN

'Someone got out of the wrong side of the bed today,' Tia commented as she walked over to his desk.

'Pack it in, Tia. I'm not in the mood,' Alex said as he switched on his laptop. Until six months ago, they had both worked from home, but on their last development they'd made the decision to convert the ground floor on an apartment block into offices. Most of the time it suited them both to have an office, as not only did it make it easier for them to collaborate, it also provided a better separation between work and home life. Although sometimes Alex felt he could do without Tia's inference.

Tia perched on the edge of his desk. 'Is it anything I can help with?'

He looked up from the screen. 'I'm just busy, that's all.'

Tia remained perched. 'I heard you'd split up with Nikki.'

'News travels fast.'

'And are you okay?'

'I was the one who called it off.'

She shifted a little closer to him. 'Oh. Only you don't seem very happy about it.'

'It's got nothing to do with Nikki. Tia, I'm busy. I need to get on.'

Tia frowned. 'Fine. I'm only trying to help. Do you want a coffee?'

He sighed and leant back in his chair. 'Please. That would be great.'

He really didn't mean to take his bad mood out on Tia. It was now Thursday and, despite repeated messages, he still hadn't heard from Liz. He'd even been round to her flat, but her van wasn't there and neither was there a reply when he pressed the buzzer for her apartment. Perhaps he'd blown it and should try to forget all about her? The problem was — he couldn't.

* * *

Jay was lying on the sofa when Liz returned from her run on Saturday morning. She shoved his legs over and plonked herself down.

'God, I'm knackered.'

'You push yourself too hard.'

'Unlike you. When was the last time you did any exercise?'

'Get lost! I get enough exercise at work. Besides, I've got a Saturday off and I'm going to do exactly as I please.'

'Which is?'

'Bit of shopping this morning, buy some new threads, pub lunch and watch the footie this afternoon. Then this evening . . .'

'This evening?'

'Ta dah!' He pulled some tickets from his pocket with a flourish. 'Two tickets to Winston's tonight, and he's DJing there himself. Fancy coming with me?'

'I'd rather have a long soak in the bath and curl up with a good book.' Liz moved off the sofa.

'Don't be an old fart. It's rare I get a Saturday night off. You used to love to dance. And you know you love Winston's.'

She stopped halfway across the living room. He was right. She did like going to Winston's, and she could definitely do with some fun. She'd had a terrible week. She kept remembering how Alex had danced with her and then, the next minute, was there with Nikki. Maybe he'd taken her there on purpose to make Nikki jealous? She wondered if she was just a pawn in his game. It didn't tally with the depth of the conversation they'd had earlier in the evening, but maybe he'd just wanted closure on his relationship with Danny? She'd had very few relationships with men and most of those had been short-lived, so who was she to know how it all worked? Maybe it was for the best. She couldn't imagine ever being comfortable with the crowd that Alex belonged to, anyway. They were far too sophisticated for her and she'd probably forever feel as though she was the country bumpkin around them. And if Nikki was anything to go by, she would always be viewed as the hired help too. But because she knew him from when she was a teenager, she'd opened herself up to him on Monday night — so much more than she had with anyone for a long time. And now it felt as though he'd thrown it back in her face. Trusting him had made her vulnerable and it wasn't a feeling she was comfortable with. Well, he wouldn't get another chance to hurt her despite his apologetic phone calls. She was better off on her own.

All week she'd thrown herself into work with a frenzy. When she wasn't cooking, she was drumming up new business, or at least trying to. She hadn't had much luck, though. She needed a good night out.

'What about Susie, though? Wouldn't you rather patch things up with her than go out with me?'

'That's just the point. I've heard on the grapevine she's going to be there tonight. I was hoping this would be my chance.'

'Oh, I see. You want my moral support, but you're intending to ditch me as soon as you can if you get the green light?' She was only teasing him, but by the pained expression on his face, she realised he'd taken her seriously.

'No! It's not like that at all.'

"I'm joking. Although if you can get it together with Susie, please feel free to dump me. I'm more than capable of making my own way home, and I'd be over the moon for you.'

'Really? So you'll come?'

'Of course I'll come with you.'

'Great! And also . . .' He paused.

'What?'

'I don't suppose you'd come shopping with me as well? I really want to buy something to impress her.'

'Sure.' She might treat herself to something new too. Although she couldn't really afford to, it might help to cheer her up.

* * *

The music was pounding and the dance floor was already full by the time Liz and Jay arrived at Winston's. Watching couples sway to the music reminded her of Monday night; of how Alex's body had felt against hers. *And that kiss*. She pushed the thought away. She needed to forget all about Alex.

'What can I get you?' Jay asked.

'White wine, please.'

She could already feel her feet tapping in time to the music as they queued at the bar and had the urge just to let go and dance. But she waited dutifully until Jay was served and they found a table.

'Look, Gary, Mark and Chelle are over there. Let's join them.'

'Good idea. Then I won't be a gooseberry when you bunk off with Susie.'

'Liz!' Jay protested, but laughed when he realised she was teasing him again.

Liz hadn't seen their friends for a while. Gary and Michelle were both chefs so it was often difficult to coordinate their nights off together. But whenever they did get together, it was comfortable — as though they'd only seen each other the day before. After chatting to them for a while, Liz tugged on Jay's sleeve. 'Come on, let's dance.'

The music was mellow and Liz allowed her body to relax into the rhythm. She was feeling confident tonight, all down to a new silver dress she was wearing and a pair of incredibly high heels. She wasn't usually a stiletto kind of girl, but she felt sexy wearing these shoes — although her feet would probably be in agony by the end of the night.

All night Liz danced, drank and laughed with her friends. Although she noticed Jay becoming more despondent as he realised Susie seemed to be a no show.

Liz handed him a drink. 'Cheer up, the night's young yet. There's still time.'

'I suppose so,' Jay said. 'But what if she's not coming?'

'Why wouldn't she? Everyone else is here.'

As if on cue, Susie walked into the nightclub. Jay's face lit up, then immediately looked as though the lights had been turned out.

'What?' Liz followed his gaze. Susie wasn't alone. A tall, good-looking, blond man led her to the bar. He stooped his head and whispered in her ear. She looked up, smiling, and kissed him on the lips.

'What the . . . ?' Jay's hands clenched and he half rose from his stool. Liz grabbed his arm and forced him to sit back down.

'Don't be stupid, Jay. You've got to play this one cool.'

'She's right, mate,' Gary said. 'Let's work this one out, shall we?'

Jay nodded, tears in his eyes. Liz put her arm around him, knowing exactly how he felt.

'Don't jump to conclusions, Jay. It could be nothing,' Gary soothed his friend.

Liz wondered if Susie was trying to make him jealous and was reminded of Monday night. She pushed the thought away. If Susie *was* trying to make Jay jealous, it was certainly working, and it was all the friends could do to stop Jay from confronting her.

'I think I'd better get you home,' Liz said after an hour of him obsessively watching Susie and drinking steadily. 'This isn't doing you any good.'

'Not yet.' Jay got up from the table before she could stop him. Susie was heading for the ladies', but Jay intercepted her on the way. They stood talking for a few minutes, or rather arguing, and then Susie flounced off. Jay stayed where he was, looking completed dejected.

'Right guys, I'm going to take him home,' Liz said, getting up.

'Need a hand?' Gary asked, but she shook her head.

'It'll be fine.' She walked over to where Jay was still standing and put her arm around him. 'Come on, let's go home.'

Jay allowed himself to be led away, but in the doorway he paused. 'I can't believe it.'

'What did she say?'

'She's been seeing this guy for months. She said she was sick of staying in at night while I was working.'

'Well, I suppose that's one of the drawbacks to the job.'

'But if I'd known she felt like that, I could have changed my job.'

Liz gasped. 'No, Jay! You love your job, and if she can't understand that then she doesn't deserve you.' Her heart went out to him. She hugged him and he gripped her. 'We'll get through this one together, I promise you.'

He pulled back, staring down at her. 'Liz, I don't know what I'd do without you.' And then, to her surprise, he lowered his head and kissed her gently on the lips. For a moment, she was stunned. His lips felt nice on hers, but there was none of the passion which Alex's kiss had ignited.

Coming to her senses, she pulled away from him. 'Hey, let's not spoil a wonderful friendship.'

'Oh, so you're rejecting me too now, are you?' He turned away from her, but she caught hold of his arm, bringing him back to face her.

'I'm not rejecting you, Jay. You're my friend and I'll always be here for you.' Slowly he nodded, and in the light of the street lamp, she could see tears glistening in his eyes. She hugged him to her. 'We're a team. Friends for life.'

She felt him nod again.

'Yes, you're right,' he finally said with a sigh.

'Come on, let's go. You need a good night's sleep.'

They walked away from the club, completely unaware of a black cab which had pulled up near to the entrance, its passenger, Alexander Sinclaire, still inside.

CHAPTER SEVENTEEN

Liz woke early the next morning with a pounding head and a tongue that felt too large for her mouth. The sun was streaming through curtains, which she'd forgotten to close, piercing her sore eyeballs. She closed her eyes and rolled over, trying to get back to sleep.

Gradually, the events of the previous night filtered in. The dancing, the drinking, Susie coming in with another man. And, finally, Jay's bumbling kiss. Back at home, he'd become maudlin, talking for hours about Susie until, to her great relief, he'd finally fallen asleep mid-sentence. She'd pulled off his shoes and covered him up with a throw from the sofa before retreating gratefully to her own room.

Now, quietly, she slipped out of bed and dressed in her running clothes. She tiptoed through the living room where Jay was still snoring away, the room fugged with stale alcohol fumes.

The run made her feel worse rather than better, and instead of going straight home, she stopped at the local café for a bacon sandwich. She needed carbs to fill her up. She wasn't used to drinking that much. *Even having fun has its consequences*, she thought morosely. Building up her business was a slog, and the rest of her life was a disaster. But she refused to be beaten.

The flat was empty when she got back home. Jay was probably at work and she couldn't help feeling sorry for him with the hangover he was bound to have. Trying to be positive, she cleaned the flat and then sat down to do her accounts. She noted down some clients whose bills were outstanding, ready to chase up the following morning. Her cash flow wasn't looking healthy, and she wondered briefly if it was worth signing on with an agency to get some temporary shifts. It was a depressing thought.

Later that afternoon, just as she was putting the paperwork away, Jay burst through the door.

'Oh.' He paused. 'You're in. Hi.'

'Hi. Yes, I'm here. Busy day?'

'Um, yeah. Liz, I'm really sorry for what happened last night. What I remember of it, anyway.' He looked at her sheepishly.

'It's okay. It was the drink and the disappointment.'

'Yes, you're right,' he said, sounding relieved. 'You know I'd never have done that if I'd been sober.'

'Yes, I know,' she said, trying not to feel offended.

'So, we're good then?'

'Of course. Like I said, friends for life.'

'Even if I move out?'

'That's sudden, isn't it?' She was shocked. 'Is it because of last night?'

'Sort of, but not how you mean. It's obvious that there's no chance of me and Susie getting back together, so I've decided I need to face facts and move on.'

'I see.' She'd been itching to get her flat back to herself, but now it felt like another loss. 'You don't have to rush into anything. You're welcome to stay.'

'I know. And thanks for everything you've done for me, but Johno, the pastry chef at work, is going back to Oz. I've taken on his lease. It's not much, but it'll be mine, and I think I need my own space.'

'I understand. But I'll miss you.'

'Oh, come here.' He put his arms around her in a bear hug. As he squeezed her tightly, tears welled in her eyes. What was she going to do now?

He lent back, noticing her tears. 'Hey, hey, what's wrong? Surely you won't miss me that much?' He rubbed away her tears with the ball of his thumb.

She shook her head and moved out of his reach. 'It's not just that. It's everything. I think I may need to get a job. The private catering isn't doing as well as I'd hoped.'

'But you've been really busy.'

'Have been. But it's hit and miss. Long-term, I need a regular income. I don't suppose you've heard anything on the grapevine, have you?'

'Yes, I was going to tell you. There's a rumour going round that Roberto's planning to open a new restaurant. Not sure how soon or whether it's definite. You always got on well with Roberto, didn't you? It was just that other idiot.'

'Yes,' Liz said, remembering his praise at Tia's. 'Could you find out a bit more for me?'

'Sure, no problem. Like I said, I'm not sure if it's definite yet. I'm surprised, though, as he's about to have a baby, but I think he's going in as part of a consortium.'

'Really? Do you know who with?' Alarm bells rang in her head.

'No, sorry.'

'Funnily enough, he was a guest at Tia's last week. I don't suppose she'd have anything to do with it?'

Jay frowned. 'I don't know, but I'm back on shift later tonight. I'll find out.'

'That would be great,' Liz said, her mouth suddenly dry. If Tia was opening a restaurant, she'd lose another part of her business. Alex was at the dinner so he was bound to be involved. And yet he hadn't said a word last Monday. Cold, hard anger settled in her chest.

* * *

Liz's hand shook as she ended her phone call. When Jay had come home from his shift last night, he'd confirmed her fears that Tia and Alex were part of the consortium with Roberto. She felt betrayed by Alex yet again. She'd been a fool to trust him and had decided that, from now on, the only person she'd rely on was herself.

But now, after that phone call, she was struggling to remain positive as she'd just found out that yet another regular customer was about to go into administration.

'I'm sorry, I can't help you,' the girl on the other end of the phone said with a quivering voice. 'You'll be added to the list of creditors.'

'And what will be the chance of me receiving what's owed to me?'

'I really don't know,' the girl said, sounding tearful. Liz thanked her and rang off. The poor girl was probably about to lose her job; the last thing she needed was angry creditors.

Liz made herself a cup of tea and steeled herself to make more calls. It wasn't a productive day. Her calls were either unanswered or she'd been given vague promises of payment — promises which she knew were unlikely to materialise. Even though she was demoralised, she was determined to fight on and find some other source of income. Because now she had something to prove, and the only way to do that was by making her business a success.

CHAPTER EIGHTEEN

Seeing Liz with Jay had wounded Alex. She'd sworn they were only friends, but what he'd seen outside Winston's on Saturday night was definitely not platonic. If she hadn't been lying before, she'd moved on incredibly quickly. He knew he probably should try and do the same, but the way she'd responded to his kiss in Crystal's taunted him. Surely that had meant something? Or did she do that with any man? Whatever her situation, it pained him to think she thought badly of him. He needed to explain to her that Nikki had manipulated the situation on Monday night. And then, if she still wanted to walk away, he'd bow out gracefully.

Thankfully, Nikki had been out of the country since their last encounter, so he hadn't had to risk bumping into her, or her turning up unexpectedly, but she'd called him frequently; calls that he refused to answer. Just as Liz was refusing to answer his own calls to her.

The door opened and Tia came in, her arms full of packages. Immediately, Alex went over to help her and put them down on her desk.

'What's all this?' he asked.

'It's the fabrics I ordered for the apartment,' she said, starting to tear open the parcels. 'I can't wait to see what they look like.' After unwrapping the first one, she picked up the fabrics and ran her fingers over them. 'They are just divine. Look!'

They were just right. Rich, vibrant and of indisputable quality. He nodded in satisfaction. 'Excellent, as usual. And you'll definitely be finished on time?'

She nodded. 'Of course. I'm looking forward to our opening. Have you had many RSVPs?'

'Yes, it should be a good crowd. I'm hoping we'll get some sales from this.'

'Great. Just one problem, though. The caterer we booked can't do the new date. I was wondering if we should see if Liz is free?'

'Good idea. Can you give her a ring?'

'Sure.' Tia hesitated. 'Unless you'd rather contact her yourself?'

'No, I'll let you do that. You know what we need.'

'Okay. I was going to phone her, anyway. A friend of mine is holding a fashion show and her caterer has also just bailed on her.'

He nodded. 'Don't forget, we've got a meeting with Roberto at four. I've found a couple of venues that I want to show you. I know that one of them in particular is going to blow your mind.'

'I can't wait. The sooner we get this project off the ground, the happier I'll be.'

* * *

Liz was working on her Instagram account when the phone rang. She'd decided to up her social media profile and make some new contacts. She needed something quirky, something that would attract attention. *But what?* It was almost a relief to be interrupted.

'Liz, darling, it's Tia.'

'Hi, Tia. How are you?'

'Busy, busy, busy, you know how it is.'

'Yes.' *Busy with your new restaurant*, Liz thought, though she did her best to keep the resentment out of her voice. 'What can I do for you?'

'We're having an open evening next Wednesday for the unveiling of the new apartments. We wondered if you could provide some canapés. Something different to get people talking?'

'We?'

'Yes, Alex and I.'

Liz bridled at the mention of his name, but work was work. She bit back her pride.

'Yes, that's no problem,' she said, knowing that the pages in her diary were empty.

'And I had a panic call from my friend Penelope today. She's organising a fashion show in aid of Cancer Research on Friday. Her caterers have just dropped out and left her in the mire. I don't suppose you could help, could you?'

'Oh, I'm not sure.' She didn't want to appear too available. 'Let me just check . . . um, that could be tight.'

'Oh dear, I was hoping you could bail her out. She does a lot of charity stuff. Could be good for business.'

'Okay, well, why don't you give me her number and I'll give her a ring? I might be able to squeeze it in. It depends on what she wants, really.'

'Thank you, darling, you really are a lifesaver. I won't forget this, I promise you. Now, have you got a pen?'

That afternoon, Liz put on her best suit and took her portfolio with her on the Tube. Normally, she drove everywhere, but today she couldn't face the hassle of London traffic or finding somewhere to park and wanted to scan the area on foot.

Penelope was a woman in her early fifties but looked much younger.

'Thank you for coming at such short notice.'

'My pleasure,' Liz said, after being shown to a sumptuous living room. Sitting down, she asked, 'So what exactly are you looking for?'

'We've got about a hundred guests coming, so we'd want canapés and drinks on arrival. And then after the fashion show, I'd like an intimate four course meal for twenty. Do you think you could manage that?'

Liz spluttered as she took a sip of her iced water. Normally, that wouldn't be a problem, but it would be a nightmare getting the staff she needed at such short notice. She hoped Emma would be free and could rope in as many of her fellow students as possible. Maybe even Jay could get a day or two off work to help her out . . .

'That shouldn't be a problem,' she replied, trying to keep the tremor out of her voice.

'Good.' Penelope clapped her hands.

'Let me show you my portfolio,' Liz said, handing over a leather-bound file. Six months ago, she'd invested in having some of her most popular dishes professionally photographed — a tool that she found incredibly useful when meeting new clients.

Penelope quickly decided on the menu and then offered to show Liz around.

The house was enormous. Penelope's high heels clacked on the marble flooring as she showed Liz to the ballroom where the fashion show was to take place. It was like something from a Jane Austen novel with wood panelling and numerous chandeliers. Then she led Liz downstairs to the largest domestic kitchen she'd ever seen.

'Do you have a housekeeper?' she asked in awe when she saw the size of it and how well fitted out it was.

'Oh no! We have a daily who does all the cleaning, but she doesn't cook. Mostly we eat out.'

'This kitchen is better equipped than some restaurants I've worked in. You have such a beautiful house.'

Penelope puffed up with the flattery. 'Well, thank you. Do you know, I might start doing more entertaining at home? So much nicer than going out all the time. Maybe you could help there?'

'I'd be delighted,' Liz said, smiling.

* * *

The day of the fashion show came round quickly, and before she knew it Liz was back in Penelope's kitchen. Penelope was fussing and Liz wished she'd go away. It was impossible to focus with her client clucking, repeatedly asking if it would all be ready on time.

She pulled two large trays of canapés from the oven and arranged them onto silver platters. Six girls in immaculate white blouses and black skirts waited patiently to take them to the amassing guests.

'Are you sure you'll have everything ready on time?' Penelope asked yet again.

'Everything is under control here.' Liz forced a smile. 'But I think I can hear your guests arriving.'

'What? Already? I'd better go. If you're sure you'll be okay?'

'I'll be fine. Don't worry.'

Penelope scuttled out and Liz breathed a sigh of relief. It had been a while since she'd catered for such large numbers. Thankfully, Jay had been more than willing to help and was busy supervising two agency chefs. Emma had brought a posse of waiting staff from her college. Throughout the morning, Emma had also been working in the kitchen and, as busy as Liz was, she couldn't help but notice a spark between her and Jay, which made her smile. They'd make a lovely couple.

She returned her focus to the job in hand and immersed herself in sending out a continuous supply of perfect trays of canapés.

* * *

After the fashion show, Liz set out twenty plates and lifted the tray of roasted poussins out of the oven. She'd added this dish to her menu following her meal with Alex, and was delighted with how well they'd turned out. She added discs of dauphinoise potatoes, a twist of cabbage and batons of carrots to the plates, and then drizzled wild mushroom sauce around the edges of each one. After signalling to the waitresses, she watched with pride as they carried away the food. Then she frowned. They'd left two plates behind. She snatched them up and hurried into the dining room, where she hoped to dispatch them to the nearest server.

'Oh, it's you.'

Liz froze at the sight of Nikki. Seeing a waitress coming toward her, she handed her the plates before Nikki could accuse her of spoiling another designer outfit. She hoped the hateful woman wasn't going to cause a scene — not here.

'Hello,' Liz said, whilst moving slowly backwards to extricate herself from the dining room.

'I'm glad to see that you've taken my advice.'

'I beg your pardon?'

'About Alex,' she said. 'Thankfully, he's seen the error of his ways. In fact, we're going shopping tomorrow. For diamonds.'

Liz's stomach dipped. The calls from Alex had stopped so she could only assume Nikki was telling the truth. Even if she wasn't, Liz decided she was better off out of it. The last thing she needed right now was to be involved in someone else's drama. Even if the thought of Alex being with someone else hurt like hell.

'I'm very happy for you,' she said, before turning and hurrying back to the kitchen. There she began to plate up the dessert, forcing herself to concentrate on her work, but she kept thinking about Nikki's announcement. The way Alex had been with her on Monday made it difficult to believe he'd been a man on the verge of popping the question. If Nikki hadn't been so spiteful, Liz would have felt sorry for her. There was no way *she* would want to marry a man she couldn't trust.

CHAPTER NINETEEN

Over the next few days, Liz threw herself into her work. The flat seemed empty without Jay. Even though he hadn't been around much, there'd been comfort in knowing that she wouldn't be on her own overnight. She'd longed to have the place to herself for ages but she hadn't anticipated how lonely she would feel. Friday had been a success, and she already had one luncheon booked because of it, but she hadn't spoken to anyone all weekend, instead trying to distract herself by creating new dishes or going out for a run. Anything to take her mind off the fact that on Wednesday she would have to come face to face with Alex again.

* * *

Wednesday came round all too soon, and as she drove into the car park of the apartment complex, she hoped she could carry off the evening with decorum. Or better still, that she would feel nothing when she saw Alex again. Perhaps tonight she'd realise he was completely out of her system. She began unloading the van, wishing that the night was already over.

'Here, let me help you with that.'

She jumped at the sound of his voice. He must have been waiting for her. She pushed the thought away. He would be too busy for that, surely?

As he lifted the tray from her, his hand brushed hers. She flinched at the searing heat of his touch and almost dropped the tray completely.

'Careful!' he warned, tilting it backwards and saving it from destruction.

'They'll need to be warmed through,' she said, ignoring the sharpness of his tone. 'Tia said I could use a kitchen.'

'Let me take you there,' he replied as she picked up another tray.

The front door to the apartment complex was already open. The hall had high ceilings and a black-and-white, marble-tiled floor. He led her into a ground-floor apartment with another wide hallway. She glimpsed the living room as she passed by — lush carpets, expensive looking furniture and a riot of colour scattered in soft furnishings. Every inch screamed executive luxury.

'This is gorgeous,' she said in awe, completely forgetting her hostility.

'Now you can see why I want Tia on all my projects. I've never met a designer with such flair. She knows instinctively what I want, but each time adds that extra twist of originality. I'm hoping we'll have some takers tonight just based on this first impression.'

'Well, I would. If I had the money, that is.'

'Thank you.'

He led her into an expansive kitchen. The floor tiles, walls and units were a brilliant white, offset by the back wall, which was a glorious petrol-blue. The black granite worktops, stainless steel appliances and glass shelving all added to the gleam.

'Wow,' Liz said. 'An amazing kitchen. But if you're showing people around, won't I be in the way? I thought I'd be using one of the other kitchens. I only need to heat things through, like I said. It doesn't need to be fully furnished, just so long as it has a working oven.'

'Ahh.' He paused. 'Well, I hope you don't mind . . . but that's part of the plan.'

'Part of the plan?' She felt the hostility creep back in.

'You know how when people are selling their homes, they bake bread and put coffee on, to give it that homely smell?'

'And you're going to use canapés and a real live chef to the same effect.'

'You don't mind, do you?'

She *did* mind. She minded a lot. And although she wanted to hate him, she knew that this would be Tia's idea rather than his.

'I'll try to make as little mess as possible.'

'I knew you'd understand,' he said. 'Is there anything else I can do to help you?'

'No, thanks. I'm sure you're very busy.'

* * *

Her sudden frostiness was disappointing. He hadn't expected it to be easy. She was only here for work. He'd noticed how she'd flinched when he'd let his hand touch hers, but he thought she'd melted a little as they'd talked — until he'd told her she'd be working in the show kitchen. He'd suspected she'd hate it, but Tia had been determined it would give an added oomph to the sales evening. He should have hung back and let Tia break the news.

The trouble was he'd been watching out for Liz, and the moment she'd pulled into the car park he'd been drawn to her side like a magnet. But she was right. He did have a lot to do. Tonight was important. If he was going to sink money into the new restaurant, he needed capital from the apartments. He didn't like to hang around in business.

He walked into the lobby, which was to be the reception area for the guests tonight. He needed to forget Liz for now and focus on work. Later, he might get a chance to win her trust back.

* * *

On Tia's instructions, Liz had made a generous number of canapés for the guests. She hated working under scrutiny, but at least there wasn't much to be done — merely heating up and assembling the platters. Tia had supplied her own waitresses to serve — all tall, glamorous girls — so all Liz had to do was to keep up production.

She worked on autopilot for the first part of the evening, listening to the echoes of Tia and Alex's presentation in the reception area as one tray after another was taken from the kitchen. Then, as the sound of clapping heralded the end of the speeches, Liz decided to take control of her destiny. If she was going to be on show, then let it be to her own advantage. Her food was her best marketing tool so she'd make herself known to some of the guests. And if they were interested, she had plenty of business cards with her to pass on.

As she mingled with the guests, a tray of canapés in hand, she watched Alex surreptitiously. She couldn't deny that he had a certain magnetism. He seemed to know what each person wanted to hear and delivered that with just the right amount of charm. He didn't lay it on too thick or sound patronising. Unlike Goldilocks, he got it just right first time. She wondered if he'd employed the same tactics on her when they'd spent the evening together. Instead of getting him out of her system, tonight had somehow pulled him closer to her. She knew he was dangerous, she knew she couldn't trust him . . . and yet she wanted to. She wanted him, she realised with horror. And now it sounded like he was engaged to someone else — if Nikki was to be believed, which she wasn't entirely sure about. Although, even if Nikki *was* lying, could she trust Alex not to hurt her?

Liz worked resolutely until the last of the food had been dispatched. She decided she would just clean up and go, slip away before either Alex or Tia could prolong her.

'I say, are you the lady who made this delightful food?'

An older, rotund man with messy grey hair and a suit jacket straining at the waist approached her as she went back into the kitchen.

'That's me.' She smiled at him.

'Well, it's all fantastic. What's in these tarts?' he asked as he picked one up from the tray.

'Caesar salad tartlets with quails' eggs and bacon.'

'Superb,' he said between mouthfuls. 'They certainly taste as good as they look. And what do you call these scallop thingies?'

Liz thought he looked like a child in a sweet shop. He couldn't choose between them, so he'd gone for all of them instead.

'Those are scallop tostadas with avocado and salsa fresco.'

'And these?'

'Pumpkin, sage and parmesan fritters. They work really well with this caramelised onion crème fraiche. Why don't you try some?' She handed him a small bowl and watched in delight as he ate and murmured his approval. This was what catering was all about — combining flavours and textures to create something amazing from nothing.

'Simply divine,' he exclaimed. 'I feel like I've died and gone to heaven.'

'Thank you,' she said. 'It means so much when people appreciate what you've cooked.'

'Appreciate?' he asked when he'd finished eating. 'If I wasn't already spoken for, I'd marry you like a shot. Did you do all this yourself?'

'I did. It's my business. I cater for every occasion — christenings, dinner parties, corporate events. I did a fashion show last week,' she added, pleased that she could now add that to her list.

'That's good to know. I've got a bit of a do on at my house in the country coming up. I don't suppose you'd like to give me a quote, would you?'

'I'd love to help if I can. Would you like my card and then we can discuss it properly?'

'Love to, love to, but perhaps you could talk to my PA? Here's my card. I'll tell her to expect your call. Don't suppose you could ring her first thing in the morning, could you? I know she's keen to get the catering booked.'

125

'I will,' Liz agreed enthusiastically. Perhaps tonight wasn't such a disaster after all. In her desire to clean up and escape, she slipped the card into her pocket without even glancing at it.

'Ah, Henry, I thought I might find you in here.' Alex strolled into the kitchen and clapped her new contact on the back. 'How are you? Did you like the apartments?'

'Indeed, I did. Lucinda's moving to town. I think living here would suit her.'

As they talked, Liz went to collect the rest of her trays. Alex's voice stopped her in her tracks.

'You're not going, are you, Liz?'

'Yes, I'm just about finished here.'

'I couldn't ask you to hang on for a bit, could I? There's someone I'd like you to meet.'

'Sure.' She kept her voice neutral, even though her heart was sinking. *Escape route blocked off.*

By the time she'd loaded everything away, the only people left were those who had nowhere else to go.

As she came back into the kitchen, Alex broke away from the conversation he was having with an overly made-up, middle-aged woman and moved to her side.

'So, who did you want me to meet?' she asked, scanning the room's remaining occupants.

'Me. I need to talk to you. I thought you were about to rush off.'

'What if I was? I've done the job I'm being paid for.'

'Liz.' He caught hold of her arm as she turned away from him and lowered his voice. 'I don't want to talk to you about work. I want to talk to you about us.'

'There is no us,' she said calmly.

'But there could be. I don't know what you saw at Crystal's, but I can assure you it wasn't what you think.'

'It looked pretty self-explanatory to me. Even if I hadn't been warned off in advance.'

He frowned. 'Warned off?'

'Nikki. She told me in the loos that you're practically engaged to each other.'

His jaw tightened in anger as she told him. 'Nikki is *not* my girlfriend. Not anymore. The only problem is she won't accept it. *She* was lying to you, Liz — not me.'

'I know what I saw, Alex, and you didn't exactly look like an unwilling participant.'

'She caught me off guard,' he exclaimed, and then, looking towards his guests, he lowered his voice. 'And off balance. I was trying to stop myself from falling.'

Liz laughed. 'Oh, I've heard it all now. Look Alex, I'm sorry, but I just don't trust you.'

She tried to move away from him but his grip tightened on her arm. 'You're a fine one to talk about trust. You lied to me too, don't forget.'

'I have never lied to you.'

'Yes, you did. You told me there was nothing between you and that chef you live with.'

She stared at him in disbelief. 'And that's the truth.'

'That's not what it looked like to me when you had your tongue down his throat outside Winston's the other Saturday.'

Liz flushed. She could imagine how it might have looked.

'Well, perhaps that wasn't what it looked like either. Jay was upset. He'd hoped to get back with his girlfriend, but she'd made it clear that wasn't going to happen. He was drunk and I was trying to give him some comfort.'

'That was plain to see.'

Her chest tightened in anger. What right did he have to judge her? 'I don't have to explain myself to you. I'm a free agent and can do what I like, unlike you.'

'I told you — I'm not with Nikki.'

'That's not what Nikki says. In fact, she told me only last Friday that you were going diamond shopping together at the weekend.'

'She did what?' he exploded.

Hearing his outburst, Tia dashed across the room. 'Alex! Keep your voice down! If you're going to have an argument, at least do it in private. Now come with me — I think I might have someone interested in an apartment, but I need you to seal the deal.'

Liz took her cue and made her escape.

CHAPTER TWENTY

Rage continued to boil inside Alex as he spoke to the client. The man seemed interested, but Alex couldn't have cared less. From the window to the side of him, he could see Liz getting into the van and he was determined not to let her go. He grabbed a brochure from a pile on a nearby table and said to the man quickly, 'Tell you what, why don't you sleep on it? I'm sure it's something you need to discuss with your wife or girlfriend. Perhaps we can fix up an appointment for a private viewing? Our contact details are on the brochure.' Not even waiting for a reply, Alex dashed off after Liz.

The engine of her van was running, but he jumped in front of it before she could move. He just hoped she wouldn't accelerate into him. But, luckily, she seemed to have spotted him and wound the window down.

'Alex! You frightened the life out of me!'

'I'm sorry, Liz, but you have to listen to me. I'm not engaged to Nikki and I never will be. She lied to you about us being together, and she's lying about this too.'

'She seemed pretty convincing to me,' Liz snapped at him.

Tia stormed across the car park and joined them.

'What do you think you're doing? I've never been so embarrassed in all my life. You realise that you've probably lost us a sale?'

'This is more important,' Alex said without breaking eye contact with Liz.

'What is? What's more important than business?'

'Liz,' he said.

The two women stared at him.

'Are you two together?' Tia asked.

'Not at the moment. Thanks to Nikki. She's been spreading lies, saying we're engaged, and Liz won't believe it's not true.'

'You? Engaged to Nikki?' Tia laughed. 'I've never heard anything so stupid in my life.' She turned to Liz. 'Alex broke up with her the evening of my last dinner party. She's in denial. At least that explains why he's been in such a filthy mood all week. I thought he was regretting finishing it with her, but it was obviously more about you. Do me a favour and put him out of his misery, will you, Liz? Because if you don't, I may just well go bankrupt.'

He watched as relief seemed to flood Liz's face.

'I'll leave you two to it,' Tia said. 'See what I can salvage of our business.' She looked pointedly at Alex before turning on her heel. Alex let her go, unable to take his eyes off Liz.

'Will you at least give me a second chance?'

'Well . . .' She frowned, and Alex dived in, not wanting to give her time to refuse.

'We've got off to a rocky start,' he said. 'But I think we can both agree there's something between us. Can't we at least talk about it, away from everyone else?'

She sighed as though in defeat. 'Yes, okay.'

'We could go out for a meal?'

She shook her head. 'No thanks. I've seen enough food for one night.'

'A drink then?'

'That would be nice. But first I need to go home. I could meet you somewhere.'

'How about I leave my car here and come back with you? Now I've got you within my sights, I don't want to leave you.'

'Don't you have stuff to finish up here?'

He sighed. 'Oh, I suppose so. I'll pick you up in a taxi in, say, an hour?'

'Yes, okay.' She smiled.

CHAPTER TWENTY-ONE

Liz unpacked as quickly as she could and jumped into the shower. She wanted to look her best, but didn't have much time. She had no idea where he was planning to take her, so she plumped for black skinny jeans, high heels and a turquoise, fitted shirt. A bit staid maybe, but it was the best she could do.

The intercom buzzed just as she was applying her lipstick, and as she looked at her watch, she realised it was exactly an hour since they'd spoken. She buzzed him in and grabbed her handbag and keys so that she was ready by the time he reached her apartment.

'As punctual as ever,' he said when she opened the door.

Feeling awkward at the closeness of him, she took a deep breath. 'Shall we go?'

'Sure. I have a taxi waiting downstairs,' he said as he led the way.

'Tower Bridge,' he told the taxi driver once they'd got into the cab.

'Tower Bridge?' She raised an eyebrow.

'I thought we'd walk along the South Bank and then go to a wine bar I know. Is that okay?'

It was more than okay. It was, Liz decided, perfect.

* * *

They walked side by side, so closely that she could smell his aftershave, but she didn't pull away. The bridge was lit up against the encroaching night sky. From the inky water, tinny music and laughter wafted up to them as a pleasure boat slipped beneath it. But it was the Tower itself which held Liz's gaze, sinister in the shadows. She shivered and Alex put an arm around her. She didn't stop him.

'Are you cold?'

'No, I was thinking about prisoners in the Tower. They brought Anne Boleyn here before she was beheaded. It must have been terrifying.'

He nodded. 'You didn't have to do much against the King to pay the ultimate price in those days. Unlike now when the Royal Family are the ones on trial by media.'

They walked across the bridge, both marvelling at the history beneath their feet.

'I really should learn to appreciate what's on my doorstep,' Liz said. 'I can't remember the last time I came here. It's magnificent.'

'I know what you mean. We rely too much on our cars and the Underground. Unless you see it, you don't really think about the river, but it used to be the main mode of transport. I often come here when I need a bit of inspiration; the architecture speaks volumes.'

Liz was silent, humbled by his speech. She hardly ever noticed her surroundings; she was far too busy concentrating on her career. Too busy perhaps. She needed to relax more.

'I almost feel like a tourist,' she admitted as they walked past the New Globe Theatre. 'Although if I was a tourist, I might actually visit the attractions. Have you ever been in here?'

'Yes,' he said, smiling. 'I came to a production of *King Lear* last month.'

'My word, cultured too. You are a bit of a catch, aren't you?'

He grinned at her. 'I like to think so. Come on, here's the bar I was telling you about.'

The bar was crowded and noisy, but Alex caught the attention of a barman straight away. As Liz scanned the room for a table, a couple by the window got up to leave. She grabbed it and sat down.

A while later, as the crisp coldness of the Sancerre slipped down her throat, Liz was buoyed up with happiness. Lights twinkled romantically on the river and she was sitting opposite a man she had been in love with since she was a girl. Earlier, she would never have believed tonight would turn out like this. The last few weeks had been a roller coaster ride, and she was worried the next part might be downhill again. She knew that Alex had the potential to hurt her, but right now she wanted to live in the moment and not fear for the future. Even so, she knew she wouldn't be able to relax until she'd confronted him about what Jay had told her.

'How's the new restaurant coming along?' she asked.

For a moment, he looked startled. 'How did you hear about that?'

'You shouldn't underestimate chefs. They're the biggest gossips.'

'Well, it's still in the early stages.' He had the decency to look guilty. 'Roberto didn't want to commit himself until we'd found a property.'

'And now?'

'We've found the perfect place. We'll need planning permission for change of use, so we need to get the ball rolling as soon as possible. Roberto wants everything up and running before his baby is born, although, to be honest, I can't see that happening. He doesn't really understand how long planning applications take.'

'I'm pleased for you,' she forced herself to say. 'Although I'll be out of a job when you open. Or part of one, at least.'

He frowned. 'Why?'

'I don't suppose Tia will be holding any more dinner parties when she has her own restaurant and neither will any of her friends.

'Oh . . . I see. Yes, of course.' He paused, then added, 'But Tia isn't your only client, is she?'

'No.' Liz took a sip of her wine, hesitating. She didn't want to reveal how precarious her business was. 'But the competition is tough.'

'And more won't help. I'm sorry, I—'

She cut him off. 'I'll just have to try harder. So anyway, tell me all about it. Where is it? What's it like? This building of yours.'

'It's an old media building in Fitzrovia.'

She nodded. 'So, was our meal out research for you too?'

He frowned. 'No. Don't think that. I wanted to show you one of my favourite restaurants. I love the area too. It has such a buzz about it. And the building we're looking at is on three floors and has massive potential.'

'Won't that take a lot of work to convert?'

'More than Roberto wanted, but I've been working on the plans and I think it could be amazing.' The enthusiasm for the project was clear in his voice and she allowed her resentment to slip away. She was determined to make her own business a success regardless of what Tia and Alex were doing. And now she just wanted to enjoy his company.

'I'd love to see your sketches sometime,' she said provocatively.

'They're at my apartment,' he flirted back.

'That's very convenient.'

'Isn't it just?' He paused. 'Do you really want to see them?'

'Yes, of course! I'm always interested when a new restaurant opens. It's something I'd like to do myself one day. If I ever had the money.'

'Wouldn't you miss the flexibility of your business?'

'Perhaps,' she said. 'But sometimes it's a bit too flexible. You never really know what's going to happen from one month to the next. But I have made some good contacts recently.'

'You made a very good contact tonight.'

'Did I?'

'If Lord Weatherton isn't a good contact, I don't know who is.'

'Lord Weatherton?' She shook her head. 'Sorry, you've lost me.'

'You know, the guy in the kitchen? Wants you to ring his PA to quote for his daughter's engagement party?'

'He hasn't asked me to quote for an engagement party, just a little do he's having at his house.'

'That's just typical.' Alex chuckled. 'Henry always likes to play things down. And his house is a country pile. He's one of the top ten richest men in the country.'

Liz choked on her drink and had to put her glass down while she recovered. 'Bloody hell! And I asked him to sort out the details direct. What must he have thought of me?'

'He probably thought you were a very down to earth and honest person. And he would respect you for that. Henry wasn't born a lord, in fact if the previous Lord Weatherton hadn't died before he'd married or had children, Henry would never have inherited. But when he did, the estate was in a right mess. The house was literally falling to pieces. He's turned it around and made it into a profitable business. He's a clever man and nice with it. He likes to give young people a leg up the career ladder. Make sure you phone his PA. You never know, he might even ask you to do the wedding itself.'

Although she knew it wasn't an attractive look, Liz stared at him, open-mouthed. 'You're joking.'

'I'm not. So, you may not have to worry about our restaurant. Although'—he paused—'if you *are* interested in seeing my plans . . .'

She had enjoyed spending time with him, and she really didn't want the night to end just yet. Feeling suddenly brave, she looked directly at him. 'I'm interested.'

* * *

Outside, Alex hailed a cab while Liz tried not to berate herself at her recklessness. She'd never normally allow herself to be taken back to someone's apartment on what was effectively a second date. But it wasn't really a second date, was it? She'd known Alex for years. If she didn't have the courage to jump now, she never would.

The taxi soon pulled up outside a huge glass-fronted apartment complex and they got out. They walked down the path which cut through manicured, landscaped gardens. He swiped his fob on the panel by large glass doors and guided her towards the lift on the other side of an impressive-looking reception area. The lift arrived immediately and swished them up to the twelfth floor. She felt like she was in another world and wondered how long it would take for the bubble to burst.

His apartment was just as flash as the communal areas — spacious, modern and incredibly neat. She thought of her own flat, which was cramped, messy and hadn't been redecorated since she'd moved in four years ago. Before she had a chance to think too much though, Alex pulled her towards him and started kissing her. She had dreamed of this moment for years but the reality was so much better, making her dizzy with desire. In danger of losing complete control, she broke away from him and stepped back. 'I thought we were coming to look at your plans. I hope you haven't brought me here under false pretences,' she said breathlessly.

He laughed. 'Of course not. I just couldn't resist. Come through to my study.'

He led her through to a smaller room, which again was immaculate and completely high tech. In the corner, on a drawing board, were a selection of sketches and photographs.

'This is the building now. And this is what it will be.' He showed her the first sketch. The downstairs dining area was open-plan. So too, was the kitchen. Liz shuddered at the thought.

'Whose idea was the kitchen?' she asked, already knowing the answer.

'Tia. You know what she's like for theatre. She thinks it will add more drama.'

'And a lot of noise.'

'You don't like it?'

'I like the restaurant floor. I'm just not sure about it being so open-plan. Sometimes that can feel a bit like a canteen. I loved the restaurant we went to. It had lots of little areas where you could be private.'

He nodded, taking her comments seriously. 'Yes, I know what you mean. Tia and Roberto lean towards the theatrical, but perhaps there's room for both?'

'You said it had three floors. You could use another floor for a different type of dining.'

'We haven't decided what to do with the other floors yet. Both Tia and Roberto are pushing to get the restaurant up and running, but I'd rather do the refurbishment as a whole to minimise the disruption. I'm meeting with them tomorrow to show them the plans so far. So maybe I can convince them to slow down a bit.'

Liz laughed. 'Good luck with that!'

Alex reached out for her, and again she allowed herself to be pulled into his embrace. The feel of his lips, the scent of citrus from his aftershave and his solid body against her made her burn with longing. At that moment, there was nowhere else she'd rather be.

'Do you want a drink?' he asked as he pulled back, breaking the spell. Her body felt cold as he moved away from her and she tried to quell her disappointment, or at least not let him see it. 'I've got some champagne chilling in the fridge.'

'Do you always keep champagne chilling in the fridge?' she asked.

He grinned. 'Not usually, but I was hoping to celebrate a successful evening. I wasn't expecting this.'

'I'm sorry to disappoint.'

'Oh, it's no disappointment,' he said as he led her back into the living room. She sat down on a large white sofa to admire the surroundings while he went to fetch the champagne.

The room was large with a thick pile carpet, which was pristine white and immaculately clean. She was already terrified she might spill something and mess it up completely. She was far too clumsy to live in a place like this.

After returning and opening the bottle, he carefully poured the liquid into a glass and handed it to her.

'So, do you like my apartment?' he asked as she sipped her drink, allowing the sharp bubbles to fizz over her tongue.

'It's lovely.' She paused. 'And I bet it has fantastic views.'

'It does. Although I sense a "but"?'

'Nothing. It's just very different from what I'm used to. You've seen where I live and where I come from.'

'I love where you come from. This place is okay, but it's not really home. You're right about the views, though. Let me show you.'

He put his glass down and drew back the thick cream curtains to reveal a French door onto the balcony.

As he opened the door, crisp spring air wafted through the room, smelling of faded sunshine mixed with the river. She followed him outside and gasped.

'Oh Alex, this is gorgeous!'

The river was in darkness but the landmarks were lit up in neon-blue. It reminded her of a postcard or print of London at night, and she could hardly believe she was looking at it for real.

'Not as gorgeous as you,' Alex said, putting his arms around her from behind and nuzzling her ear, sending a thousand volts of electricity through her body. Then he kissed her again, leisurely at first, but with increasing passion. She pushed herself into him, wanting to be even closer. He led the way back into the living room and they landed softly on the sofa, his hands exploring, sending trails of heat wherever he touched. She'd waited for this moment since she was a lovesick teenager. She should be in heaven. And yet. *And yet*. Gently, she put her hands over his to stop him from going any further.

'Alex.'

He pulled back and looked straight at her. 'It's too soon, isn't it?'

She nodded, her throat constricting as tears stung her eyes. She felt so childish — the complete opposite to the sophisticated woman she wanted to be.

'Hey, it's okay,' he whispered.

'It's not that . . .'

'Hush.' He put his finger on her lips and then kissed her gently. 'I understand. This has all happened very quickly.' He moved away and she sat up and straightened her clothes. He topped up her glass and passed it over. 'From the moment I saw you again, I knew you were something special.'

'You did?'

'Yes, and I've not felt like that since I met Kas.'

'Oh.' She was dying to ask about Kas, wanted to know everything about the woman he had loved so much. But now was not the time.

'Nikki's very attractive, but I didn't really connect with her. Tia's crowd can be fun to be with and that's what I thought I needed. At first being with Nikki *was* fun, but then I realised that she had deeper feelings for me than I could ever return. That's when I finished it. I thought I was letting her go before I hurt her too much . . . but I think I left it too late.'

'And now she doesn't want to let go,' Liz said.

'She doesn't, but it's all one-sided. There's nothing going on between us because I want to be with you, Liz, and I'm prepared to wait for you until you're ready.'

He leaned across and wiped away the tears on her face with his thumb. She hardly even realised she was crying. Her throat felt tight, and at first she couldn't speak, but eventually she managed to choke out a few words. 'Thank you, Alex. Not many men would understand. I thought I was ready, but it looks like I need more time.'

He put his arms around her and whispered gently into her hair, 'We have all the time in the world.'

CHAPTER TWENTY-TWO

While the coffee was brewing the next morning, Alex stepped out onto the balcony. The sun was shining, glinting off the Thames, and the air was warm, its smell reminding him of honey. He felt lighter than he had in a long time and he couldn't help smiling.

He'd meant what he'd said last night. He was prepared to take it slowly with Liz. She was like a young deer, fearful of trusting, but over time, he knew he'd be able to persuade her that she could believe in him. He hoped he'd proved last night that she had nothing to fear from Nikki, and he'd paved the way so that gradually they could build up their relationship.

Smelling the coffee, he went into the kitchen to pour himself a cup. He took it back out onto the balcony and sat down. He should get ready, but for once he was in no rush. For so long he'd kept himself busy, not allowing himself time to think or dwell on his loss.

He could scarcely believe how much his mood had changed since meeting Liz again. He didn't miss Kas any less, and she was constantly in his thoughts, but now Liz was too. Last night, he'd gone to sleep dreaming of Liz and she'd still been on his mind when he'd woken up. Before she'd left, they'd made arrangements to see each other again tonight, and he couldn't wait.

With a sudden flash of guilt, he walked over to Kas' photograph and picked it up.

'I won't ever forget you,' he said, talking to the picture as he often did. 'But for the first time since you left me, I feel as though I might have a future.' Liz was very much like Kas in personality, and he enjoyed just talking with her, especially about his business. Not only did she listen but she inspired him too, which was exactly what he wanted from a long-term partner.

He went into the study to have another look at his drawings for the proposed restaurant. The outline of the building didn't lend itself to small intimate areas, but it would be perfect for functions, with space for socialising before dining. He also knew who would be the perfect function chef to partner with — especially after Liz had voiced her concerns about her business last night. She hadn't gone into detail but the way she'd quickly changed the subject made him think that things were worse than she was letting on. He would have to get the idea past Roberto and Tia first, so he decided not to tell Liz anything yet. The last thing he wanted was to build her hopes up if he couldn't make good on it.

* * *

The traffic was slow as Alex travelled to his meeting, finally arriving ten minutes late.

'Punctuality is so important in business. Meeting deadlines is the key to a successful restaurant,' Roberto complained when he finally arrived.

Roberto's tone annoyed him, and he was about to tell him so when he caught Tia's glare and bit back his retort. He needed to keep them both on side.

'Let's get straight down to business then, shall we? I have some ideas about the efficient use of the first floor.'

He showed them the plans for the ground floor, which were all received favourably albeit with a few minor changes.

Alex moved on. 'If we used both the ground and the first floor for restaurant purposes, I think we would struggle to fill it. So, I propose we redesign the first floor to hold private functions. That way we could maximise potential and give function guests privacy away from the main restaurant.'

Roberto shook his head, frowning. 'You'd need a large staff to cater for both functions and normal service, and they wouldn't always be utilised.'

'Not if you contracted out the functions. It could be fee earning rather than salaried.'

Tia grinned. 'And I bet you have just the person in mind.' Roberto looked puzzled, until Tia added, 'Liz Cartwright. She cooked for you the other week.'

'Ah yes.' Roberto nodded. 'Do you think she could cope with the pressure?'

'What do you mean?' Alex bristled. He'd seen Liz work under extreme pressure without batting an eyelid. Tia gave him a look, but he ignored it.

'I'm sure she has the practical skills,' Roberto said. 'My doubts are whether she has the emotional resilience. The reason she left my restaurant was because she had a personality clash with my second in command, Louis. And I intend to ask him to help get this restaurant up and running.'

'I can see why that might be a problem,' Tia agreed.

'From what I've seen, she's extremely professional,' Alex said, feeling the need to defend Liz. 'Besides, she wouldn't be working for Louis, she'd be working for herself.'

'She already has her own business, though,' Tia said. 'I'm not sure she'd be able to provide the commitment we need. Besides, I'd like to put forward my own ideas for the first floor.'

'Which are?' Alex asked, annoyed at how quickly she was dismissing his plans.

'We could use the first floor as a bar area, attract the after-work drinkers who then might want a meal. It could also be used as a reception area for those who have already booked. If we maximise the turnover in alcohol, we'll create a much higher profit margin, and those drinking wouldn't be cluttering up the dining space.'

'I thought we were worried we wouldn't fill the space, not that it would be cluttered?' Alex cut in.

'I'm looking to the future. I envisage this restaurant being a tremendous success.'

'I'm sure we all hope that.' Alex gritted his teeth. 'But I think that functions would be a more efficient use of the space than a bar area, and they would offer an additional string to our bow.'

'There's still the second floor,' Tia said, surprising him. 'It's smaller I know, but I think it would work. We could give it a completely different look to differentiate it from the main restaurant. The middle floor could be the reception for both the floors. What do you say?'

Alex nodded thoughtfully. 'Yes, that might work. I'd need to take another look at the top floor. See how much a conversion would cost.'

'And don't forget we need to think of the timing issues,' Roberto reminded them, looking at his watch. 'And for now, I need to go. Why don't you two carry on and email me later to let me know how you get on? But let's not get carried away. You see a dream, I want reality. Let's meet at the building at nine o'clock tomorrow morning.'

'Agreed,' Alex said. 'Tia, do you want to go to the property now? We can discuss structure and ideas for internal redec and put together some drawings.'

'Okay,' Tia said. 'Let's go.'

* * *

At the venue, Alex and Tia explored the three floors, with Alex eventually agreeing to Tia's plan. The sticking point came with the kitchen though as, true to form, Tia insisted on yet another open-plan kitchen.

'No, absolutely not,' Alex argued, remembering Liz's comments from the previous night. 'You can't have the crashing and banging of mass catering on view at functions. An enclosed kitchen here would be better.'

'You seem to be an expert on the subject suddenly,' Tia commented drily. 'How did last night go?'

'Fine,' he said, not giving anything else away, and changed the subject. He didn't want to discuss this fledging relationship with Tia.

'Emotional and working relationships don't always work, Alex. You should remember that as you're recommending her to be involved in this. You have no idea how things will play out. It's already had a bumpy start.'

'That's all sorted out now,' he flung back at her, watching as she flinched. 'Sorry, that sounded harsh, but I think I know what I'm doing.'

'Well, we can discuss the finer points at a later date. We don't even know if it's something she'd be interested in. But I do worry about your personal involvement.'

'Point noted,' Alex muttered.

'I suppose it could work on a function-by-function basis. And if your relationship starts to affect the restaurant, we'll find another chef.'

'Fair enough,' he said. It irritated him that Tia always had to be the one in control. He concentrated on the practicalities. 'It will mean a lot of changes to the plans and to the planning application.'

'You'd best get on with it then, hadn't you?' Tia said as they left. She looked at her watch. 'I've got a meeting with some suppliers. I've got great ideas for the interiors, so the sooner I have your plans, the better.'

CHAPTER TWENTY-THREE

On the dot of nine, Liz phoned Lord Weatherton's PA.

'Ah yes, I've been told to expect your call. I'm afraid I'm busy today, but I could see you first thing in the morning.'

'That would be perfect.'

'If I give you the details of what we're looking for, perhaps you can prepare some menu suggestions. We'd like a buffet style menu for three hundred people.'

'Three hundred,' Liz repeated. Lord Weatherton certainly was the master of understatement.

'Is that a problem?'

'No, of course not,' Liz said hurriedly, thinking she was going to need a huge support team. 'It's just that Lord Weatherton implied it would be a small affair.'

'Oh, it is. You should see the numbers for the wedding.'

'Right,' Liz replied, but covered up her shock by asking, 'Did you have any particular food in mind?'

'Yes. Game, seafood, oysters, if you can get them, quails' eggs — Lord Weatherton is particularly fond of those. Let me have your best ideas and I'll see if we can work from there. Can you come to Lord Weatherton's office tomorrow morning at nine-thirty?'

'Of course. Where are you based?'

'We're right by the Palace of Westminster, handy for the House of Lords.'

'Perfect. I'm looking forward to meeting you.'

'Me too. Lord Weatherton was quite taken with you. If it was down to him, you'd get the work straight away, but I do believe in doing a job thoroughly.'

'I agree. It's best to get several quotes.'

She put the phone down with a surge of adrenaline. *Three hundred.* Quails' eggs, oysters. She was going to enjoy putting this menu together.

She cast her eyes around her living room. As usual, books were strewn everywhere. She shook her head as she remembered Alex's pristine flat. She needed a clear space to be able to focus today.

After her tidy up, she sat down with a cup of coffee, her portfolio and recipe books. This was going to have to be her best work.

She was so deep in concentration, she jumped when her mobile rang, but looking at the screen brought a smile to her face.

'Hello,' she said, unable to keep the delight out of her voice.

'Hi. How are you?' His voice was deep and chocolaty and sent shivers down her spine.

'I'm fine. Busy. What about you?'

'I'm busy too. In fact, I don't think I'm going to be able to make it tonight.'

'Oh.' Her voice fell flat along with her mood. She hoped this wasn't just an excuse.

'It's not that I don't want to see you,' he rushed on. 'In fact, it's the thought of seeing you that's keeping me going. The plans have changed for the restaurant and I need to get the drawings done as soon as possible.'

'I see. Well, I'm pretty busy myself. I've got a meeting with Lord Weatherton's PA in the morning.'

'That's brilliant. So, you're not too disappointed about not meeting up then?'

'A little,' she lied. She didn't want him to know just how disappointed she actually was. 'What are these changes, anyway?'

'You were right about planning the other floors, and we've got some pretty interesting ideas.'

'Sounds intriguing. Tell me more.'

He paused. 'I'd rather tell you face to face. How are you fixed for tomorrow evening, about eight?'

'That's good for me,' she said, wondering what he couldn't tell her over the phone.

When her phone rang again five minutes later, she grabbed it, hoping that Alex had changed his mind about tonight, but it was only Jay.

'Hi.'

'Hi, Liz. Are you busy?' He sounded upset.

'Well, I am, but . . . what is it?'

'Can I come round? I could do with a chat. Or rather a moan.'

'Oh dear, bad day?' she asked, wondering if it was work or whether he was still pining for Susie.

'Oh yes.'

'I'm in all day so call round whenever you want.'

'Great. I finish my shift at three, so I'll see you after.'

* * *

Liz was still knee deep in recipes when Jay rang her doorbell.

'You *do* look busy,' he commented.

'I really am,' she agreed. 'Can I get you a coffee?'

'Love one.'

He was peering at her notebook when she brought the coffee in.

'I've been asked to quote for Lord Weatherton's daughter's engagement party.'

Jay whistled. 'Get you! You've really hit the big time.'

'Maybe,' she said, remembering the reason for his visit. 'But never mind that. What's up?'

Jay sighed and sat down. 'You know Roberto's planning on opening a new restaurant?'

'Yes.' She considered telling him about her conversation the previous night but didn't want to interrupt him.

'I thought it might give me some opportunity for promotion, but I've been completely overlooked.'

'Are you sure? I mean, the restaurant is only an idea at the moment. Surely Roberto hasn't finalised the staffing arrangements already?'

'It's not Roberto who's the problem. It's Louis.'

'Louis?' Liz shuddered at the memory of the man who had delighted in bullying her when she worked at La Emporium. 'What's he done now?'

'He's going to be in charge of the new restaurant and he's made it clear there's no place for me.'

'I see.' Typical that the nasty people rose to the top. 'But what about La Emporium? If they're moving people around, what about promotion there?'

Jay shook his head. 'Nope. Louis is in charge of staffing overall. I need to face facts, Liz. I'll have to look for another job.'

'But I don't understand. I thought you always got on okay with Louis. What's made him go against you?'

'Ah yes, well . . .' He picked up his coffee cup and drank, unable to look her in her eye.

'Jay?'

Jay looked up. 'You know that function you did at Tia's with Roberto?'

'Yes.' She still glowed whenever she remembered his praise.

'He was telling Louis how much you'd improved. Louis was seething and I couldn't help bragging about how well you were doing. I really enjoyed seeing the look on his face, but it's backfired now.'

'Oh, Jay! I'm so sorry.'

'Don't be. I'm glad I said what I did. He's a bully and I hated what he did to you.'

'But now he's bullying you. Can't you say something to Roberto?'

Jay shook his head. 'No point. Louis will always be Roberto's golden boy. I'll find something else. Somewhere they'll appreciate my considerable talents.' He grinned at her, but she could see that he was masking his sadness. She tried to be positive too.

'Maybe that's what you need. No point staying somewhere where there's no chance of promotion.'

'Maybe. I'll just have to ask Roberto for a reference, not Louis.'

'If I get this engagement job, I'm going to need some extra chefs. It's at the end of June if you fancy taking some holiday?'

'Yes, I'm up for that. I really enjoyed working at the fashion show. I can easily book holiday for anything else you might need me for as well. I've got enough owing.'

'Oh, I will. And as you will have worked for me, you can put me down as a referee.'

'Thanks, Liz,' Jay said, leaning over and giving her a hug.

After he'd gone, she went back to her menu planning. She felt guilty that he'd stuck up for her and lost himself a chance of promotion. But it made her even more determined to get the engagement job, to give him a chance to put something else on his CV.

* * *

Liz woke up at six the next morning. After a night of tossing and turning, she got up and went for a run. Already it looked like it would turn into a beautiful sunny day. The air was crisp and fresh, with the dew coolly shining on the grass. If the meeting went well, she decided, she would spend a leisurely afternoon browsing the shops. She could do with a treat.

Mrs Anderson, Lord Weatherton's personal assistant, was a middle-aged, slim lady with blonde bobbed hair and an immaculate dress sense. The office was as stylish as she was, and Liz could sense that she ran it with quiet efficiency.

She was welcoming, though, and it wasn't long before Liz was entirely comfortable with her. The previous evening, she'd Googled Lord Weatherton's country home to get a feel for the place, and she'd come up with a plan.

'We'd like the event to be held in the grounds, weather permitting of course. But we'll need a back-up plan just in case. You never know with the British weather,' Mrs Anderson commented.

'I can't guarantee the weather but I do have some ideas. I was thinking of a typical Edwardian-style summer garden party — you know, marquees, croquet on the lawns? We could do a champagne and oyster bar outside, a Pimm's and strawberry tent, seafood and game platters, and the obligatory cucumber and assorted sandwiches, canapés and cake. I've put together a portfolio of dishes in here.' Liz handed her the folder she had compiled. 'Of course, if it does rain, we can set these up in the house. We can serve the champagne, oysters and Pimm's in the orangery. The rest in the main hall. How does that sound?'

'It sounds perfect, and just what we're looking for. You've obviously done your homework. Now to costings.'

'Yes, I wasn't sure of your budget, so I've priced at different levels and then you can choose what you want. I haven't costed drinks either.'

'That's fine. Lord Weatherton will provide all the champagne direct from his own cellars and I will source the rest. Now, does this price include staffing?'

'No, but I can provide as many waitresses as you want at a competitive hourly rate.'

'Really? You have that command at your fingertips? That's very enterprising for someone who works on her own.'

'I'm on very good terms with local catering colleges — students are always looking for extra income.'

'Won't it interfere with exam timetables?'

'The exams will be finished by then. I'm sure it won't be a problem.' Liz kept her fingers crossed as she said this. If she had to drag people in off the streets, she'd make sure the function was fully staffed.

'Well, that all sounds satisfactory. I have another company to see, but I'll let you know by tomorrow.'

'Perfect.'

Mrs Anderson got up to shake her hand. 'I hope we'll be seeing each other again. I think we could work well together.'

Liz smiled as she left. She was glad she'd worked so hard yesterday on her presentation — hopefully it would pay dividends. Even if she didn't get this job, there might be others in the future.

She decided to treat herself to a jaunt in Covent Garden where she did some shopping and ate a lazy lunch as she watched the street performers. Her phone was ominously silent, and although she was tempted to phone Alex, she resisted the urge. If he was busy, she didn't want to interrupt him. Neither did she want to appear too keen. She would just have to wait. To take her mind off waiting for his call, Liz wandered through the back streets of Covent Garden, pausing as a woman retrieved a large tray of vegetables from a nearby van and then crossed the pavement in front of her. She stopped in her tracks.

'Eleni?' she asked, suddenly recognising her.

The woman turned to her, a beaming smile lighting up her Mediterranean features.

'Liz! How lovely to see you.'

'And you! I thought you were in Greece?'

Liz and Eleni had trained together in Manchester and then moved to London together to work and share a flat. Homesick for her beloved Greece, Eleni had eventually decided to go home and had later married a Greek man. The two women had kept in touch sporadically but Liz hadn't heard from her for a while.

'It's a long story,' Eleni said. She pointed to what looked like a closed restaurant. 'Come inside so I can put this down, and then I'll tell you all about it.'

Together, Liz and Eleni emptied the rest of the van and placed everything onto a counter top inside the restaurant.

'Let me introduce you to Dimitri,' Eleni said. She disappeared into the kitchen and came out a few minutes later, followed by a tall, dark-haired, very handsome man.

Dimitri took Liz's hand and kissed it while Eleni explained further. 'Dimitri got the travel bug and I wasn't about to let him go off on his own. So, we travel together, doing pop-up nights to pay for our journeys.'

Dimitri hugged Eleni to him. 'Not that I would travel without her,' he said.

'That sounds amazing,' Liz said, feeling just a little bit envious.

'It's good, yes, but our travelling will be coming to an end soon. We want to try for a baby and home is the only place I want to bring up my family.'

'Ah yes, of course.'

'It has been nice to meet you,' Dimitri said when they had chatted for a while. 'But we open tonight, one night only, so there is a lot of work to do.'

'I won't keep you from it then,' Liz said.

'Why don't you come tonight?' Eleni asked. 'We won't be able to chat much but I guarantee you good food'

'I'd love that.' Crossing her fingers that Alex hadn't made other arrangements, Liz booked a table for two.

* * *

She was nearly home by the time Alex rang her. He sounded tired but happy to hear her voice.

'How are you? How did your meeting go?' he asked.

'Fine. Well, it seemed to anyway. I'll know tomorrow.'

'I'm sorry about last night but I was so snowed under.'

'That's okay.' She tried to keep her voice light. 'And have you finished it now?'

'Yes. The first drafts, at least. We had another meeting with Roberto, and of course he wants some changes. But I'm still free tonight.'

'That's great,' she said. Knowing that he wanted to see her again made her heart sing. 'But let me choose the restaurant this time.'

'Oh . . . okay then,' he said.

She smiled at the surprise in his voice. 'Meet me outside the Punch and Judy pub in Covent Garden at eight. That okay for you?'

'Sure. See you then.'

CHAPTER TWENTY-FOUR

When she reached the stone facade of the Punch and Judy, she was delighted to find Alex already waiting for her. He was dressed in what seemed to be his usual evening attire of a shirt and chinos.

He greeted her with a hug and she had the urge to sink into his embrace and stay there forever, but reluctantly she pulled back. His lips were only inches away from hers. She was desperate to kiss him but was hesitant to make such a bold move so early on in the evening. Alex moved away but reached for her hand.

'So, where are you taking me then? I must say I'm intrigued,' he said.

She smiled. It was nice to be taking the lead. Tonight would be very different. Certainly not the posh meals out he was used to with his model friends.

'There and back to see how far it is,' she said. It was something her father had always said to them when he'd taken them on one of his magical mystery tours as children.

'Lead on then,' he replied.

Smiling, she led him across the square and down a side street. Unlike this afternoon, the restaurant was lit up, and from a brief glimpse in the window looked really busy. As she pushed open the door, she was immediately immersed in the cacophony of a full restaurant, warmth, and the delicious smell of garlic, herbs and tomatoes. Eleni greeted them, embracing Liz in an exuberant hug.

'I'm so glad you came,' and after acknowledging Alex with an appreciative smile said, 'Let me show you to your table. The celebrations are just about to begin.'

They sat down and Eleni went off to get them some drinks.

'Celebrations?' Alex asked.

'Greek night,' Liz explained. 'It's a set menu, but if I know Eleni, the food will be wonderful.'

As she spoke, a man dressed in a white shirt, waistcoat and pantaloons walked around the restaurant with his bouzouki, followed by exotic women dancing behind him in their long, flowing skirts. Liz and Alex sat back, sipped the drinks Eleni had brought over, allowed themselves to become absorbed in the music, and watched the dancers. Liz smiled as one of them paid particular attention to Alex, much to his embarrassment.

'Well, that was fun,' Alex commented, as the dancers finally retreated.

'It's certainly different,' Liz replied, hoping this would be a night they would remember for all the right reasons.

'I wonder when they'll start the plate smashing,' he remarked with a laugh.

'Probably not until we've finished eating, otherwise they might not be able to serve the food.'

Alex ordered a bottle of wine, and a mezze starter was brought to the table. The food was a delicious platter of breads, dips, olives, feta cheese, lamb koftas and stuffed vine leaves.

'So, this is a hidden gem. How did you find it?'

I popped into Covent Garden earlier and literally bumped into Eleni. We trained together in Manchester then moved here. We shared a flat for a while but then she moved to Greece. I hadn't even realised she was back in England.'

'That was a nice surprise for you,' Alex said, before adding, 'She certainly knows her stuff. This lamb kofta is delicious.'

'She should do. It was the food she grew up with, and she was taught how to make it by her grandmother.'

'Shame this is only a pop-up. I'd definitely come back.

'She said she'll be moving back to Greece soon. She and Dimitri are planning on starting a family.'

She watched as a flicker of a frown crossed his face before he swiftly changed the subject. 'You didn't tell me properly — how did your meeting with Lord Weatherton's PA go?'

'I think it went well, but she's seeing someone else and said she'd let me know tomorrow. All I can do is keep my fingers crossed.' *And pray*, she added silently because she *really* wanted to get this job.

'I don't think you'll need to worry,' Alex said, taking a sip of his wine. 'It's a done deal if Henry's got anything to do with it. I spoke to him today about an apartment he wants to buy for his daughter and he couldn't sing your praises highly enough.'

She felt a thrill of excitement at his words.

'I certainly hope so. It's the kind of function that could really put me on the map.'

After the waiter cleared away their plates, she moved on to the topic she was most interested about. 'You were going to tell me about the restaurant?'

'Oh yes.' His eyes lit up as he explained. 'I had a good meeting with Tia and Roberto today and we've decided what to do with all three floors.'

'There's a lot of space to fill.'

'There is.'

The waiter approached with steaming plates of beef stifado, creamy mashed potato and green beans. They were silent as he served the food. Liz was eager to eat, the smell of the garlic and tomatoes making her mouth water. When the waiter had gone, Alex continued his conversation.

'That's why we've decided to turn the top floor into an area where we can cater for functions.'

She dropped her fork in shock, suddenly feeling sick, yet Alex was grinning as though he should be applauded.

'More competition.'

'What?' The smile slid from his face. 'No, Liz, you've got the wrong end of the stick.'

'Really?' She couldn't believe how angry she was. Just when she thought their relationship was progressing, he was jeopardising it yet again. It was one step forward and two steps back with him.

Eleni came over to the table. 'Is everything alright with your meals?'

Liz pinned a smile on her face. 'Yes, it's delicious.' She forced herself to pick up the abandoned fork and ate some more. Although she still felt nauseous, the food tasted wonderful.

'Good.' It was clear Eleni realised something was wrong from her frown. 'Well, if you need anything, let me know.'

After she'd gone, Alex took hold of her hand. 'Liz, just hear me out.'

She desperately wanted to snatch it away but found she couldn't. She willed him to say what she wanted to hear, that somehow, even though he was setting up in direct competition with her business, it didn't mean the end of them.

'The building is far too big to fill with casual diners itself. We're going to use the ground floor as a restaurant, as we originally decided, and the first floor as a bar and meeting point.'

'Go on,' she said through gritted teeth.

'That just leaves the second floor, which we'll advertise for private functions.'

She tried to move her hand away from his, but he held onto it a little more tightly.

'We can't afford to have staff on salary to cater for ad hoc functions, and using the restaurant staff would put too much pressure on a busy service, so we would want to outsource the function catering. Do you know any reputable chefs who might be interested?'

He was smiling again, but she couldn't smile back. When she didn't reply, he added, 'You said last night you were worried about the competition and that your business can be a bit hit and miss, so this is the perfect solution for us all.'

'I see.'

Slowly, she began to eat, not wanting to waste the food but also giving herself time to reply. She wasn't sure how she felt. Happy that her business wasn't in the jeopardy she had first thought it was, or angry with him for assuming she needed his help?

'I thought you'd be pleased,' he said, frowning in confusion.

'It's a lot to take in.'

Perhaps she was being too harsh. It was clear he only had good intentions, but he was steamrollering her. She placed her hand over his and forced herself to smile.

'Thank you for thinking of me. But there's a lot to consider and tonight isn't the best time to do that.'

'No, probably not. I appreciate that this may have come out of the blue for you, but I can see this working for both of us.'

'Perhaps.' She paused. 'It took a lot for me to move away from the safety of employment. And although it can be tricky at times, I enjoy being my own boss. I don't want to lose that.' She was thinking about Tia and how controlling she could be. And then there was Louis . . .

'But you wouldn't be taking orders from anyone. We'd just provide the space. You'd liaise with the client and do everything else.'

'And it would be completely independent from the restaurant?'

'Completely.'

She nodded. Perhaps there was merit in it. 'I can see how it might work. But let's leave it for tonight.'

'You're right. And, anyway, it's probably way down the line. We've got to get planning permission before we can do anything.' He looked uncertain. 'I haven't ruined tonight, have I?'

'No. And I'm sorry. You caught me by surprise. I'm used to doing everything for myself, at my own speed. You move at a much faster pace. I'll have to get used to that.'

'I hope you can.'

She tried to put their conversation to one side and enjoy the rest of the evening. But as she joined in with the obligatory plate throwing, her mind was elsewhere.

* * *

Lying in bed that night after Alex had dropped her off in a taxi, she couldn't stop thinking about it. Alex was right. It could work for both of them. With the extra business, she would have to employ more chefs — maybe give Jay a full-time job, even a partnership. She enjoyed her independence, but if she was going to be in a partnership with anyone, Jay was her man. It might be nice to share the burden and have someone on her side to stand up to the personalities involved. One thing was for sure, if she was going to do this, it would be on her own terms.

CHAPTER TWENTY-FIVE

'Earth to Alex,' Tia said, and Alex jumped at the sound of her voice.

'Sorry. I was miles away.' He sighed.

'You can say that again. You've been staring out of the window for the last ten minutes at least.'

'I've got a lot on my mind.'

Tia got up from her desk and walked over to the coffee machine where she made them both a cup of coffee.

'Want to talk about it? You know what they say, "A problem shared".'

Alex took the coffee from her gratefully. 'It's not really a problem. We're still waiting for the Planning Department to give us consent for the change of use for the restaurant, and yesterday I sold the last of the apartments. So, I haven't got much on at the moment.'

'Ah, so that's it — you're already looking for a new venture.'

'Actually, I'm thinking of getting rid of some old ones,' Alex said, deciding it was time to confide in Tia. 'I'm going back to Dubai for a few weeks.'

Tia spluttered inelegantly as her coffee went down the wrong way. 'Wow, that's a big decision. You haven't been back to Dubai since you first moved back here.'

'I know. Dad's been brilliant looking after the properties I own over there, but he wants to retire, and it's not fair on him. So, I've decided to go over and get things sorted.'

'And how do you feel about that?'

'Mixed, really,' Alex admitted. 'It feels as though it's time to move forward.'

'This wouldn't have anything to do with your new relationship, would it?' Tia gave him a knowing look.

Alex had been seeing Liz, as often as their busy schedules allowed, for almost a month now — and every time he saw her, he felt as though he fell a little bit more in love with her. He paused before answering. 'Sort of. I came here because I couldn't bear to be in the same place where Kas died. Because everywhere and everyone reminded me of her. And I couldn't live with the guilt.'

'Oh Alex, we've been through this before. You have absolutely no reason to feel guilty.'

'But if I'd paid attention, and not been so focused on work, I might have realised—'

'She contracted sepsis, Alex. There was nothing you could have done.'

'But if I'd got Kas to hospital earlier, then maybe she would have survived.' He paused again, and through a throat that felt like it was choking with tears, whispered, 'Maybe our baby would have too.'

Tia put her hand over his and squeezed gently. 'You can't live on "if only's".'

He sighed. 'I know. But the truth is I've been thinking about it a lot recently. Maybe it's because I feel guilty about Liz.'

'You've really fallen for her, haven't you?'

'I have. I just feel complete when I'm with her. I haven't felt like that since . . . well, since I met Kas.'

Tia nodded. 'And that's why the guilt has come back, is it?'

Alex nodded. 'I feel like I'm betraying her.'

162

'You're not betraying her.' She put her hand on Alex's arm. 'Look Alex, I know we've only known each other since you came back from Dubai, but I'd like to think we've become friends as well as business partners.'

'Of course we have. I don't know how I would have made it through the last couple of years without you.'

'So, trust me when I say that although I didn't know Kas, from what you've told me about her, I'm sure she'd want you to be happy.'

'You think so?' he asked hopefully.

'Yes,' Tia replied.

He nodded and decided that, while he was being so open, he would confide in Tia about the other thing that was bothering him, 'I also feel guilty about the fact that I still can't bring myself to tell Liz that Kas was pregnant when she died.'

Tia sighed. 'I know you find it really difficult to talk about, but if Liz is that important to you, you need to tell her. You can't have an honest relationship if you keep it from her.'

He took a deep breath. 'I know.'

'Tell her, Alex, before you go to Dubai. Until you can put the past fully behind you, you'll never be able to move forward.'

* * *

'Do you fancy a glass of wine?' Liz stood in the kitchen doorway the following Sunday evening. She smiled at the sight of Alex sprawled on her sofa, reading the paper. Whilst Alex's apartment was the height of luxury, she still preferred it when they spent time at hers, where she felt more relaxed. At his, she was always afraid of spilling something on the plush white surfaces.

'I'd love one,' he said, looking up from the newspaper.

Fortunately, Alex enjoyed spending time at hers, which he'd been doing quite a lot in recent weeks. Since the night at the Greek restaurant, their relationship had gone from strength to strength. They had spoken little since then about his and Tia's restaurant and she'd been glad to leave it there. She preferred to keep her business and her relationship with Alex separate. The only fly in the ointment was that he was going away for two weeks tomorrow to sort out his affairs in Dubai. She hoped it was a good sign, but part of her was afraid that once he was over there, he wouldn't want to come back.

Today they'd spent their Sunday afternoon at the cinema followed by an early dinner in China Town, and now she was looking forward to a cosy evening in together. Although they still hadn't slept together, she felt as though they couldn't be any closer.

She poured the wine and, after handing him his glass, snuggled on the sofa next to him.

'This has been the perfect way to spend a Sunday.' He sighed with contentment.

'It's not over yet, although I wish you didn't have to go away tomorrow.'

He put his wine glass down and pulled her into his arms. 'Me too, but it's got to be done.'

'How do you feel about going back to Dubai?' she asked cautiously.

'Bit mixed, really. I'm looking forward to seeing the family, but as for the rest, well, it all seems a little final.'

'Yes, I can imagine.'

He shifted slightly and held her closer.

'And you'll be gone for two weeks?'

'Yes, I'll be back for Lucinda's engagement party.'

'I'm glad about that.' She'd been delighted when Lord Weatherton's PA had phoned to say they wanted her to cater for his daughter's engagement party, and she was determined to make it a success. Her good reputation was spreading and business was picking up.

'I wish I could take you with me,' Alex interrupted her thoughts. 'But I know how busy you are.'

'It's probably better you go back on you own, this first time anyway.'

'True.'

She sensed a drop in his mood but couldn't help asking, 'Do you think you'll be able to get all your business done in two weeks?'

'Probably not. I imagine it'll take a few visits.'

'You might even decide to stay.' She kept her voice light, even though she was expressing her worst fear.

'There's no chance of that,' he said, squeezing her arm. 'My life is here now.'

She kissed him lightly on the lips but soon their kiss grew deeper. She would never grow tired of kissing him; it set every nerve ending tingling. She didn't want it to stop, but there was something else she needed to know, so reluctantly she pulled away.

'Will you tell your family about me?'

'Definitely.'

'What will they say?'

'I think they'll be happy for me. I hope so, anyway. When I lost Kas, I didn't think I could ever love again . . . I'm so glad that I met you again and you proved me wrong.'

'I'm glad we met again too,' she said.

When he didn't reply, she looked at him. 'Is there something else?'

He hugged her closer to him. 'I'm sorry . . . I know I should have told you before. I just find it very difficult.

'That's okay. I understand.'

He sighed. 'When Kas died of sepsis, she was fourteen weeks' pregnant. We'd only just told everyone.'

Liz wrapped her arms around him, not knowing what to say. He had a faraway look in his eye, clearly lost in his memories.

'When she told me she was expecting, I couldn't have been happier. It wasn't planned but it didn't matter. I vowed on the day I found out that I'd do everything I could to protect her and our baby. But I didn't, did I? I thought she just had a bit of cold, and I had to get to a meeting about a property I was buying. She knew how important the meeting was — that property was going to make us the money we needed for our future. She told me she would be fine . . . she'd take some painkillers and sleep it off. By the time I got back, the fever had taken hold. I rang an ambulance and got her straight to hospital . . . but it was too late.'

'Oh Alex, I'm so sorry.' She leaned over, pulled a tissue from a box on the table and handed it to him. He took it from her and wiped his tears away.

'No, *I'm* sorry. You must think I'm daft crying like this after all this time.'

'I'd be more surprised if you didn't cry.'

'If only I'd realised how serious it was, she and our baby might have lived.'

'How could you possibly have known what would happen?' She paused, riddled with guilt herself. 'I'm so sorry for what I said when I first met you again.'

'Don't be. You weren't to know. We've both been through the mill, losing people we love.'

'Yes, but I haven't dealt with it half as well as you have.'

'You look like you've dealt with things pretty successfully to me.'

She sighed. 'I didn't for a long time.'

He shifted position. 'Want to tell me about it?'

It was something she also found difficult to talk about, but seeing as Alex had shared his innermost feelings with her, she didn't want there to be any secrets between them.

'Do you remember when you used to come and stay with us on the farm? she asked.

'Of course I do. I used to love coming to stay with your family.'

'I had a massive crush on you, you know?' She noticed his lips twitch. 'Wait, what are you laughing at?'

'I knew all along.'

'You never let on.'

'No, I didn't want to hurt your feelings.'

'Why? Because I was so fat and ugly?' Anger bubbled up inside her at the memory of Danny's friends' words. Words she had never forgotten. She turned her face away as tears threatened. Gently, he turned her face back towards him and looked at her intently. The tenderness in his eyes nearly sent her over the edge.

'You were never fat and ugly. It was just the age gap between us seemed much more prominent then.'

'That's kind of you to say, but all the others thought it.'

'They were just silly boys,' he said, frowning.

'And I was a "baby",' she said, repeating what he had called her. He gasped and she continued. 'I overheard them teasing you one Christmas Eve, about me having a crush on you and about how disgusting I was.'

'You overheard that?' he asked, horror in his voice.

'Yes, I was in Dad's study.'

'Oh, you poor thing.' He hugged her closer.

'That's when I started dieting in earnest. I thought that if I was ever going to get anyone to notice me, then I was going to have to be a lot thinner.'

'I did notice you, but you were Danny's little sister — I saw you as a sister to me too.'

She sighed, and then in an attempt to lighten the conversation asked, 'I hope I'm not like a sister to you now?'

'What do you think?' He kissed her on the lips, gently at first but then with growing hunger.

She pulled away, not wanting to be distracted when she had more to tell him. 'After Danny died, I took dieting to another level. He was my confidant but with him gone, I felt as though I had no one. I decided the only person who could fix things for me was me. Dieting became the only way I could control anything in my life. I couldn't see how much weight I'd lost because all I could see was the fat girl in the mirror. Mum and Dad were too wrapped up in their grief to notice, and Mel had just moved in with Simon. Then one day I collapsed on a run. Mel found me. If she hadn't called an ambulance, I probably wouldn't be here today.'

'That must have been awful,' Alex said quietly.

'Like you, I find it hard to talk about. Mel was brilliant and I'll never be able to thank her enough.'

'I'm so glad you had her.'

'Me too. It took me a long time to recover, but it never really goes away.'

'You mean it could happen again?' He looked horrified.

'I hope not. But it's the reason I left La Emporium. I don't say it lightly, but Louis, the deputy chef there, is a bully. He bullied me in that kitchen and I felt myself slipping back. My anxiety was through the roof, and although I was working with food, I couldn't eat. I had to leave because I couldn't risk staying there.'

'How come you didn't tell Roberto?'

'Roberto is old school. Although he's a brilliant mentor himself, he doesn't see anything wrong with chefs who shout at their team. It's the way things used to be done. I think the saying, "If you can't stand the heat, get out of the kitchen" was designed for chefs. I couldn't stand the heat, so I got out and I'm glad I did.'

'That explains why you were hesitant about getting involved with the restaurant.'

'It's one of the reasons, yes. But I'm relieved to have told you now. I don't want there to be any secrets between us.'

'I don't either. I'm glad to have found someone I trust so much.'

'Me too. Alex?'

'Yes.'

'Will you stay tonight?'

'You mean . . . ?'

She nodded, got up from the sofa and held her hand out to him. 'Stay with me?'

'You don't need to ask twice,' he said as he followed her into the bedroom.

As she closed her bedroom door behind them and turned to face him, her nerve almost faltered. He took her in his arms and kissed her lightly on the lips. 'Are you sure you want to do this?'

She nodded, unable to speak as a lump formed in her throat. She had a much better perspective on her body image these days, but as she compared herself to Nikki, she wondered if she would be enough for him. It had been a long time since anyone had seen her naked body.

'If you want to stop at any time, just tell me. Don't be afraid.'

She nodded and then, summoning all her courage, she kissed him. Their kiss deepened and she could feel her limbs turning to jelly. She stepped backwards, her knees folding against the edge of the bed. She shifted across to make room for him and he lay down beside her, barely breaking their kiss.

'I've dreamed of this for so long,' he said eventually. He was staring at her intently, his eyes filled with longing, and she realised she had never wanted anyone more.

'I hope I won't disappoint you.'

'Oh, you won't,' he said huskily as he began to kiss her neck, slowly moving down towards her collarbone; small butterfly kisses which made her shiver with anticipation. Slowly, he began to undo her shirt buttons until her bra was exposed, kissing down her chest to the top of her breasts. He stroked her through the silkiness of her bra and her longing for him exploded. Wanting to feel his skin on hers, she tugged at his polo shirt, lifting it up, and then he pulled it off roughly and threw it on the floor before reaching behind to unclasp her bra in one swift movement. And suddenly she was free.

'Oh,' he moaned as he cupped one of her breasts gently in his hands and stroked her nipple, which immediately sprang to attention. 'Oh, you're so beautiful.'

'No, I'm not,' she said, her automatic defence kicking in. He stopped stroking and lifted his head to look her in the eyes.

'Yes, you are. You're beautiful inside and out, and don't let *anyone* tell you otherwise. It's about time you started to believe in yourself.'

Instead of replying, she kissed him again, running her hands down his strong, sturdy back. He began to caress her, swirling his fingers down to her stomach and to the waist-band of her jeans. She was now so filled with desire that she wanted to be free of her clothes completely. Being naked in front of him no longer made her anxious, and she peeled off her jeans and her knickers whilst he also quickly undressed. They lay side by side, skin against skin as they kissed and she moaned in desire. She felt his erection against her thigh and reached to stroke him, his skin silky beneath her fingers. His own fingers were stroking between her legs, slipping in and out of her, tantalising her. Suddenly, she could stand it no more.

'Now, Alex, now.'

He reached for a condom from his jeans pocket, and then he was inside her, his weight pressing down on her. She clutched at his buttocks wanting him to be closer still. He filled her up and made her feel complete. And then, suddenly, there was no way back. She cried out as her orgasm mounted and then exploded, rippling through every part of her body.

* * *

Later, as they lay limp and exhausted, their fingers gently stroking each other, she thought about what he had said to her about being beautiful inside and out. Maybe, with Alex by her side, she could finally start believing in herself?

CHAPTER TWENTY-SIX

Alex whistled as he walked into the office the next morning, filled with the euphoria of having spent the night with Liz. It had shocked him when she'd told him about her anorexia, but it explained a lot about her, and he was glad she trusted him enough to confide in him, as he had in her. He'd promised himself that he would be patient with her and wait until she was ready to commit to him and he was glad that he had. Their lovemaking had been better than he could have ever imagined, their bodies fitting together in perfect unison, and the depth of emotion he'd felt as they came together had been like nothing he had experienced since being with Kas. He just wished he wasn't about to go to Dubai, that he could be with her tonight and every night, rather than having to spend two weeks so far away. But it had to be done. Finally, he was ready. He was looking forward to seeing his father and some of his old friends, but he would miss Liz like crazy.

'Someone looks happy.'

He stopped short as he saw Nikki draped across the sofa in the office reception area.

'What are you doing here?'

'That's a friendly welcome, I don't think.' She unfurled herself and walked forwards as if to embrace him.

He stepped back. 'Again. What are you doing here?'

They hadn't spoken for weeks and he thought she'd finally got the message. Seeing her here in his office made him uneasy.

'I must admit; I'm surprised to see you in this early too. Surprised you could tear yourself away from your new girl-friend's bed.'

He was startled, wondering how Nikki knew about last night, and then realised — of course she didn't. She was just making assumptions.

'I don't think that's any of your business,' he said. 'What exactly do you want, Nikki?'

She put her hand on his arm and he fought the urge to shrug her off. 'Can we go somewhere private? I don't want anyone to overhear this.'

'Overhear what?'

'In private, if you don't mind,' she repeated, and with the sense of uneasiness mounting, Alex led the way through the communal office and into the room they used for private meetings.

When he'd closed the door behind him, he looked at her sternly. 'Whatever it is, can we get on with it, please? I've got a meeting to go to.'

'Darling, please don't speak like that. It sounds so unfriendly.'

'It's meant to.' In the confines of this room, it was less easy to avoid her.

She pouted. 'That's no way to speak to the mother of your unborn child.'

Her words stunned him. 'What?'

'I'm pregnant, Alex.'

He shook his head, unable to take it in.

'Are you sure?' He'd always been so careful.

Again, she pouted. 'Of course I'm sure. We're going to have a baby.'

A baby? A baby with Nikki? He sat down with a thump, completely unsure how to react.

'I'm sorry. I suppose this is a bit of a shock for you.'

'It's one hell of a shock,' he said faintly, thinking not just about this unborn child, but also the one he'd lost.

'It was a shock for me too, when I first suspected,' she said, putting her hand on her stomach. 'But now I'm delighted.'

'I thought you didn't want children. You were very disparaging when Roberto made his happy announcement. "It's not a beginning, it's an ending" — that's what you said.'

Nikki looked away from him and shuffled uncomfortably. 'That's how I felt then.'

'It wasn't that long ago, Nikki.'

She took a deep breath. 'No, it wasn't — but now that it's happened to me, I've changed my mind. I've realised that this is something I really want.'

'What about your career?'

'I can take a break. It won't be easy, but I'll just have to work hard to get my body back after the baby's born. Other models manage it.' She paused. 'What are you trying to do, Alex? Convince me to have an abortion?'

He gasped. 'No! Of course not.'

'Because that's not an option.'

'And I wouldn't ask you to do that.' He could never ask that. The irony of the situation suddenly struck him. He had another chance to become a father, but it was with the wrong woman. He'd even be happy if Liz said she was pregnant — despite the fact they'd only just properly got together. But Nikki? He shook his head, almost forgetting that she was there with him.

'I hope that when you get used to the idea, you'll be as pleased as I am. This changes everything.'

He looked up, startled. 'What do you mean?'

'Well . . . obviously we'll get back together.'

'No,' he said quietly.

'No? What do you mean no?'

'I don't want to get back with you. I'm with Liz.'

She scowled. 'Well, yes, but only just. And like I said, this changes everything. We're having a *baby*.'

173

'And I'll be a good father. But we can co-parent without being together.'

'No, Alex, I don't want that, I don't want to bring this child up on my own.'

'And you won't. I've already said, I'll be a good dad.'

'But that's not what I want.'

He thought for a minute that she was actually going to stamp her foot. Instead, she sat down next to him, put her hand on his arm, and with tears in her eyes said, 'I need you with me, Alex. We were good together once, we can be again.'

Before he had chance to reply, the door opened and Tia walked in. She stopped short when she saw the two of them together.

'Oh, I'm sorry. Alex, I thought you were ready for our meeting?'

'Not quite. I've just got to discuss a few things with Nikki. Can you give me ten minutes?'

Tia looked at her watch, a puzzled expression on her face. 'Of course. Take as much time as you need.'

When she'd gone, he turned back to Nikki. 'How far along are you?'

'Six weeks, or there abouts.'

'And have you seen a doctor, or a midwife?'

'Not yet.'

'Right. Look, Nikki, I'm sorry but I'm going away tonight for two weeks . . .'

'What? I've just told you I'm having a child and you're going away?'

He shook his head as he heard the petulant tone in her voice, and he knew from experience that he would have to keep very calm to stop her from having a meltdown. 'I can't change it now. I've got meetings set up. But why don't you make an appointment to see a midwife and then, when I get back, we can sit down and talk about this properly? Until then, I think we should keep this between ourselves.'

'You'd like that, wouldn't you? Brush it all under the carpet.'

'I'm not trying to do that. It's just a lot can happen before twelve weeks, so most people keep it to themselves until then before telling anyone.'

'You seem to know a lot about it. Have you done this before?'

'Yes,' he said simply.

'I bet you've got lots of little Alex's all over the place, haven't you?' she asked spitefully.

'No,' he snapped. 'My baby died, along with my wife.'

She gasped. 'Oh Alex, I'm sorry. I never meant—'

'Never mind.' He cut her dead, all thoughts of pacifying her flown out of the window. 'Please can you do as I ask and go and see your midwife? And we keep this to ourselves until we've made a few decisions.'

'Okay, if that's what you want. But don't think you can fob me off.'

'I don't think that for a minute.'

He watched as she left, still as graceful and attractive as ever. Only now he didn't find her appealing. He'd bought himself some time, but only a little. Eventually, he'd have to face facts. It seemed as if he was going to be a father. He'd have to tell Liz. But not now. Not when he was about to go away and she was busy. Or when he was still in shock. He couldn't believe how much had changed in just a few short minutes. Earlier he'd been at the top of the ladder, but now he was sliding back down the snake.

CHAPTER TWENTY-SEVEN

The morning of the engagement party dawned bright and clear. The day before it had rained heavily, and although the forecast for today promised sunshine, and right now there wasn't a cloud in the sky, Liz crossed her fingers and hoped it would stay that way. The party would be so much better if it remained dry.

It had been a busy few weeks. Once word had got around that she was catering for Lucinda Weatherton's engagement party, the phone hadn't stopped ringing. She couldn't be happier that the business was finally taking off, and she thrived on being busy. And then there was Alex. The night they'd slept together had been one of the best nights of her life, and it wasn't just the memory of their lovemaking — the secrets they'd shared proved how much they trusted each other. She felt that the spectre of Nikki and her past with Alex had been vanquished.

She'd missed him dreadfully since he'd been away, but he was due back today and she couldn't wait to see him. He'd be a guest at the party later on, and although she'd be busy, at least he would be there. Then, when the party was over and everything had been cleared away, well, she didn't care how tired she'd be — seeing Alex would rejuvenate her.

She shook herself out of her reverie. She'd better get a move on. The last thing she needed today was to start off late. Not when she'd planned everything so meticulously.

Thankfully, she had a full complement of staff. She'd booked a coach to take them to and from the venue to make sure there were no travel hiccups. Jay and Emma were travelling with her to get there early. Yesterday, they'd shyly announced they were seeing one another. They'd seemed so loved up she couldn't help but be happy for them. At least with Emma, Jay would have someone who could understand the unsocial hours he worked, and they seemed made for each other. They'd arrived together half an hour earlier and were now helping her check everything off her list as the food was loaded into the van, ready to be transported to the party.

'Right, that's it, we're ready,' Liz said finally.

The motorway was clear and they speeded down with little trouble. Jay, who could sleep anywhere, immediately dozed off, his head lolling on Emma's shoulder, and Emma could clearly barely contain her grin at being so close to him.

Liz smiled and ran through her to-do list in her head. Today had to be perfect.

* * *

The morning passed in a frenzy of preparation as Liz set up and organised the food. The marquees were already in place and, supervised by Emma, the waiting staff polished the silverware and glasses. Knowing she had Emma to rely on meant that she could concentrate totally on the food.

By one o'clock, just as the first of the guests were arriving, they were ready. As long as they could keep up the production of food, everything would be fine.

'Jay, can you keep things moving here? I'm going to oversee outside.'

He gave her a mock salute. 'Will do, boss.'

It had been fun working with Jay again, and it was so good to be able to share the load. She opened the door to what she suspected had once been the butler's pantry and shrugged on her jacket which was hanging there. It was far too hot to be wearing a jacket, but she felt it distinguished her from the rest of the staff. She was just about to enter the fray when Alex poked his head around the door.

'Hello, gorgeous. How are you?'

'Alex!' She flung herself into his arms, delighted to see him again. 'I've missed you so much.'

'Not half as much as I've missed you.' And, as if to prove it, he pulled her closer to him and kissed her passionately.

Eventually, she pulled away. 'Don't do that, not when I've got so much to do.'

'Shame.'

'I know, but—'

'Sshh . . .' He put his fingers to her lips. 'Don't worry. I know how important this is to you, so I'll stay out of your way today. But tonight — tonight is a different matter, and I want you all to myself.'

'Your wish is my command,' she replied, smiling at him as they walked back into the kitchen together.

* * *

Liz surveyed the gardens, checking that everything was running smoothly. The grounds looked fantastic, and she almost had to pinch herself to make sure she wasn't dreaming. A quartet was playing on the veranda so above the tinkling laughter came the soothing sounds of classical music. The earlier part of the afternoon had flashed by as they'd all been so busy. At one point, she'd thought they wouldn't be able to keep up, the food was disappearing so quickly, but Jay and the other chefs worked as though they were on fire. The tartlets with quails' eggs that Lord Weatherton was so fond of had run out, but not before Liz had made sure his Lordship had had his fix.

The champagne bottles were still popping, and those with room had moved over to desserts. Fresh strawberries, caramelised nectarines and berries in a mint julep syrup were in plentiful supply, and for those with a sweeter tooth there were mini gateaux, profiteroles and cheesecakes.

On the terrace, Lucinda, the bride-to-be, was holding court, her arm wrapped around her aristocratic looking fiancé. She was wearing a stunning dress in oyster chiffon, which gathered in at the waist to show off her hourglass figure. Lucinda hadn't had much involvement in the planning of the party, which had surprised Liz. If it had been her engagement party, she'd have wanted to be involved in every detail, but she supposed Lucinda was used to having staff to do everything for her. She seemed pleased today, though.

Liz was also surprised at the number of people she knew. Lucinda and Tia had many friends in common; designers, musicians and models alike. Over by the Pimm's tent, Liz spotted Susie, Jay's ex and Nikki's friend. Susie was very much of the same ilk as Nikki and had always seemed to look down her nose at Liz. Apart from that, no matter how many times Liz had assured her that she and Jay were only friends, she never felt that Susie truly believed her. She thought about the night at Winston's and shuddered. She was glad she and Jay had got their relationship back on a platonic footing.

Susie caught her eye and Liz walked over to her.

'Can I top you up?' she asked, gesturing with the champagne bottle she was carrying towards Susie's glass.

'Liz . . . oh, er, hi? I didn't realise this was your job.'

'Well, it is,' Liz said, determined not to let Susie make her feel inferior.

'I didn't know you worked on such a large scale.'

'Oh, I can cater for most events.' Liz forced a smile. 'How are you?'

'I'm fine.'

'And your boyfriend?'

'Richard? We split up.'

'I'm sorry.'

'Really?' Susie raised a sceptical eyebrow. 'Have you seen much of Jay recently?'

179

'I have, yes. In fact, he's here today.' Liz noticed a quickening of interest in Susie's eyes.

'Oh? Has he left La Emporium?'

'No, he's just helping me out.'

Susie narrowed her eyes. 'You two have always been close, haven't you?'

'We've always been good friends, yes.'

There was a pause. 'I saw you outside Winston's.'

Liz flushed, wondering how many other people had seen them. 'Jay was upset about you and Richard. He was very drunk and unhappy. About you. I was just trying to get him home.'

'Really?'

'Yes, really.' And then, in an effort to convince Susie that there was nothing between them, she said, 'That's why I'm so happy he's moved on.'

'Moved on?' A shadow flickered across Susie's face.

'Yes, he's going out with my head waitress.'

'He's going out with a waitress?' Susie couldn't have sounded more horrified if Liz had said Emma was a stripper.

'She's actually doing a degree in hotel management. They seem very happy together — she understands the unsocial hours he works.'

'Good for them,' Susie said, but she looked like she was sucking a lemon. Liz couldn't help thinking that Susie and Nikki really *were* cut from the same cloth. 'I heard you were seeing Alex Sinclaire for a while?' she continued.

'I still am.'

'Oh? I thought he was back with Nikki?'

Liz laughed. 'No, I think you've got the wrong end of the stick. He's not back with her.'

'Are you sure about that? They seem to be doing a pretty good impression of being together. Look.'

Liz followed Susie's gaze and felt her skin go cold, even though the sun was still ferocious. Nikki had walked over to Alex and put her arm around him. *Is she up to her old tricks again?* Liz wondered. But Alex wasn't pushing her away. In fact, it looked as though he had moved closer to her. And the way he was looking at her . . . Her stomach wrenched at the sight of them.

'I know it must hurt, but it's good that he's doing the honourable thing by her and the baby, isn't it?'

'Baby?' Suddenly, she was lightheaded and the ground beneath her didn't feel very stable.

Susie gasped. 'Oh, don't say you didn't know that Nikki's pregnant? I *am* sorry, Liz. I thought Alex would have told you. Especially when it's the main topic of gossip in our social circle. Still, I don't suppose you're really included in that, are you?'

Liz was struggling for breath.

'Oh dear, are you alright? You've gone awfully pale.'

'Y-yes, I'm fine. It's just very hot. I need to check on things in the kitchen.' She stumbled away.

On her way back to the kitchen, Lord Weatherton intercepted her. 'Elizabeth dear, I must congratulate you. Today is an unmitigated success.'

She forced a smile. 'Thank you. It's very kind of you to say so.'

'Kindness has nothing to do with it. I'm so pleased with your work. You've really added all the personal touches that other bigger companies wouldn't care about. So thank you, my dear, you've made me a very happy man.' And to her surprise, he took her hand and raised it to his lips to kiss it.

'It's been an honour. I'm so pleased you're happy with the way everything has gone,' she said. 'I was just on my way to see if there are any more desserts. Perhaps I could send some out to you?'

'That would be delightful.'

As she walked away, she did her best to pull herself together. *Nikki was pregnant!* She didn't think there was any way Alex and Nikki were back together again. But a baby? An innocent child who needed a mother and a father? A child who was depending on Alex? She couldn't think about that now or she'd fall apart. That couldn't happen. Not today.

* * *

Alex had been looking forward to getting back to England and seeing Liz again. He had spent the last two weeks longing to feel her in his arms, and the kiss they had shared in the kitchen had only inflamed his desire. He couldn't wait until later when they could be alone. As he looked around the grounds, he couldn't believe what she'd pulled off. The food was exquisite and everyone was commenting on it. This event would really put her on the map. He was so proud of her.

He'd been anxious about going back to Dubai. Even if Nikki's news hadn't been hanging over him, it would still have been a difficult visit. Surprisingly, though, it hadn't been as traumatic as he'd feared. Standing on the balcony of his father's apartment thinking about both Kas and Liz, a rare breeze had wafted over him. It was as though he was receiving his wife's approval. He remembered his conversation with Tia. She was right — Kas would want him to be happy, even if it meant that he was with someone else. She had always put other people first. The trip had cemented his conviction that he and Liz had a future together. Even his father had noticed the difference in him. Over a relaxing dinner one night, he'd told him all about Liz. His father had seemed pleased, and Alex had promised to bring her out for a visit. Business had gone well too. He would need to go out again, but soon he would be free to fully concentrate on his life in England. Even if that did involve Nikki.

He accepted a glass of champagne from a passing waiter and went to mingle. But the strange thing was, as he approached people, they seemed to turn their back on him, or drifted away. Puzzled, he looked away and then, there in front of him, was the last person he wanted to see.

'Alex! You're back!' Nikki threw her arms around him. He tried to subtly extricate himself, but she was like a limpet and pulled him closer to her.

Eventually, he managed to release himself from her grip and looked down at her. 'How are you?'

'I'm okay,' she said. 'Although I'm as sick as a dog in the mornings.'

He nodded. 'Have you been to see the midwife?'

'No.' She seemed to falter. 'Not yet.'

'But Nikki, I thought we'd agreed—'

'I know, but I didn't want to do it without you.' She held onto his arm and he did his best not to pull away from her.

'Well, I'm back now for a few weeks at least, so you can make an appointment. The sooner we can make sure that everything's okay, the better.'

'You're right, Alex,' she simpered. 'I knew I could rely on you to take charge.'

Alex cringed inwardly. Nikki certainly wasn't going to make this an easy ride for him. He wanted to do the right thing by her, but he just hoped that it wouldn't jeopardise his relationship with Liz.

'Alexander, my dear boy.' Henry Weatherton clapped him on the back. 'Nice to see you back.'

'I wouldn't have missed this, Henry. What a fabulous event.'

'Yes, it is, and a lot of it is thanks to that lady chef you introduced me to.'

'She has put on a fantastic spread,' he agreed as he watched Nikki scowl. Well, Nikki could scowl all she liked. Liz more than deserved the praise.

'She certainly has and I've just seen her to tell her myself. And I believe you are to be congratulated too?' Henry looked at him questioningly.

'Me?' Alex asked, puzzled. 'What for?'

Henry chuckled. 'Why, I hear you're going to be a father.'

'I'm what?'

'I'm sorry, Alex,' Nikki whispered, looking contrite.

'I thought we'd agreed not to say anything just yet,' he hissed. He turned to Henry. 'I wanted to wait until twelve weeks, just to make sure that everything's okay.'

'I know, but it just slipped out,' Nikki said quietly behind him, not really sounding sorry at all.

'And I do hope you're going to do the right thing by this lovely young lady?' Lord Weatherton looked to Nikki, who smiled back at him.

'I beg your pardon?' Alex said.

'Marriage of course, my dear boy. You'll want to make an honest woman of her, won't you?'

Alex stared at him in disbelief, completely lost for words.

'Now, I must circulate. Congratulations again to both of you.'

Alex waited until Henry was out of earshot and then turned incredulously to Nikki. 'Just what the hell have you been saying to people?'

'Nothing much,' she said. 'Just that we were expecting, but that you were away.'

'And how many people have you told?'

She shrugged. 'Just a few.'

Which he assumed meant everyone. And judging by their reaction to him today, she hadn't been presenting him in a favourable light. *Oh God! What a mess!* And then it struck him — if everyone else knew, how long would it be before Liz found out? He had to find her and tell her himself before anyone else did.

* * *

Liz was taking some empty food platters back to the kitchen when she bumped into Alex.

'Congratulations, Liz. You did a fantastic job today,' he said, attempting to give her a hug. 'You should be proud of yourself.'

She stepped back to avoid him. 'I am.'

'Are you okay?' he asked. She thought he seemed on edge. *And so he should be!*

She shook her head. 'Come with me.' She led him into the kitchen, put down the platters she was carrying, and then walked into the butler's pantry. She turned to face him. 'Is there anything you need to tell me?'

She watched as guilt flashed across his face. 'Oh,' he said.

'Yes, oh! And just when were you going to tell me that Nikki's pregnant?'

'I only found out the day I went to Dubai. I didn't want to tell you over the phone, especially before today. I didn't want to mess this up for you.'

'I *really* wish I hadn't had to find out through the grapevine.' She still felt nauseous from the shock of hearing that he was having a child with Nikki.

'I'm sorry. I asked Nikki not to say anything until we'd had a chance to sort things out, but she blabbed to everyone while I was away. I was going to tell you tonight.'

He reached out to take her hand but she snatched it away from him.

'Look, this doesn't have to change anything between us,' he said.

She stared at him in disbelief. 'How can you say that? Nikki will always be in our lives. On the side-lines, trying to split us up. And your child, her child, will always have to come first. Which is as it should be. But I wouldn't put it past her to use that to get what she wants.'

'I won't let her do that. I've told Nikki that I'll support her and the child, but it's you I'm with.'

'And you think she's going accept that, do you?'

'She won't have any choice. I'm *not* getting back with her.'

Liz shook her head, lost for words. Even from the little she knew of Nikki, she was convinced she wouldn't let him go that easily. Not when there was a child to keep pulling him back to her.

He sighed. 'Look, I know you're busy now and this is hardly the place. Can we talk about this tonight? At yours?'

'No, Alex. Not tonight. I'm sorry, but it's been a very long day, and this has all been a shock. I need some time to think. Maybe we can talk about this tomorrow?'

'If that's what you want?'

'It is.'

'Fine. But I promise you, Liz, the only way Nikki will split us up is if you let her.'

Liz watched as he walked away from her. She had the sickening feeling that this was the end. When she was sure he had gone, she returned to the kitchen and stacked the empty trays.

'Everything okay?' Jay asked.

She nodded and swallowed back the tears. She desperately wanted to confide in Jay but she had a job to finish, so she'd have to keep a lid on her emotions and be professional. 'Fine, thanks,' she managed in a strangled voice before returning to her work.

There was the muffled sound of a mobile ringing.

'That's yours, isn't it?'

'What?'

'Mobile? In your jacket on the door?'

'Oh . . . yes.' Numbly, she walked towards it. If it was Alex, she would switch it off. But it wasn't Alex. It was Mel. Liz hesitated. Mel would be able to tell that something was wrong with her, but it would be nice to hear her sister's voice.

'Mel, hi, how are you?'

'Liz, you need to come home.'

'What?' The desperation in his sister's voice startled her. 'What's wrong? It's not one of the kids, is it?'

'No, it's Dad. He's been in an accident.'

Liz staggered backwards and then grabbed hold of a work surface to stop herself from falling.

'Oh my God! Is he . . . is he . . . ?'

'He's alive, but he's in intensive care and it's touch and go. You need to hurry.'

'I will. I'll be there as soon as I can.'

CHAPTER TWENTY-EIGHT

Liz stood clutching the phone, unable to move. Her dad. The man she'd wasted so many years needlessly blaming. A sob escaped her and suddenly Jay was there, holding her as tears slid down her cheeks.

When she was calmer, he handed her a tissue. 'What's wrong?'

'It's my dad. He's been in an accident.'

'Oh God, is he going to be okay?'

'I don't know. Mel said to come quickly. It's touch and go.'

'Right.' He gently pushed her in the direction of the butler's pantry. 'Get changed.'

'What?'

'Get yourself ready. I'm taking you to the nearest train station. You're going home.'

'But . . .' She looked wildly around the kitchen.

'Don't worry about this. The others can finish up here. I'll come back after I've dropped you off. All you need to think about is getting back to your dad.'

'But Lord Weatherton—'

'Will understand. I'll explain everything. I've still got a spare key to yours, so I'll drop the stuff back there later. Just go and get changed.'

Wordlessly, she nodded and did as she was told.

* * *

Liz stared out of the train window. The journey to the station, organising the ticket and getting on the train were all a blur. She couldn't have managed it without Jay. Now, though, the shock was wearing off. If her dad died before she got there, she'd never be able to forgive herself. She was glad she'd made her peace with him recently, and they'd spoken since her last visit, but it wasn't enough. Not to make up for all the years she'd shut him out.

She closed her eyes and offered a silent prayer. If her dad recovered from this, she vowed she'd be a much better daughter. She couldn't make up for the past, but she could change the future.

The future. Did it include her and Alex? Another relationship founded on mistrust. She believed him when he said that he wanted nothing to do with Nikki, despite the fact that she said she was having his child. But he'd kept it from her, hadn't trusted her enough to tell her. If Nikki had this baby, no matter how Alex felt about her, there would be a connection between them forever.

As the train finally pulled into Crewe station, she'd made up her mind. She wouldn't get in the way of an innocent life. Alex and Nikki needed to sort themselves out and concentrate on the baby. Alex was already haunted by the loss of one child, now he had a second chance and he needed to get it right. If they did manage to get together in the future, she was painfully aware that she might not be able to have children due to her past — this might be his only chance of becoming a father. She felt sick at the thought of giving him up, but deep down she knew it was the right thing to do.

* * *

The man lying in the hospital bed didn't look like her father. He looked like a frail old man. She'd thought he'd looked a lot older when she'd seen him last, but at least then he'd still been robust. Now his face was grey against the brilliant white of his pillow, his skin papery and thin. Monitors were attached to his chest and the machine at his side bleeped constantly, proving that he was alive at least, even if he didn't look it. The sight of him almost made Liz cry out in anguish, but she took a deep breath to steady herself and walked towards the bed. On one side sat her sister and on the other, also looking shrunken and tired, her step-mother.

'Oh Liz, you're here. Thank God!' Mel said, rushing to embrace her. Liz clung on to her tightly.

'How is he?'

Mel shook her head. 'It doesn't look good. His injuries are so bad they've had to put him into an induced coma.'

'What happened?'

'It was a car accident,' Mel said quietly, and Liz gasped in shock. *Not again? Twice in one family. It's just too cruel.*

'But he was always a careful driver . . .' *Unlike Danny.*

'It was a Range Rover coming down a county lane too fast.' Ruth spoke for the first time. 'The police said it looked as though your dad swerved to avoid it, but there wasn't enough space and . . .' She started to sob, and instinctively Liz reached out to hug her. It was an unfamiliar gesture. Until now she had always pushed Ruth away, but seeing her like this emphasised how selfish and thoughtless she'd been. It was obvious Ruth loved her father very much, and Liz found herself overwhelmingly ashamed of the way she had treated her step-mother in the past.

Mel rose to her feet. 'I'll get the tea. I think we could all do with one. Have my chair, Liz. You look like you could do with a sit down.'

Liz slipped into her sister's seat, which was still warm.

The two women watched the man lying so still in the hospital bed, listening to the machines as they kept him alive.

'I'm glad you made it up with your dad,' Ruth said eventually. 'Your forgiveness meant a lot to him. He's been so happy since your last visit.'

'I should have done it sooner,' Liz said, full of regret. 'I was stubborn and selfish . . . I wasted so much time.'

'We just have to hope that there will be plenty of time ahead of us.'

Liz nodded, unable to bear the thought of the alternative. Then she pulled herself together and took a deep breath. 'I'm sorry for the way I've treated you too, Ruth. You didn't deserve the cold shoulder. I've seen for myself how happy you've made Dad and I'm glad you found each other.'

'Thank you,' Ruth whispered back. 'I never blamed you. You went through so much, it must have been so difficult to deal with, but what you've just said means a lot to me.' She reached out over the bed and they held hands across her father, both silently willing him to survive this.

* * *

'How are you?' Liz asked Mel later that night. They'd persuaded Ruth to go home for a few hours with the promise that they'd phone her if there was the slightest change. At first, she'd refused, but they could see she was exhausted and they'd continued to press her until she'd caved in and allowed Simon to come and pick her up. 'I mean, with Simon and with the business?'

Mel shrugged. 'The business is struggling and we've had to make two staff redundant. It was awful. I know they blamed me.'

'I'm sure they didn't.'

'Well, I would in their shoes. It looked like I'd come waltzing in and started the firing squad. But we simply couldn't afford to keep them. I've learnt pretty quickly what it's like to run a vet's practice. Sophie's been great too — she loves spending time with the animals. And as for Ben, well, as long as he's got his Xbox all is right with the world.'

'And Simon?'

'Working all hours as we've had to let one of the vets go, and feeling incredibly guilty for re-mortgaging the house without telling me. We're going to have to sell it and buy something smaller.'

Liz gasped. 'But you love that house.'

'It's only bricks and mortar. If Simon had spoken to me earlier, maybe we could have turned things around sooner, but I can't just blame him. I was living in my own little bubble, completely oblivious to the real world.'

'I'm so sorry, Mel,' she said eventually.

'Don't be. We're closer now than we've ever been. We've just got to keep our heads above water.' She paused and sighed. 'I don't want to think about that now. The only thing that matters is Dad. I'm so glad you're here, sis. Do you have any idea how long you can stay?'

'No. I haven't even thought about it. Jay just pushed me on a train and here I am. I was doing a function at Lord Weatherton's estate in Hampshire. I don't even have a spare pair of knickers with me.'

Mel raised her eyebrows. 'Was that the engagement party for Lucinda Weatherton?'

'Yes, it's going to be in *Hello!* magazine, would you believe?'

'Oh God, and you had to leave in the middle of it? I didn't realise.'

'We were at the clearing up stage by the time you rang.'

'Thank God for that. How did it go until then?'

'Okay, I think. Although, actually, no.' Liz smiled for the first time since receiving Mel's phone call. 'It went really well.' She was determined to concentrate on the success of her food rather than dwell on Alex and Nikki.

'Good for you. But if the business is on the up, you'll need to get back to London, won't you?'

'Not straight away. I've got nothing on for a few days at least. I just wish it was longer.'

Mel reached out and gave her a hug. 'You're here now and that's the important thing.'

* * *

Alex stood on the balcony of his apartment watching the sun set slowly over the London Eye, brooding over the whole sorry situation. Financially and professionally, he was successful, but it meant little when the woman you loved didn't want to know you.

He'd been devastated when Liz had turned him away, but he understood. It was the shock. He'd stayed away last night, but by lunchtime he'd been desperate to speak to her, to reassure her that nothing would change the way he felt about her. Her phone had gone straight to voicemail, and even though he'd left a message, and several more since, she still hadn't returned any of his calls.

It was almost as though she wanted Nikki to split them up. He'd thought they were stronger than that, that they had a future together. Perhaps he was just a useless judge of character where women were concerned. He'd got it wrong with Nikki, hadn't he?

Nikki. The last person he wanted to be involved with for the rest of his life. But a child? He couldn't turn his back on that. Not after losing Kas and their baby. He sighed. He *would* be a good father — he was determined about that. He would just have to learn to manage Nikki's expectations of what she thought their relationship would be, because it was obvious that she wanted more than he was prepared to give. Liz was right on that.

But there was something else bothering him too. Nikki had been more than happy to tell everyone about their news but, as yet, had still not made an appointment to see a doctor or midwife. That was the first thing Kas had done after showing him the pregnancy test as she'd wanted to make sure that everything was okay. So why hadn't Nikki? Unless, of course, there was no baby? Unlike Kas, she hadn't shown him the pregnancy test either.

He shook his head, trying to work it out. What would be the point of lying about this? Before long it would be obvious whether or not she was pregnant. What could she hope to achieve? He remembered Henry Weatherton's comment at the engagement party about him making an honest woman of Nikki and wondered if she was hoping to get him down the aisle before she started to show. Would she go as far as lying about a miscarriage? He shook his head. Not even Nikki could be that devious . . . *could she?* Well, if that was her game, she wasn't going to win. There was no way he was going to marry Nikki. Ever.

Alex closed the patio doors and locked them firmly behind him. He wished it was just as simple to lock Nikki out of his life. What a mess. The woman he wanted didn't want him and the woman he didn't was having his child. As he walked into the living room, he double-checked his phone. As he suspected, there were no missed calls.

CHAPTER TWENTY-NINE

The day dawned hot and humid. The country was going through a mini-heatwave, leaving London limp and exhausted. After a night of fitful sleep, Alex felt the same. But it wasn't just the heat that had kept him awake. In his disturbed dreams, he'd found himself chasing something which continually slipped through his fingers. *It doesn't take a genius to interpret that*, he thought when he woke.

After a shower, he switched on the coffee machine. He was going to need caffeine to get through the meetings he had lined up for today.

As he reached for a mug, the buzzer to his apartment sounded. He pressed the intercom, wondering who could be calling at this time in the morning, hoping against hope it was Liz.

'Alex darling, it's Nikki. Let me in.'

Disappointment flooded through him.

'How are you, darling?' She flung her arms around him and pressed herself into him as soon as she walked through the door. Firmly, he prised her arms away and took a step backwards.

'Don't!'

'What? Can't you hug the mother of your child?'

'I've told you before. We don't have that kind of relationship.'

'We did once.' She smiled up at him. 'Maybe we could again.'

'Not going to happen, Nikki.'

'Oh, don't tell me you're still in a mood about me letting it slip to a few people?'

'I'm not in a mood. But I'm not going to let you mislead everyone into thinking we're playing happy families. I'm already in a relationship, don't forget.'

'Ah yes, the lovely Liz. And how has she taken the news?'

'It's none of your business.' It had been three days now since the party and she still hadn't returned his calls. She'd obviously decided that their relationship was over, and he was both hurt and angry that she hadn't tried to give them a chance. He wasn't going to tell Nikki that, though. 'I want you to do a pregnancy test.'

Her eyes rounded in surprise. 'But I've already done one.'

'Not in front of me you haven't. I only have your word that you're pregnant. And let's face it, you've lied before, haven't you?'

'I didn't lie. I only told that chef an embellishment because she was sniffing around you.'

'What?' He couldn't believe how little grasp she had on the truth. 'You told her we were *engaged*!'

'And we will be, won't we? Call me old-fashioned, but I'd prefer to be married before I have a baby.'

And now he was convinced that his suspicions were correct.

'I won't marry you, Nikki, so you can get that idea out of your head. Now, about that pregnancy test, shall I go to the chemists and you can do it while you're here?'

'I don't know how you can be so cruel, insinuating that I'm not even pregnant!'

'I'm not being cruel. I just can't understand why you haven't been to see a midwife. Don't you want to make sure our baby's okay?'

'Of course I do. I told you, I was waiting for you to come back so we could go together. But if you're going to be like that, I think I'd prefer to go on my own!'

'And that's meant to make me less suspicious? Because if you had nothing to hide, you'd be more than happy for me to come along.'

The anger was back in her eyes, always a bad sign, but today he didn't care. If she was playing games, he didn't want any part of it, especially if it meant losing the one person who was important to him.

'You'll soon see that I *am* pregnant, but for now you'll just have to take my word for it,' she said before slamming the apartment door behind her.

* * *

'Mum? What are you doing here?'

Liz had been dozing in a chair beside her father's bed when her mother came onto the ward. The pungent smell of her perfume was the first thing Liz noticed. Then that her mother was immaculately turned out, even though she must have travelled on an overnight flight from Spain to get to the hospital so early. After the radio silence from Diane over recent years, Liz couldn't be more shocked at the sight of her now.

'Ruth phoned me.'

'She did?'

Her parents' divorce had been bitter, each blaming the other and fighting over money. And when her mother had finally gone to Spain, Liz assumed that her father had cut all contact with her. That Ruth even had her number or had wanted to tell her about the accident was astounding.

'I was married to him for nearly twenty-five years. That doesn't just go away.'

'No, but you've not exactly played an active part in any of our lives recently, so forgive me for being surprised.'

Diane tutted. 'We've more important things to discuss than the past. Anyway, don't I get a hug after coming all this way?'

Liz allowed herself to be wrapped in her mother's arms. When she was released, Diane looked over to the bed where her ex-husband lay motionless. 'How is he?'

'Not good. Although he's stable, he's in an induced coma. The doctors will try to bring him out of it when he's ready, but they don't know when that will be.'

'It was a car crash, Ruth said?'

'Yes, there was a Range Rover driving too fast towards him. He swerved to avoid it.' Her throat constricted at the words and the impact they would have on her mother. Although there was little love lost between them, it must be hard for her to face that again after Danny's death.

'Another crash,' her mother whispered, blinking rapidly.

'Mum, you don't have to be here if it's too much for you.'

'Nonsense,' Diane replied, sniffing away the tears and standing straighter. 'I wanted to be here for you and Mel. Where is she? I thought she'd be glued to his bedside. And Ruth?'

'They've gone home to get some sleep. No point in us all keeping a vigil. I said I'd phone them if there was any change.'

Diane nodded. 'Yes, well, I suppose it's easier this way, anyway. At least I can get my foot through the door before Mel turfs me out again.'

'Mum! Mel wouldn't do that.'

'I wouldn't bank on it. She always did take your father's side.'

'It's not about sides,' Liz said. Her sympathy for her mother immediately diminished as Diane went into the prickly mode Liz remembered all too well. 'At least not now, anyway.'

'No, but she could never see any wrong with your father and I don't suppose that's changed since. At least you saw through him.'

Liz was silent, trying to form the words to explain how she felt. Eventually, she said, 'I did at the time, yes. But I think I was too harsh. There are two sides to every story.'

Diane huffed. 'So, Mel got to you too eventually, did she? I knew she would. You always did let her boss you around.'

'No, Mum, it's not like that. I've just grown up, that's all. And don't forget, Mel was there for me when I needed her.'

'Ah yes, your anorexia. I wondered when I'd get the blame for that one.'

Liz sighed. 'I was ill, Mum. There's no need to blame anyone. But if all you've come for is a row, it'd be better if you left.'

'I'm not going anywhere. I've got as much right to be here as anyone.'

Not for the first time, Liz wondered how her father had picked two completely different wives. Right now, she had a lot more respect for Ruth.

'Then at least consider other people's feelings. It's a difficult time for everyone.'

'Thank you, Elizabeth, I am aware of that.' Her mother smoothed down her skirt and sat down. Their conversation lapsed into silence as Liz listened to the monitors beeping and watched the steady rise and fall of her father's chest. Eventually, her mother spoke again. 'So, how are you these days? Still living in London?'

'Yes.'

'Still working in catering?'

'Yes, I run my own function business.'

'Really?' Her mother raised her eyebrows.

'Yes, I'm doing okay.' *Which you would have known if you hadn't taken Carlos' word over mine,* she thought. 'How's Carlos?' She might as well get it out of the way.

There was a pause before Diane spoke. 'Gone. Run off with the cleaner.'

Liz fought back the urge to say, "I told you so". Instead, she managed a quiet, 'I'm sorry.'

'No, you're not. You tried your best to split us up.'

'I didn't try to split you up, Mum! He couldn't keep his hands to himself. I literally had to fight him off, but you made me out to be the liar.'

'Well, you were right all along,' Diane snapped. 'So I'm better off without him.'

Part of her felt sorry for her mother; it wasn't easy being made a fool of by a man at any stage of life, but she imagined it would be harder the older you were. Although it did also make her question the real reason for her mother's sudden return.

At the sound of footsteps, Liz turned to see her sister carrying two cups of coffee.

'Hi, sis. I've brought you—' Mel stopped short when she saw her mother calmly sitting by her father's bedside. 'What are you doing here?'

'Well, that's a nice welcome. That's exactly what your sister said, although not quite in the same tone. How are you, Melissa?'

'Doing just fine without you, Mother.' She turned to Liz. 'Did *you* tell her?'

'No!'

'Ruth told me. I'm glad that someone had the decency to.'

'I don't see what it has to do with you. You've made it perfectly clear that we're not part of your life.'

'That's not true. You can come and see me whenever you want.'

'Yes, and when's the last time you visited us? Or even sent cards to your grandchildren on their birthdays? That's how good a mother you are.'

'Mel, please! Not now. Let's not argue by Dad's bed-side,' Liz urged, falling into her previous role of peacemaker between her mother and sister.

Mel scowled. 'Fine, but don't ask me to speak to her. She's probably only come over because she's trying to sniff some money out, just like she did during their divorce.'

'Melissa!'

Mel ignored her. 'How's Dad? Has there been any change?'

Liz shook her head. 'No. No change.'

'Why don't you go to ours and get some rest? I'll ring you if there's any news.'

Liz nodded wearily. 'Thanks, Mel. I think I will.' The thought of sitting there listening to her sister and her mother bicker was too much for her. She couldn't help thinking it might have been better if Diane had stayed away.

Outside the hospital, as Liz waited for a taxi, she switched her phone back on. There were several missed calls from unknown numbers. She listened to the voicemail messages in turn. They were all from people who wanted her to cater for them following Lucinda's engagement party. Her wish for her business had finally come true, but what lousy timing. Who knew when she'd be able to deal with them, or even if she would? It all depended on her dad.

The other two calls were from Jay and Alex. She listened to the voice message from Alex, asking her to call him. He sounded pretty desperate, and the sound of his voice tugged at her, but she was far too tired and confused to speak to him at the moment. She'd have to face him soon, but not yet. Right now, all she really wanted was to sleep.

CHAPTER THIRTY

'Alex, are you even listening to me?' Tia's voice burst through Alex's thoughts and he looked up in surprise.

'What?'

Tia sighed dramatically. 'I just said that I've spoken to my contact in the Planning Department and it looks like we'll get permission for the restaurant very soon.'

'That's quick!' Alex perked up, immediately interested.

'Yes, well, it helps when you know that right people.'

'Tia, you haven't done anything—'

'No, I haven't done anything illegal, if that's what you're about to ask,' she interrupted him. 'I just have a few contacts who can speed things along a bit. So, as soon as it all comes through, I'll need you to be firing on all cylinders, not mooning about the women in your life.'

'I'm not mooning,' Alex lied. He still hadn't heard from Liz and he was beginning to wonder if he should just let it go. What they had, or what he thought they'd had, obviously hadn't meant as much to her as it did to him.

'Have you got all the contractors on stand-by?'

'Yep, ready and waiting to go.'

'Good, because the sooner we get the renovations on the way, the better.'

'You do know I've got to go back to Dubai next week, don't you?'

'What, again? What for this time?'

'I told you, the contracts are ready to be signed. Once that's done, I won't have any more business over there and I can concentrate on my life here. Such that it is,' he added with a sigh.

'Ah yes, Nikki. You need to do something about that woman. She's talking loud and clear to anyone who'll listen and making it sound as though you've had your fun and cleared off.'

'Tell me about it! It's payback for me asking her to prove she's pregnant.'

Tia gasped. 'You mean you think there's a chance that she's not?'

Alex explained why he was suspicious and Tia looked thoughtful. 'Well, then you need to get proof one way or another. If she is lying, and I'm not saying she is because that's a terrible thing to lie about, then you need to get it out in the open as soon as possible. If you don't, your reputation will be in tatters. And the reputation of the restaurant will be tarnished before it's even opened.'

'Oh, I see.' Alex nodded. 'It's the restaurant you're concerned about, not me.'

'It's not like that. I'm just trying to give you some advice, that's all.'

'Advice? Sounds more like a lecture.'

'And you're beginning to sound like a petulant schoolboy.' Tia sat down on the desk and put her hand on his arm. 'Alex, this isn't like you. You're completely unfocused.'

'I know.'

'It's not just Nikki, is it?'

'No,' he admitted. 'If she is pregnant, I'll support her and the baby. But I will not be forced into any other kind of a relationship with her. Those days are gone. Besides, she's not the person I want to be with.'

'And how's Liz taking it?'

'Who knows?' Alex sighed again. 'No one's seen her since she found out about the pregnancy and she's not returning any of my calls.'

'And you wanted her to be involved in the restaurant? I've always told you it's a mistake to mix business with pleasure.'

'Oh bloody hell, Tia, all you think about is the restaurant. It's becoming an obsession.'

'A lot safer than relationships, if *you're* anything to go by. Now, enough about the women in your life. We have work to do.'

CHAPTER THIRTY-ONE

Alex still hadn't heard anything from Liz by the following Monday, and before his flight to Dubai that afternoon, he decided he needed one more chance to speak to her. He didn't want to leave the country without convincing her that Nikki wasn't a threat to their relationship.

As he looked up towards the window of Liz's flat, he thought he saw movement and pressed the buzzer again. To his surprise, a male voice answered, 'It's Alex Sinclaire. I've come to see Liz.'

'She's not here.' There was a pause. 'You'd better come up.'

The door to her flat was open when he reached it, and Alex recognised the man standing just inside as the person who'd let him in the first time he'd visited.

'Hi. We haven't met properly, but I'm Jay.' He held out his hand. 'I'm just checking on things while Liz is away. Messages on her phone mainly.'

'Liz is away?' Alex asked, surprised. Perhaps that would explain why she hadn't returned his calls. 'She never mentioned it.'

'No, it was very sudden. Her dad was involved in a car crash.'

'Oh God! When was this? Is he okay?' Alex could feel his heart pounding at the unexpected news. He'd thought she'd given up on their relationship. It hadn't occurred to him there would be another reason.

'It's not good, I'm afraid,' Jay said. 'He's in a coma. It happened the night of the engagement party. She's been with him ever since.'

'That explains a lot,' Alex said. 'She must be going through hell.'

'She is. But she's coming back tomorrow.'

'And I'm going to Dubai tonight.'

'Listen, why don't you come in for a minute?' Jay beckoned him.

Alex hesitated. He wasn't in the mood for a heart-to-heart with someone he'd previously mistaken for competition.

'It won't take a moment,' Jay said, so Alex followed him into the living room. 'Do you want to sit down?' Jay gestured towards the sofa. Alex looked at it, remembering the wonderful hours he had spent on it with Liz. Reluctantly, he sat down. 'I've heard on the grapevine that Nikki's pregnant.'

'I think half of London has by now.' Alex sighed. 'That's why I'm so desperate to get in touch. Liz hasn't spoken to me since she found out. Not even to tell me about her dad.' As he spoke, he realised how wide the gulf between them had become.

'I've known Liz a long time but she's always played things very close to her chest. She's been different since she met you but this is bound to bring her barriers back up.'

'I understand that. But I don't want a relationship with Nikki, although I will support my child if she's pregnant. The only person I want is Liz.'

Jay whistled. 'I see. It's one hell of a situation to be in.' He paused and added, 'You said, "if she's pregnant". Is there any doubt?'

'I might be clutching at straws, but when I've asked for proof, she wouldn't give it to me.'

'I used to go out with one of her friends.' Jay looked thoughtful. 'She's a tricky character, and I wouldn't want her to get between you and Liz.'

'Wouldn't you?' Alex asked, surprised.

'No. I think you two are good together. For a while there, she was the happiest I've ever seen her. I hope it works out for you. It won't be easy though, as I'm sure you know.'

'Oh, I know that,' Alex agreed.

'If it helps, I'll tell Liz what you've told me. She's got a lot on her plate, but I think the two of you should talk at least.'

'I'd be very grateful if you did,' Alex said, wishing that he didn't have to go away. But one thing he was sure of now was that he wasn't going to give up on his relationship with Liz without a fight.

CHAPTER THIRTY-TWO

Liz opened the door to her flat with mixed feelings. It would be nice to spend time in her own home, but she didn't want to be so far away from her father. She needed to be there when he woke up. *Or worse?* No, she wouldn't think like that. She had to be positive. She was here to work. The sooner she could get it done, the sooner she could be back with her dad.

She walked through to the bedroom and dumped her bag on the bed. The sheets were rumpled, and although the last time she'd slept here had been on her own, she couldn't help remembering the night she'd spent here with Alex. The sense of longing overwhelmed her for a few moments before she pulled herself together. What she felt for Alex wasn't important now. He was in the past. It was the future that mattered.

The intercom buzzed, and with some trepidation, she went to answer it. She hoped it wasn't Alex. She wasn't ready to face him just yet. To her relief, it was Jay, and she buzzed him up.

'I come bearing gifts,' he said, handing her a coffee when she opened the door.

'Thanks, that's exactly what I need right now.'

'And'—he said, opening his backpack and pulling out a carton of milk and a loaf of bread—'provisions. I had to throw out everything you had in your fridge.'

'Thanks, Jay. I haven't even thought about going shopping yet.' She slumped down onto the sofa and took a sip of her coffee. 'And thanks for everything you've done for me. I owe you big time.'

'Not a problem,' he said, sitting opposite her.

'I've had so many phone calls since the engagement party, it's overwhelming, and I just don't know what I'm going to say to them. It's heartbreaking, really. All this time I've been desperate for bookings and now I've got them coming out of my ears.'

'How's your dad?'

She shook her head. 'No change. There's nothing anyone can do. We just have to wait.'

She felt the tears welling in her eyes as guilt and sadness overwhelmed her. Jay put his arm around her and hugged her to him. 'I'm here for you, Liz. We'll get through this together.'

She squeezed his arm. 'Thanks, Jay. Like I said, I don't know what I'd do without you.'

'Just take one day at a time.'

'I know, but my head's in a mess.'

'I'm not surprised,' he said. 'That's why I'm here to help. Let's go through these messages and see what we can do.'

She nodded. 'You're right. There's so many of them, though. I'm not sure I could cope even without all this going on.'

'Let's just have a look, shall we?'

A while later, after having made a list, Liz shook her head. 'I'm going to have to tell them to find someone else.'

'You can't do that,' Jay protested. 'Not when you've spent so long building up your business.'

'But what about Dad? What if he takes a turn for the worst? I can't suddenly drop everything if I have bookings. And I can't not be there.'

'What you need is a business partner,' Jay said quietly.

'You're right, I do. But that's not going to happen.'

'It's not impossible.'

'What do you mean?' The penny dropped. 'Do you mean you? But what about your job?'

Jay sighed. 'I've decided that I'm definitely going to hand in my notice.'

'Louis not getting any better then?'

He shook his head. 'Worse if anything. The idea that he'll be in charge of two restaurants has completely gone to his head. He's impossible to work with and I've just about had enough.'

'Well, I know what that feels like.'

'It's not just that,' Jay said. 'Honestly, I've really enjoyed the last few functions I've done with you, and we work well together. I know it's risky, but I'd like to help you out, even if it's just for the short-term.'

'You're serious, aren't you?'

'Completely. Look at these enquiries. We can work it out between us. That would give you the freedom to spend time with your dad.'

She nodded. 'I enjoy working with you too. But what about our friendship? I don't want to ruin that.'

'I see your point. But I'd hope that if we had any problems, we'd be able to talk to each other about them.'

'We'd have to make sure we did. And we'd need to have a proper contract.'

'Agreed. So, is it something you think we could make happen?'

'It would make sense, but it's difficult to make any long-term decisions at the moment.'

'I understand. But you will think about it?'

'Yes, I will.'

'Good.' He paused, 'And if you decide you don't want a partnership, I won't be offended. I'll sign up with an agency until I find something else, or just fill in for you if you need me and you can pay me the going rate.'

'You'd do that?'

He laughed. 'I'll need the money.'

For the first time in ages, Liz smiled. 'Well, in that case, we'd better take a closer look at these enquiries.'

Together, they worked with complete concentration until Liz's stomach rumbled.

'Fancy going out for something to eat?' Jay asked.

'Not sure if I'm up for going out, but I could eat.'

'Takeaway it is then.'

It was later, when they were sitting eating chicken and noodles, that Jay said, 'I saw Alex while you were away.'

She paused, fork midway to her mouth. 'Really? Where?'

'Here. He came round to see you.'

She put the fork down. 'Oh.'

'He wanted to see you before he headed back out to Dubai.'

'He's back there, is he?' She wasn't sure whether she was disappointed or relieved that there was no chance of seeing him. 'He said he'd need to go back to complete his business there so he could commit to being in England. That will be even more important with a child to bring up.'

'He's not convinced there even is a child. Nikki's being all cagey about going to the doctors and he's asked for proof that she's actually pregnant.'

Liz frowned. 'Surely even Nikki wouldn't lie about that?'

'Who knows? But he needs to find out for sure. If she's pregnant, he says he'll be a good dad.'

'He said the same to me.'

'But he was adamant you're the woman he wants to be with. Love like that doesn't come along very often, you know?'

'Love? Neither of us has actually said the "L" word yet!'

Jay laughed. 'Well, it's obvious to me. Before this, you've been the happiest I've ever seen you. And as for him, well, pining for you doesn't even begin to describe it.'

'Really?' she asked, surprised. Her heart began to flutter at the thought that Alex might love her, but then realisation crept back in.

'It doesn't really matter if he loves me, or if I love him. I don't feel as though I can trust him. Or Nikki. He knew she was pregnant before he went to Dubai last time, but he didn't tell me.'

'Maybe he had his reasons?'

'He said he didn't want to tell me when he was away and that he didn't want to distract me with the engagement party coming up.'

'So, he was thinking of you then?'

'Maybe. I don't know. I can't get my head around any of it.'

'That's not surprising. But maybe, when he's back from Dubai, you could at least speak to him. Let him tell you his side of the story and you can tell him how you feel. It doesn't even have to go anywhere from there, but at least you'll both know where you stand.'

Liz smiled, grateful to have Jay as her friend. 'That's good advice. But I really don't think I should get in the way of him being a good dad.'

'Maybe he can do both. In time.'

'Maybe. And in the meantime, there's always business. Let's get to it.'

Later on, completely worn out, Liz decided to have an early night, but despite her tiredness, she couldn't sleep. Alone in her bed, her thoughts drifted automatically to Alex. She wondered what he was doing. Until the engagement party, she'd really thought she'd found her soulmate. He was the man she'd always dreamed of, even when she thought she hated him, and to finally be with him properly had meant everything to her. To have it snatched away was worse than not knowing what it would be like in the first place . . .

* * *

Standing on the balcony of his father's apartment in Dubai, Alex was thinking about Liz too. Finding out about her father's accident had been a massive shock. He knew she regretted the time she'd missed with her dad. What if she didn't get a second chance? He'd done her an injustice when he'd assumed she'd gone to ground because of him and the situation with Nikki. He should have realised she was better than that.

Even though it was the middle of the night, he couldn't sleep. He'd hoped a glass of whisky might help, but the first glass was now empty and he was still wide awake. He poured a second drink and swirled the amber liquid around as he contemplated his situation.

Not being able to speak to Liz was eating away at him. Although it was late in England, he decided to bite the bullet. She hadn't picked up any of his calls during the day, but calling now might catch her off guard. He hoped a phone call at this time of night wouldn't send her into a panic, thinking it was about her dad, but he really needed her to know that he was thinking of her.

* * *

Liz jumped as the landline rang. Praying that it wasn't anyone bringing her bad news about her father, she picked it up straight away.

'Hello,' she answered breathlessly.

'Liz, it's Alex.'

'Alex.' Relief flooded through, but then her heart started to beat a little faster at the sound of his voice.

'I'm so sorry about your dad. Are you okay? Or is that a silly question?'

'I'm fine,' she said. 'Well, you know . . .'

'How is he?'

'Not good. He's in an induced coma because his injuries are so bad. It's just a waiting game, hoping that he'll get well enough to come round.'

'I'm really am sorry. I wish there was something I could do to help.'

'There isn't. And I'm sure you've got enough on your plate.'

'Liz, I don't want to be with her. And I don't want Nikki to come between us.'

'Alex, don't. I'm sorry, but I just can't deal with this at the moment. I've got enough to cope with, trying to spend time with Dad and run my business. I don't need any more complications in my life.'

'I see.' The hurt in his voice tore at her, although she knew she was doing the right thing. But he continued speaking. 'I'll get this sorted, Liz, I promise you I will. And then maybe you might think again?'

'We'll see,' she said before putting the phone down. If only it was that simple. Alex might think that Nikki was lying about being pregnant. But what if he was wrong? Then it would be about a child's life; not something that could be simply "sorted".

CHAPTER THIRTY-THREE

Liz was ploughing through a pile of paperwork the following Friday when her phone began to ring. It was Jay.

'Liz, I've done it!' he said, the joy obvious in his voice. 'I've handed in my notice.'

'And?'

'And you wouldn't believe! I have to tell you in person. Do you fancy going out for a drink?'

Liz thought about going out to a noisy bar with people celebrating the end of the working week and realised she couldn't face it.

'Jay, I'm sorry. I don't want to go out, but maybe you could come here?'

'Sure, no problem. I'll pick up some wine along the way. I'll be there as soon as I can.'

As Liz sat waiting for her friend to arrive, she wondered what he was so excited about. If Jay had something to celebrate, she'd do her best to show that she was happy for him. He'd been there for her, and even though she was in no mood to celebrate anything herself, she wouldn't want to deny him his moment.

Jay burst through the door when she opened it. 'Have you got glasses?' he asked straight away, and she smiled at his enthusiasm.

'In the living room, ready and waiting.'

When he had poured them both drinks, he said, 'So, this afternoon I gave Roberto my letter of resignation.'

'And?'

'And he was furious. Said I was one of his best younger chefs, and with the new restaurant opening he was hoping to promote me.'

'I thought you told me Louis said there was no chance of any promotion?'

'He did, but apparently he had no right to say that. He's not in charge of staff. Roberto said he's still the one making those decisions. So, then he asked me if I would reconsider my resignation if I did get a promotion.'

'But that's brilliant news! I hope you said yes.'

'Nope,' Jay said, still grinning.

'What, because of Louis?'

'Partly. But when I refused, I decided to tell Roberto exactly why I couldn't work with Louis anymore.' He paused. 'I hope you don't mind but I also told him the real reason you left.'

'Oh!' Liz was shocked. When she'd left La Emporium, Roberto knew that she and Louis had clashed but she hadn't told him the extent of Louis' bullying. If she had, she'd known she would have also had to tell him she was afraid of having a relapse with her anorexia, and that was something she didn't have the strength to do at the time. But she had often regretted it, knowing that Louis would get away with doing it to someone else, as he now had with Jay.

'That is okay, isn't it?' Jay asked, looking concerned.

'It's more than okay,' she replied, smiling. 'I'm glad you told him. He needs to know what's going on under his name. I'm just ashamed I didn't have the guts to tell him myself at the time. So, what did he say then?'

'He was horrified. I'm afraid I've really dropped Louis in it. He'll be lucky to have a job at the end of this. I know I shouldn't celebrate someone's downfall, but he's got away with his behaviour for far too long.'

'That's true. But what happens now? Surely that means you can accept Roberto's offer of promotion.'

'I could, but . . .' Jay paused.

'What?'

'Look, I don't want to put any pressure on you, but have you thought any more about our partnership?'

'Yes, I have,' Liz replied, taking a sip of her wine, deliberately leaving Jay in suspense.

'And?'

'Jay, are you sure you want to do this? I don't want you to if you're doing it out of compassion for my current situation. I'd hate to think that you'd turned down promotion because you felt you needed to help me out.'

'I don't think that. Not at all. Well, yes, I want to help you out, but I wouldn't turn down a promotion because of it.'

'But you loved working at La Emporium.'

'Yes, I did,' Jay agreed. 'Until I did those functions with you. I don't want to be cooking the same things, night in night out. I want more variety, more creative input. I want to design my own menus. With your help, of course.'

Liz laughed. 'Of course, that goes without saying. I know we've had a lot of enquiries recently, but the business can be very up and down. It might be difficult to create an income for the both of us, long-term.'

'That's the other thing I need to tell you.'

'What?'

'Roberto's asked us to tender for the function contract at the new restaurant.'

'Ah.' Liz paused. 'I'm not sure about that.'

'Why not? It would complement the business we already have and could provide us with the extra income we could definitely do with.'

'I know but . . .' She sighed. 'Okay Jay, if we're going to be business partners, we need to be completely honest with each other. When Alex first mentioned it to me, he thought he was doing me a favour because my bookings were down. I felt as though it was a pity decision, and that didn't sit well with me.'

'I can understand that, but the situation's completely different now.'

'It is, which might make working with Alex even more difficult.'

'I can see why you might think that, but I doubt Alex will have anything to do with the day-to-day running of the restaurant. That will be down to Roberto and Tia.'

'Tia, yes, but have you ever worked with Tia? She does like to get her own way.'

'Oh, I can deal with that,' Jay said confidently. 'I bet she's a pussycat underneath. Look Liz, I understand your concerns, I really do. What if we agreed that I would be the face of the functions in the restaurant and you could concentrate on the private stuff? The restaurant won't be up and running for a good while yet, so it won't affect the time you need to spend with your dad now.'

Liz smiled. It would be so nice to share this with someone else, and especially someone who worked the way she did. 'In that case, partner, I think we need to toast our new business.'

'Really? You mean it?'

And when she nodded, Jay put his glass down. 'Never mind a toast. I need a hug!'

CHAPTER THIRTY-FOUR

Roberto was not the kind of man who let the grass grow under his feet, so within a few days Liz found herself and Jay facing him and Tia in Roberto's office in La Emporium. The way Tia kept glaring at her, though, made Liz feel that the other woman didn't want her there. Was she annoyed that Liz had asked Alex to leave her alone? If she was, it was really none of her business. Liz tried to shrug off her uneasiness and concentrate.

'So,' Roberto said, 'we're here to discuss your tender to become our catering partner for functions.'

'We'd be delighted to be considered,' Liz said.

'Are you sure it wouldn't get in the way of your personal life?' Tia asked, straight to the point.

'I'm sorry, what do you mean?'

Tia ignored her question. 'I suppose that having both of you will provide some back-up if one of you is suddenly unavailable.'

Liz frowned. Did Tia know about her father? If so, why was she being so frosty?

Tia sighed as though she was about to explain herself to a child. 'The success of this restaurant is vital. I need professional chefs, not ones who disappear when a personal relationship gets a little tricky. I tried to call you last week but your phone was switched off. And you disappeared after the engagement party. I assumed it was to do with the whole Nikki situation.'

Enlightenment dawned, and with it a sense of outrage that Tia was bringing this all up in front of Roberto. 'Yes, I have been away. But it had nothing to do with Alex. Or Nikki for that matter,'

'Really? I find that hard to believe.'

Liz pictured her dad lying in his hospital bed and felt tears welling in her eyes. For a moment, she was speechless. Jay came to her defence.

'On the afternoon of the engagement party, Liz's father was involved in a serious road traffic accident in Cheshire. He's been in intensive care ever since.'

'Oh,' Tia said softly. 'I'm sorry, I—'

'Jumped to conclusions?' Liz said, finally finding her voice.

'Well, yes, but—'

'I suppose the timing didn't help. Just for the record, though, if Alex and Nikki are having a baby together, that's nothing to do with me. Whatever my personal life is, my professional life will always be separate.'

'Yes, of course—' Tia tried to say, but Liz spoke over her.

'I'm sure you can appreciate that while I was at the hospital, I had my phone switched off. If you needed to talk to me, you could have left a message. I would have called you straight back.'

'I'm sorry. I just assumed . . . well, I just hope your dad gets well soon.'

'Thank you.' Liz slumped back in her chair, feeling deflated. She didn't want sympathy. She just wanted to keep going. Since meeting Alex again, she'd allowed her feelings to come to the surface, and that had left her vulnerable — something she couldn't afford to be right now.

'How is he now?' Tia asked.

'He's still in a coma. So, in between jobs for the foreseeable future, I'll be travelling back up to Cheshire. But I'll return all of your calls if you need to talk to me and leave a message. And, of course, I'll give you Jay's number, who will cover for me if the circumstances don't allow me to be here in person.'

'That sounds like a good plan.' Tia nodded.

'I was also sorry to hear about your father,' Roberto interjected. 'And obviously you'll need to spend time away from London. But I believe that you and Jay will make a good partnership and I have no questions about your professionalism. Now, shall we focus on business?'

'Yes, please go ahead,' Liz said, surprised at the rather barbed comment towards Tia. One thing was for sure, Tia wouldn't always be able to get her own way as far as Roberto was concerned.

* * *

For the next week, Liz divided her time between London and Cheshire, performing any functions she already had booked in alone whilst Jay was working out his notice. In their free time, they worked on the tender for Roberto, either together if she was in London, or over Zoom and email if she was with her father.

Above all, she tried her hardest not to think about Alex; not to remember how they'd been together. She tried to forget how his lips had felt on hers and how the slightest touch from his fingers made her skin tingle. She tried not to think about how good it would feel to share her fears with him. But, most of all, she tried not to think of his unborn baby.

In Cheshire she sat by her father's bedside for hours on end, willing him back to life. She also tried to support Mel, who seemed to be crumbling in front of her eyes. Mel had always been the one Liz leant on when things went wrong, but now it was the other way round. Mel had been so much closer to their father. Liz could only hope for a future when all this was behind them.

In the darkest hours, she would lie awake worrying. And in moments of complete weakness, she would wonder what Alex was doing. No matter how much her head told her she was better off out of the complicated situation, it didn't stop her yearning for him. In the rare moments she could sleep, she would wake up after having the most erotic dreams about him. The emptiness of the other side of the bed left her feeling overwhelmingly lonely. Although she was a person who enjoyed her own company, now she realised there was a vast difference between being alone and being lonely.

'You look tired, sis,' Mel commented when she picked her up from the train station on one of her trips to Cheshire.

'You don't look much better yourself.' Liz reached out for a hug. 'Any change?'

Mel shook her head despondently. 'Nope. The doctors are talking about reducing his medication, hoping to bring him out of the coma.'

'That's good news, isn't it?' Liz felt a surge of hope.

'It depends on how well he copes with it. It could go either way. But they're going to leave it for a few days yet. Mother's still hanging around like a bad smell,' Mel added.

'Mel!'

'She's after something, I can tell. Money probably, although she's got a cheek if she is. She squeezed enough out of Dad during the divorce.'

'No, I don't think so. The night she arrived she seemed genuinely concerned. I'm sure she's just staying until there's some kind of change.'

'Either that or she has nowhere else to go.'

'She's staying in a hotel, isn't she? That must be expensive.'

Mel shook her head. 'Not anymore. She asked to stay at mine.'

'What did you say to that?'

'I told her no, of course. I don't need her hanging around when we're trying to sell the house. And the less she knows about our problems, the better. She never wanted me to marry Simon in the first place; she'll only say I told you so.'

'Where's she staying then?'

Mel laughed. 'Would you believe she's staying with Ruth?'

'You're joking!'

'I wish. They seem to have some cosy little double act going on. I can't get my head round it. I always thought Ruth was kind, but to welcome your husband's ex-wife into your home? That's just too nice for her own good. I can't understand why Mother doesn't bugger off back to Spain and leave us alone.'

Liz sighed wearily. 'I'm not sure I should tell you this. She didn't exactly tell me not to, but I think you should know. Carlos has left her. Run off with someone younger from the sounds of things.'

'Ah well, that does make sense,' Mel said. 'I wondered how long it would take him. I don't suppose you could have a word with her and find out how long she's planning on sticking around? We need to find out what's going on. Before Dad comes round.'

'I'll try,' Liz replied, although she didn't relish the idea of a heart-to-heart with her mother, especially on the subject of Carlos.

Later, Liz sat beside her father's bed, holding his frail hand in her own. He looked at peace, as though he was just sleeping, but she wished he would wake up.

Ruth came into the ward and sat down on the other side of the bed.

'Any change?' she asked quietly, without any real expectation in her voice.

Liz shook her head. 'No. No change.' She'd grown so bored of those words recently.

'Why don't you go and get some rest? You look done in.'

'I think I might.' Liz had been sitting beside the bed for hours now. 'Is Mum at yours?'

'Yes.'

'Is she cramping your style?'

Ruth laughed. 'No, not really. Although I don't know what your dad would say if he knew.'

'He'd have a fit.'

'Probably. But she's got nowhere else to go. Let's just say we've come to an understanding. She'll be moving on before long.'

'Moving on? Back to Spain?'

Ruth shook her head. 'Ah no, I think that part of her life may be over.'

'What do you mean? She's coming back?'

'It's not for me to say but, reading between the lines, I'd say it's not worked out over there quite as she expected.'

'Okay, well, I'll let you have some time alone with Dad,' Liz said as she got up from her chair and stretched out her cramped limbs. If their mother was planning on staying, life was about to get a whole lot more complicated.

Rather than going straight back to Mel's, Liz took a taxi from the hospital to her dad's house. She walked round to the back door, which was usually open. When she stepped inside, her mother was pottering around the kitchen, looking as though it belonged to her. Liz stopped in the doorway, staring in disbelief as Diane wiped down surfaces whilst singing along to the radio. Then she turned round and visibly jumped as she spotted Liz.

'Liz! What are you doing standing there? You didn't half give me a fright.'

'Sorry.' Liz couldn't believe her mother. Not only had she chosen to live with her ex-husband's wife, she looked so happy doing it.

'Have you been to see your dad?' Diane asked.

'Yes.'

'No change?'

'No change,' Liz confirmed, and decided to bite the bullet. 'Mum, how long are you planning on staying here?'

Diane shrugged. 'I don't know. I want to support you both.'

'But Mel won't speak to you and I'm living in London.'

'Yes, well, at least I'm here if you do need me.'

'But your life is in Spain. Won't people be missing you there?'

'Hardly.' Diane walked over to the kitchen table and slumped down in a chair.

'What's wrong?'

'You know I said that Carlos had left me?'

'Yes.'

'Well, that's not the only thing. Before he left, he re-mortgaged the apartment and didn't keep up the payments. He also cleared out the bank account. He's left me with nothing. Less than nothing, in fact.'

'Oh God, Mum! I always knew he was slimy, but that takes the biscuit.'

Diane wiped away a tear which had spilled onto her cheek. 'It's my own fault. I should have been more independent. Stood on my own two feet. But I loved him, and I thought he loved me back.' She laughed cynically. 'They're right about what they say, you know? There's no fool like an old fool.'

'You're not old. And you're not the first to be betrayed by a man.'

'It still leaves me up the creek without a paddle.'

'I don't know what to say.'

'I didn't want to worry you, but I've nothing left, Liz. Nothing at all.'

'You could always stay with me,' Liz said, almost against her own will.

'Thanks, love, and it's a very kind offer, but I need to stand on my own two feet. I'm going to get a job.'

'Doing what?'

Diane shrugged. 'I have absolutely no idea. And there's not exactly a lot in the job market these days, especially for someone like me. The only thing I can do is cook. Remember how we used to cook together when you were little? Maybe that's where you got if from?'

'Maybe.' Liz didn't have the heart to tell her that it was recovering from anorexia that had given her the cooking bug, not her mother. But Diane was right about one thing — she *was* a good cook, so maybe she could get a job involving that somewhere. 'I think you need to tell Ruth,' she continued.

'Not yet. It's kind of her to let me stay, but she thinks it's only temporary.'

'Don't underestimate her. She's a lot more tuned in to people than you realise.'

'Maybe.'

'I'll lend you some money if you need it,' Liz offered, knowing she had little to spare.

Diane hugged her. 'Maybe as a last resort. Like I said, I need to sort this out myself.'

Liz was quietly impressed by her mother's wish to stand on her own two feet, but how she was going to do it was anyone's guess.

CHAPTER THIRTY-FIVE

By eight-thirty, Alex had showered and was ready to leave the flat. It had been a long night flight from Dubai, but he was on a mission. It was time to get some answers.

Whilst he'd been away, he'd visited Kas' parents. He still kept in touch and felt a part of their family, even though Kas wasn't there. He'd been sitting on their balcony with Lena, Kas' mother, watching the sun slowly dip down in the sky, casting an amber glow, when Lena had turned to him.

'It's been so nice to see you, Alex. It's been a long time.'

'I know, I'm sorry. At first, I couldn't bear to be here because everything reminded me of Kas. And the longer I left it, the harder it was to come back. I've never stopped thinking about her, though.'

'I doubt you ever will, no matter what happens in your life. She'll always be part of it.'

'She will,' Alex said quietly.

'But what's happened to bring you back? I get the feeling you have something on your mind. Something you want to share with me?'

'Is it that obvious?' He wondered if Lena would think he was being disloyal to Kas because his heart was full of Liz.

Or worse, that he couldn't be with Liz because someone else was pregnant with his child. *What a mess!*

'Have you met someone else?'

He nodded slowly. 'Yes. But it's not quite that simple.'

'In that case, I'll get us a glass of wine.'

Alone, Alex looked out to the sunset. Maybe, out there somewhere, were the answers to his problems. Or perhaps they were right here on the balcony. Lena returned and Alex listened to the soft glugging of the wine as she topped up his glass.

'There is someone in London. A girl I met years ago when she was just a teenager.' And then, slowly, he told her the whole story and explained what a sorry mess he was in. When he'd finished, he added, 'It all feels wrong. What Kas and I had was so special. If she hadn't been taken from us, in time, we'd have had a whole brood of children running around at our feet and I would've been the happiest man alive. But the thought of having a child with Nikki, well, it just doesn't feel right.'

'And what if it was Liz? How would you feel then?'

He grinned. 'I'd be over the moon.' He stopped himself when he realised how his words might wound his mother-in-law. 'I'm sorry. I didn't mean to be insensitive.'

She put her hand on his arm. 'You're not. I can tell you're very much in love with her, and I'm glad. It's time you moved on. And Kas would want you to be happy with someone else, not grieving for her for the rest of your life. You're a good man, Alex, and you'd make a good father too. Of course, I'm sad that I'll never be a grandmother to your children, but that doesn't mean to say you shouldn't have any yourself.'

Alex shrugged. 'Yes, but not with Nikki. Liz and I were getting on so well when Nikki dropped her bombshell. Now Liz won't speak to me. I can't blame her really. Who would want to be in the middle of this?'

Lena sipped her wine and let the silence stretch out. Eventually, she said, 'Perhaps it isn't such a lost cause. Maybe Liz is giving you some space to sort yourself out? Just give it time.'

He nodded in agreement. 'She probably is. And she has problems of her own. But she was scarred emotionally as a teenager, and I'm worried she'll back off completely.'

'If it's meant to be, it will work out eventually. You have to sort things out with Nikki first. If you really believe she's lying, you need to get medical confirmation about the pregnancy.'

And so here he was, acting on her advice, armed with a pregnancy test he'd bought at the chemist. Lena had made everything sound so simple, and whilst he didn't think it would be, he knew he couldn't run away from this. If things ever worked out between him and Liz, then he'd take her to meet Lena. He had a feeling they'd really get on.

* * *

Nikki sounded groggy when she answered the buzzer to her apartment.

'Nikki, it's Alex. Can I come up?'

'Oh, um . . . okay.'

As the door clicked, he bounded up the stairs. Nikki looked flustered as she opened the door. 'What are you doing here at this time in the morning?'

'I just got back from Dubai. I wanted to know how you were. And the baby.'

'Why the sudden concern?'

He ignored the hostility in her voice. 'While I was away, I did a lot of thinking. If I *am* going to be a dad, I want to be the best one I can be. But I need to be sure first.'

'I don't know why you can't just believe me.'

'Because you've lied to me in the past. I've bought a pregnancy test for you. All you need to do is to pee on the stick, and if you're telling me the truth, as you insist you are, you have nothing to worry about.'

'I have nothing to worry about,' she said defiantly. 'And I'm not peeing on the stick, Alex — not at your command. I went to see the midwife and everything's fine.'

That was something at least. 'Have you booked your twelve-week scan? I want to be with you for that.'

She looked away from him, unable to meet his eyes. 'I'm not having one. That scan is just to work out dates. I'm sure of mine, so I don't need it.'

He frowned. 'Well, I want you to have one. I want to know that this baby's okay and I'd have thought you'd want that too.'

'You know I hate hospitals — the less I go, the better. I'll be seeing enough of them before long.'

'I can book a private appointment if that helps.'

She sighed. 'You're not going to let this drop, are you?'

'No. I need to be sure my baby's okay. Sorry if I sound like a stuck record, but it's very simple really.'

'Okay then, but I don't need you to be there.'

'Oh no! I'm coming with you, Nikki. Because if you don't want me there, then I can only assume you don't want me in your baby's life at all.'

'Fine!' she snapped. 'You can come. Can you go now? I've got things to do.'

Alex almost skipped down the stairs. Her reluctance to go to the doctors and her refusal to do the test had convinced him his instincts were right. But now that he'd insisted on booking a scan and going with her, he'd find out for certain if there was a baby.

CHAPTER THIRTY-SIX

Liz placed buttered cabbage in the centre of the plates, positioned the slow-roasted duck leg on top, and then carefully spooned the gooseberry jam around it. The addition of celeriac puree completed the dish. She gave the rims of the plates a quick wipe and nodded in satisfaction. This was the last of the main courses to go out, and it was definitely her favourite.

Roberto had accepted their tender and they were now officially the function caterers for the new restaurant. He'd asked them to produce some sample menus, and so they'd arranged the tasting session. It was a shame that Jay wasn't here with her, but he had already booked in another function before Roberto had insisted this was the only date he could do. She was confident about their dishes, but was nervous about seeing Alex again.

Carefully, she picked up the three plates and took them to her diners. She'd been shocked when Alex had turned up at the restaurant earlier that morning, throwing her into a tailspin. He was tanned from the sun and looked positively glowing with health. His dark brown hair had grown a little and was curling around the nape of his neck. It made him even more attractive. Her stomach had taken a roller coaster dip when he'd walked through the door, and she'd realised with horror that none of her feelings for him had gone away — if anything, they'd intensified. Her hands ached to reach out and touch him, and she almost reeled with longing at the thought. Instead, she turned away to concentrate on the food and tried to put all thoughts of being caressed by him out of her mind.

Her hand was shaking as she put the plate in front of him. She was so close to him she could smell the citrus of his aftershave, reminding her of when they'd been together. She put the other plates down quickly and stood back as everyone began to eat.

'God, that's delicious,' Tia enthused as she chewed slowly. 'The gooseberries really complement the duck, don't you agree?'

Alex nodded. 'All the dishes are excellent, but this is the best.'

'Yes, definitely one for the menu. I don't think I could grow tired of eating that,' Tia exclaimed while Roberto laughed in agreement, and Liz breathed a sigh of relief. Although she was confident about her and Jay's ideas, it was nerve-wracking waiting for a reaction, and she realised she'd been chewing her lip nervously.

Tia sat back in her chair. 'I'm stuffed — and there are still the desserts to come!'

'I've done them in trios,' Liz said. 'So that you can taste them but not be overwhelmed. I thought about putting the option of a trio on the menu. I find it works well, especially for large functions.'

'Good idea,' Tia replied. 'But could you give us a break for about fifteen minutes? I want to do them justice — and besides, I've got some phone calls to make.'

'No problem.'

Roberto's phone began to ring and he walked away to answer it. 'I'm sorry, I've got to go. There's a problem at La Emp.' He turned back to Tia. 'I'm sure I can trust your judgement as far as the desserts are concerned.'

'Oh, definitely,' Tia replied, and then looked at Alex. 'I'll be back in fifteen.'

Liz was about to go back to the kitchen when she heard Alex's voice behind her. 'Liz. Please can we talk?'

As she turned, her legs began to shake. How was she going to convince him they had no future when all she wanted to do was run into his arms?

'I think we said everything on the phone, didn't we?'

'I don't want to leave it like this, but I respect that you need space. You won't rule out us being together in the future, though, will you?'

It would be so easy to say she wanted him, that she needed him. To fall into his arms and forget all the complications. Just wish them away. But life wasn't that simple, and she couldn't relent now.

'I'm sorry. I just can't think about that right now.'

'Okay, I understand. How's your dad? Any improvement?'

She shook her head. 'No, I'm afraid not.'

'Is there anything I can do?'

His sympathy made her want to cry. She stepped back. 'Look Alex, I need to get on.'

'I understand. But Liz, if you need me, I'm here for you. Just call me.'

'Thank you,' she whispered as tears sprang to her eyes. She really wished it could be different. But it was impossible.

Leaving him, she forced herself to focus on putting the finishing touches to the desserts: a chocolate tartlet with caramel snap and crème fraiche, raspberry and honey panna cotta squares, and baked lime cheesecake.

'Ooh, they look fabulous,' Tia said when Liz finally put the desserts in front of them. 'I really do like the idea of trios.' She eagerly forked some of the chocolate tart into her mouth. 'Lovely and gooey, but not too rich,' she exclaimed when she'd finished. Then she dived straight into the panna cotta, followed by the cheesecake. Liz watched her, smiling. She was like a child at Christmas. When Tia had cleaned the plate, she spoke again. 'Well done, Liz. The combination of the panna cotta and the raspberries and honey is brilliant. I can't see anyone not liking these, and you can change the fruits according to the season. What do you think, Alex? You've been very quiet.'

Alex, who was looking stony-faced, cleared his throat. 'Yes, excellent. But I need to check up on the builders. I must go.' He flicked his jacket off the back of the chair and strode out of the restaurant.

Tia frowned and turned to Liz. 'What's eating him?'

Liz shrugged. 'I wouldn't know.'

'Are you sure?'

'Of course I am. I told you, Tia, anything between me and Alex is firmly in the past. It's strictly business from now on.'

'Alright, sweetheart. No need to snap my head off.'

'Sorry. Have you finished with those plates? I need to get cleared up before I go back to Cheshire. I'll be gone for a few days, but if you need to speak to me just give me a ring.'

'Okay. I hope your dad's improving.'

Liz forced a smile. It was really hard to accept people's sympathies whenever her father was mentioned. 'Well, not at the moment, but I'm keeping my fingers crossed.'

* * *

Liz checked her mobile when she got back in the van.

'Damn!' she muttered when she realised she was out of battery. She pulled open the door to the glove compartment and plugged in her charger. Then she set off towards her flat, where she would drop off the van and head straight to Euston station to get the train back to Cheshire. She needed to get away from everything which reminded her of Alex. She wished everyone else would let her forget about him because she wasn't doing a very good job of it on her own.

As Liz pulled into the car park, the phone rang. Her blood ran cold as her sister's name flashed up.

'Mel?' she answered fearfully.

'Liz, you need to get here as quickly as you can.'

'I'm getting on the next train. What's happening?'

'I think Dad might be coming round. The doctors say his vital signs are responding and they're going to reduce the medication.'

'That's amazing! I'll be with you as soon as I can. Don't bother picking me up from the station. I'll get a taxi.'

'Okay, sis. I'll see you soon. Fingers crossed.'

'Give me a ring if you have any news.'

Liz ran into the flat as soon as she got home and picked up a bag which she kept ready packed before rushing to the Tube station.

She could hardly contain herself on the train, urging it faster and faster towards her father. Perhaps she was being given the chance to make up for all the time she'd wasted? She'd do everything she could to look after him, spend every spare minute in Cheshire until he was back on his feet. Part of her cursed the distance and her move to London. If she hadn't gone, they might have overcome their differences a long time ago. She hated feeling torn between her work and her family.

Finally, the train drew into Crewe, and as soon as she could she elbowed her way off it in her haste to get to the hospital. She stopped short when she saw Mel at the end of the platform. What was she doing here? She said she'd meet her at the hospital! But then she saw her sister's stricken face, and she knew.

'Watch where you're going!' A man in a business suit snapped as he almost walked into her. Liz barely heard him but kept her eyes on Mel as she walked towards her in a daze. When she got closer, she realised that Mel's face was ravaged with tears.

'Mel?'

'Oh Liz, I'm so sorry.'

Liz stared at her sister, dumbfounded, as tears slowly trickled down her own cheeks, both of them oblivious to commuters rushing past them. Eventually, she wiped them away with the back of her hand. 'What happened?'

'He just slipped away, not long after I phoned you. It was all very peaceful.'

Liz nodded, unable to speak, and Mel put her arm around her and edged her forward. 'Come on, Simon's waiting in the car. Let's go home.'

CHAPTER THIRTY-SEVEN

Liz was numb for the next few weeks. She felt as though her body belonged to someone else. It devastated her that she hadn't had the chance to say goodbye. It seemed incomprehensible that she'd never be able to speak to him again, especially when they'd thought he might recover.

'He knew you loved him. Hang on to that,' Simon had told her when she'd been inconsolable.

Unable to believe his conviction, she'd asked through her tears, 'Did he?'

'Yes, he did. He told me just before the accident how glad he was that you'd made it up.'

'Don't!' She couldn't bear to think of all the lost years. Years that could never be regained. Simon's words hadn't helped as he'd intended. They'd just proved that she'd wasted so much time.

And now, here they were on the day of the funeral. A day Liz had been dreading.

'Are you okay?' her mother asked. They were in the living room of her dad and Ruth's cottage, waiting for the hearse to arrive.

'I don't know,' Liz answered blankly. If the thought of burying her dad wasn't enough, memories of another funeral, years earlier, were slowly surfacing. The desolation was over-whelming. In the distance, the doorbell rang and someone went to answer it.

'You'll get through this, we all will,' Diane said, putting her arm round Liz. Mel glowered at them.

'She's only hanging around to see if he left her anything in his will,' Mel had predicted earlier in the week. Liz hadn't the heart to tell her that Diane would be sticking around for a lot longer than her sister realised.

Instead, she'd concentrated on taking it a day at a time, and finally the morning she'd been dreading had dawned. After a sleepless night, she felt itchy-eyed and hollow inside. If she'd tried to eat anything, she was sure she'd have been sick.

'He's here,' a voice said beside her. She looked out of the window as the hearse pulled up alongside the gate. Liz swallowed back the tears, fighting to keep control. They weren't even at the church yet and already she was falling apart. She couldn't help but wish that Alex was with her.

And then, almost as though she'd conjured up his image, he was standing in front of her. She smiled. Was she going mad? Alex couldn't be here, so obviously her imagination was providing him for her.

'Liz?' His voice startled her, and she realised that this wasn't a hallucination.

'What are you doing here?'

'I wanted to pay my respects.'

Whilst waiting for the funeral, Liz had gone back to London, but she'd refused to see or speak to Alex, even though he had tried to get in touch on several occasions. Her head was full of grief for her dad, and she knew if she had seen him, she'd have been unable to resist him. Right now, resisting him was the most difficult thing of all. She wanted him to take her into his arms and run away with her. Run away from this, from Nikki, from everything. But that was just impossible. She took a deep breath and blinked back her tears. 'That's kind of you.'

The cortege of cars parked behind the hearse and people organised themselves into groups.

Alex let go of her. 'I'll go in my car, leave you to your family. But I'll be in the church and I'll see you afterwards. Okay?'

She nodded and swallowed back the tears once more. *Afterwards*. After they had buried her father. When he would be truly gone. Despite knowing that, she kept expecting him to walk through the door laughing, 'Ha ha! Fooled you.' Now she could see the coffin, she realised it wouldn't happen. This was it. His last journey.

Mel came to her side. 'We're to go in the funeral car with Ruth.'

'Diane, will you join us?' Ruth asked. Mel stared at her in horror. Liz put a hand on her sister's arm to stop her from protesting. Now was not the time.

In the car, they spoke in stilted conversation, but Liz didn't want to talk. She remembered when they were little, when her dad would grab her in a bear hug when he came through the door and swing her round. Or when they would walk the fields together and he'd point out the different trees and vegetation, talking about the time when he was a boy himself on the farm with his father. He'd never lost the love of the country and had declared he couldn't live anywhere else. It hadn't rubbed off on her, though. Although she loved to come back, and missed the farm, she'd realised after college that she was a city girl at heart. She'd always longed to live in London when she was little — a yearning that came from watching films like *Love Actually* and *Four Weddings and a Funeral*. Although she realised the London of the films was fictional, she'd hankered after her own city lifestyle. Reality wasn't a big song and dance like in the movies, though. Instead, it was a rather solitary existence. Although she had some good friends, they were all busy in their careers as she was with hers. But coming home had stamped on her the meaning of family. Would she be able to settle now when she went back? She didn't want to stay here, but she wanted something more from her life than just work and an empty flat.

The car stopped and Liz realised they were sitting outside the pretty village church; the church where they'd attended many happy family weddings in the past, and also the church where Danny was buried. Father and son would be reunited, and she hoped they could make peace with one another.

She bit her lip as they lifted the coffin out of the car and onto a trolley. The men gathered round — Simon and some distant cousins — six strong men who would carry her father to his final resting place. A sob escaped her and she stemmed it with a hand to her mouth. Mel put her arm around her, and when Liz looked up, she saw a single tear travelling down her sister's face unchecked. She squeezed her tightly and wondered how they were going to get through it.

The service passed in a complete haze. She remembered a few of the hymns and bits of the eulogy delivered by Simon. She admired him for having the strength to stand up there and talk about her father's life. He'd always been very close to his father-in-law, and she knew he'd miss him deeply. As they all would.

Once outside, they walked in quiet unison behind the coffin towards a sunny spot in the churchyard. Her brother's headstone had been taken away and a large gaping hole had been dug for their father. At the sight of it, Liz felt the tears flowing from her eyes and she did nothing to stop them. Perhaps crying would ease the huge shard of grief which seemed to be lodged in her chest.

* * *

After the burial, her mother lingered by the grave.

'I don't know why she's suddenly looking so concerned,' Mel whispered viciously.

Liz pulled her away out of earshot. 'Mel, don't. She's grieving too. She lost her son.'

'She didn't seem that bothered before. Just legged it away with her fancy man.'

'Before Danny died, she was a good mum. We can't imagine what she went through — everyone deals with grief differently.'

'I still don't see how she could do that to Dad. Didn't she care what he was going through?'

'I don't think she could see it. She blamed Dad for that last argument with Danny. She blamed him for losing her son. She was wrong, and I think she realises that now. I know it won't be easy, and it's going to take time, but maybe we should try and forgive her for what happened in the past.'

Mel began to cry and Liz led her further away from the crowd. 'But she left me, Liz. She left me when I needed her. When I got engaged and married. When I was pregnant with Sophie. She should have been there for me. But she was too busy living out in Spain. With that man. He was more important to her than any of us.'

'I don't think he was. But by then she'd made the move and, even if it was a mistake, she couldn't undo it. Maybe she thought we'd be better off without her?'

'Well, I wasn't.'

'I know,' Liz said softly. 'And I know you'll never get that time back. But we've lost our dad — maybe we shouldn't lose any more time with our mum?'

Simon joined them and Mel turned to him, sobbing quietly. Liz stepped aside to give them some time to themselves. She hoped Mel would listen to her and one day, soon, find it in her heart to forgive their mother.

CHAPTER THIRTY-EIGHT

Alex watched as the two sisters attempted to comfort each other. It had shocked him to see how devastated they were by their father's death. He'd known, of course, that it would hit them hard — but this? They both looked crushed. He'd always been fond of Mel. She'd been a spirited twenty-some-thing when he'd visited; a girl who knew what she wanted and how to get it. He'd admired her for her tenacity and her determination. It seemed she was also loyal. Liz had told her how Mel had single-handedly pulled her through her illness when she was too wrapped up in grief to help herself. He found himself hoping that her father's death wouldn't trigger Liz's anorexia. He'd do anything he could to protect her from that happening . . . if she'd let him. Today, he'd wanted to pay his respects to a man he'd looked up to as a youth, as well as to make up for not being at Danny's funeral. But most of all, he wanted to show Liz how much he cared for her. That he wanted her in his life, baby or no baby. He had to prove the depth of his feelings for her somehow.

As he saw her break away from her sister, he went over to her. 'Are you okay? Sorry — silly question.'

She leaned into him, as if needing his support, and he instantly pulled her closer, eager to feel her in his arms after the long weeks apart.

'No, not really,' she said. 'But we'll get there. We have to. Life has to go on, doesn't it? Even if you don't want it to.'

His breath caught in his throat at her words. 'Don't say that.'

'Oh Alex.' She put her hand on his arm reassuringly. 'I didn't mean it like that. I'm not about to go off the rails. It's just that no matter how sad you feel, you have to do the normal day-to-day things.'

He nodded and tried to push back the memories of how he'd felt after first losing Kas.

'It's Mel I'm worried about, actually,' Liz continued, breaking the awkward silence. 'She blames Mum for everything and won't have anything to do with her. It's not good to foster such hatred.' She half laughed. 'I've learnt that the hard way.'

'Well, you can always talk to me. You know that, don't you, Liz? I'll be here whenever you need me.'

'Won't you be a little busy?'

'I'll make time for you. Always.'

'Thank you.' She smiled up at him. 'That means a lot.'

* * *

The wake was held in the local pub, rather appropriately called The Farmer's Arms. It was a place where Liz's father had spent many a happy evening. The turnout was good, with people chatting happily, telling stories they remembered about him, and the atmosphere was often punctuated with the sound of laughter. It was, Alex reflected, the kind of funeral he would want for himself; one where so many people had kind thoughts and happy memories. He hoped it would help Liz to know how much her father was liked and respected. During the day she seemed to have rallied a bit. A little colour had returned to her cheeks and occasionally she'd even managed the odd chuckle.

'It's kind of you to come.' A voice at his shoulder startled him out of his thoughts. It was Liz's mum.

'Diane, it's so nice to see you again.'

'After all these years. There's no need to guess what's brought you back into our lives. You can't take your eyes off her.'

Alex felt the colour rise in his own cheeks. 'I do like a woman who says what she thinks. She must get that from you.'

'Touché. Well, I'm glad she has someone to look after her in London. How did you two meet up again?'

'She was working for a colleague of mine. In fact, we're opening a restaurant together, and Liz is going to run the functions for us.'

'Well, well, well. So, how come she's never mentioned you?'

'We've had a bit of a falling out.'

'Nothing that can't be resolved, I hope?'

'I hope it can be, but your daughter is a very stubborn woman.'

Diane flicked her ash-blonde hair out of her eyes. 'Now, *that* she gets from her father.' The laughter seemed to die in her throat even as she said the words. 'I probably shouldn't have said that. I seem to be putting my foot it in rather a lot today. I've never been any good at handling these sorts of situations.' She looked over at Mel.

'Liz is worried about Mel,' Alex said.

'I know. She won't even speak to me, but I'm sure that will change when she realises I'm not after her father's money, and that I'm not going anywhere. However much she might want me to.'

'Now who's stubborn?'

'Okay, so that might come from me. Both girls can be stubborn when they want to be, but maybe one day Mel will let me back into her life.'

'I'm hoping for the same from your daughter.'

'Then make sure it happens.'

'Mmm,' Alex replied wistfully. 'I wish it were that simple, but it's . . . well, it's complicated.'

243

'It's only as complicated as you make it,' Diane replied. 'It's been lovely to see you again, Alex, but I must go. Ruth looks like she needs some support.' Alex followed her gaze to where a buxom woman was leaning against the bar, looking completely drained.

'Ruth?'

'Yes, Andrew's second wife. We've struck up a rather curious friendship over the last few weeks. She helped me out when I needed her and now it's my turn to do the same.'

'Well, it's been nice to see you again despite the circumstances,' Alex replied, thinking about what an amazing family Liz had. He'd always thought it in the past, but today had confirmed it.

'And you.' She pecked him on the cheek, engulfing him in a waft of perfume. 'I do hope you come back soon.'

'Me too,' Alex whispered as she walked away from him.

* * *

He reflected on her words as he drove back to London. Perhaps it wasn't so complicated after all? There was nothing like a funeral to make you seize the day. He pulled over into a layby and dialled Nikki's number. Just as he thought it would go to voicemail, Nikki picked up.

'Hi Nik, how are you?'

'Fine, thanks.' She sounded guarded.

'You haven't forgotten the date of the scan, have you?'

There was a long silence at her end of the phone before she spoke again. 'I'm sorry, Alex. I can't make it. I've been offered a modelling job and I need the work.'

She sounded so blasé that something within him snapped. 'No, Nikki, that's not good enough. I'll pay you what you would have earned from the job, but I want you there at that appointment. And if you don't turn up, you need to drop this pretence and tell everyone that I'm not the father of your imaginary child.'

CHAPTER THIRTY-NINE

'He really loves you, you know?' Mel said as she poured herself and Liz a glass of wine.

'Who does?' Liz was only half listening. Gradually, the mourners had left the pub, along with Ruth, who was emotionally exhausted. Diane had taken her home. It amazed Liz how close the two women had become. They were like chalk and cheese. The only thing they had in common was the loss of the man they'd both loved. Liz wondered what her mother would do now. Now the funeral was over, she'd have to make a start on her future. Whatever that might be.

Soon after, she and Mel had left the stragglers to it and were now sitting at Mel's kitchen table, the children safely in bed. Simon had been dispatched to pick up a takeaway, even though no one was particularly hungry.

'Alex. He didn't take his eyes off you the whole day.'

'Oh . . . I see.' Her stomach flipped at the sound of his name. *Alex*. It had been wonderful to see him today, to feel that he had been there to support her. But that was here. London was a very different situation — one where he had a child to bring up, and a woman who didn't want to let him go. He'd already lost one child and this was his chance to be a good father. He couldn't do that if he was constantly being torn between her and Nikki. She would just have to get on with her own life. Without him.

'Don't tell me you don't feel the same.'

Liz took a sip of her wine, allowing the sharp, fruity tang to roll over her tongue. She hadn't dared have a drink earlier in the day, afraid that the alcohol would make her lose her grip on her emotions and she'd make a fool of herself. But now, alone with her sister, she didn't need to keep her guard up. If she drank too much and lost her composure, she was in safe company.

'It doesn't really matter now. It's over.'

During the long hospital visits, sitting beside their dad, she and Mel had had plenty of time to talk, and she'd told Mel all about her relationship with Alex, as well as Nikki's involvement in it.

'I can see why you wouldn't trust her or want her near your relationship. But you can deal with that. It's obvious that you're both head over heels in love with each other, and love like that doesn't come along very often. Why don't you fight for that?'

Liz sighed. 'Because of the baby. He lost a baby with his first wife and I don't think he really got over it. He needs a chance to be a good dad, and he can't do that if I'm there reminding Nikki that he loves me not her.'

'Sounds to me like she needs to grow up and move on. Aren't you just playing into her hands? He can still be a good dad and be with someone else. Lots of people do it. And what if you decide to have children? Then he can be a dad with you.'

'But what if he can't?'

'Can't what?' Mel asked, looking puzzled.

'Can't have the chance to be a dad with me.' The words caught in her throat. 'What if I can't give him a child?'

'Who's to say you couldn't?'

'Because of the anorexia. Don't you remember they told me there was very little chance I'd be able to conceive?'

'Oh, Liz! That was years ago. Medical science has moved on since then. And so have you. Look at the way you look after yourself now. I can't think of a healthier person.'

'Even so.'

'So, be honest with him. Tell him what the doctors said and let him make that decision for himself.'

'I don't have the strength.'

'You might think you don't, but I believe you do. Look Liz, love isn't about playing safe. It's about realising that no matter how bad your life is, it's much worse without the person you love in it. It's about taking a chance and risking everything because being without that person is unthinkable.' Mel paused. 'So . . . just you think about that.'

Liz did think about it, long into the night, staring at the ceiling in the spare bedroom. And just before dawn broke, before she finally fell asleep, she made her decision. She was going to fight for her man. She loved him, and even though he hadn't actually told her himself, everyone said he loved her. And life without him was unthinkable. If he decided that he didn't want to be with her because she might not be able to have children, then Mel was right — that had to be his decision. She was going to be brave and finally let herself trust him, even if she lived to regret it.

CHAPTER FORTY

It was early evening by the time Alex reached his apartment, tired and hungry. He parked in the underground car park and got straight in the lift. Nearing his front door, he was surprised to see a figure hunched up outside it. *Nikki.* He wasn't sure he had the energy for another fight with her. But as she looked up, he realised she was crying.

'Nikki, what are you doing here?' he asked, more gently than he'd spoken to her on the phone.

'I needed to speak to you. Where have you been? You've been gone for hours.'

'I was at a funeral,' he said as he put his key in the door.

'Oh, I'm sorry. Was it someone close to you?'

'Someone from the past,' he said quietly, thinking of both Liz and her father as he stepped back and let Nikki enter his apartment ahead of him. 'Can I get you anything to drink?' he asked as she sat down on the sofa in his living room.

'A glass of water would be good. Thanks.'

Once back in the living room, he handed her the glass. She took a sip, and as she put the glass on the coffee table, he noticed that her hand was trembling so much that she nearly spilled the contents. He sat down opposite her.

'Why are you here, Nikki? Because if it's about the scan, I won't back down.'

She didn't reply, but just as he was about to ask again, she said, 'It's not about the scan. There's no easy way to say this.' She paused. 'I'm sorry, Alex, but I lied to you. You were right. There is no baby.'

Although he had suspected it, hoped for it even, her words still shocked him.

'Say something,' she said as he sat there, dumbfounded.

'Why? Do you hate me that much?'

'I don't hate you, Alex. I love you.' She was staring at him so beseechingly he almost felt sorry for her. Almost wanted to take her in his arms and comfort her. *Almost*.

'You don't do that to someone you love, Nikki.'

'I'm so sorry,' she said as she sobbed. 'I saw you and that chef getting closer and closer, and I just couldn't bear it. I had to do something to split you up.'

'Well, congratulations. You got your wish. Liz and I are in the past.' As he said the words, he wanted to cry too. Because for the first time since Nikki had announced her supposed pregnancy, he realised it *was* over between him and Liz. She'd wanted to be with him — maybe she even loved him — but she didn't trust him. And you couldn't build a life on mistrust. Nikki had just proved that.

'I'm so sorry. You have to believe that I just wanted us to be together. I had this stupid idea that, if you thought there was a baby, you'd change your mind. You're a good man and I know you'd have taken that responsibility seriously. You'd have made a brilliant dad.'

'Once, maybe, but not anymore.' There would be no babies for him now. Not without Liz.

'Oh God, Alex. I'm so sorry. I never meant . . .' She couldn't finish the sentence because she was sobbing so much. He handed her a tissue, but this time he felt no sympathy. He'd lost something very important because of her.

'Look, I know you're upset, and I know that you're sorry, but I'd like you to go now. I need to be on my own.'

She nodded and scrubbed at her face with the tissue. 'I understand. But what do we tell people?'

'Tell people whatever you feel is best.'

'You really don't mind what I say?' she asked.

'No. It doesn't really matter anymore. But there is one thing: Liz. If I get a chance, I will tell her the truth. I won't lie to her.'

'I understand.'

'Before you go,' he said as she turned away, 'tell me, how long were you going to keep this up? I mean, pregnancy? It's not something you would have been able to pretend about for very much longer.'

She bowed her head. 'I didn't really think it through,' she mumbled. 'At first, I thought if I told you I was pregnant that you'd come back to me. I suppose I hoped you'd offer to marry me and then . . . I don't know, maybe I'd have told you I'd lost the baby.'

'You were going to trap me into marriage based on a lie?' Although he'd had his suspicions, the reality of what she was saying stunned him.

She began to cry again, and this time he didn't even offer her a tissue. He couldn't believe that someone who said she loved him could act so cruelly.

'Please go now.'

CHAPTER FORTY-ONE

At Euston station, Liz strode across the concourse and down to the Underground. As it was mid-morning, the trains were only half full, and she was grateful for a seat as she realised how much she was shaking. But despite her nerves, she was resolute. She would go and see Alex and tell him how wrong she'd been; how she should have fought for him. She'd convince him that whatever the future, they would face it together. The train seemed to take forever as she swayed from being positive to wondering if Alex would even listen to her. After weeks of her pushing him away, she wouldn't blame him if he didn't want to know. Had she left it too late? She hoped not.

A little later, she nervously buzzed on the intercom outside Alex's apartment block. When there was no reply she buzzed it again, then waited until someone walked through the main doors and followed them in. There was still no reply when she reached his apartment door. She glanced at her watch. Of course, he'd be at work. She'd been so focused on seeing him, it hadn't even occurred to her that he wouldn't be there. She fished in her handbag for her phone. When he didn't answer, she hesitantly phoned Tia. She'd know where he was.

'Liz, hello. How are you?'

'I'm fine, thanks. Um, you don't know where Alex is, do you?'

'I don't, I'm afraid,' Tia said. 'He was actually supposed to meet me at the office this morning, but he didn't turn up. I can't get him on his phone either. I really don't know where he's got to.'

'I'm at his apartment but he's not answering the door,' Liz said, pressing the buzzer once more. There was a faint noise on the other side. 'Oh, hang on! I think I can hear something.'

He opened the door and she gasped. She'd never seen him looking anything less than immaculate, but the man in front of her was still wearing the clothes he'd worn to her father's funeral. His hair was tousled and a dark shadow of stubble covered the lower half of his face.

'Alex, are you okay? You look awful.'

'Tell him to ring me. ASAP,' Liz vaguely heard Tia say before she hung up the phone.

* * *

Alex couldn't believe the apparition before his eyes. He'd spent the night drinking and trying to push her from his mind. He'd eventually fallen asleep on the sofa where he had dreamt about her. *Am I still dreaming?* he wondered.

'Liz,' he croaked, his voice hoarse from lack of use. 'What are you doing here?'

She frowned at him and he realised the state he was in.

'I'm sorry. I must look a sight. Come in.'

'Are you okay? You look like you've slept on the sofa.'

He tried to laugh it off. 'Well, something like that.'

He led her into the living room and hastily removed the empty glass and half bottle of whisky.

'Heavy night?' she asked.

'Sort of. Nikki came to see me.'

'I don't suppose she was doing any of the drinking?'

'No, she wasn't. In fact—'

252

'Alex, sorry, but I need to tell you something,' she interrupted him. 'I have to say it now or I might lose my nerve. I'm sorry for pushing you away these last few weeks. My head's been all over the place.'

Despite his thoughts last night that it was definitely over between them, his heart was now thudding with hope.

'About Nikki,' he tried to explain.

'No, Alex, I'm sorry — again. I don't mean to keep interrupting you, but if I don't say this now, I never will.'

'Say what?'

'That I love you. That I don't care about Nikki or the baby or anything . . .'

Before he could even think twice, he'd covered the space in the living room between them and pulled her into his arms. As he kissed her, euphoria flooded through him. When he eventually let her come up for air, he said, 'Liz, you don't know how long I've waited to hear you say that. I've wanted to tell you so many times that I love you too, but I thought I'd lost you . . . that Nikki had come between us.'

'I thought so too,' she gasped. 'But I realise now that I love you too much to let you go. Nikki, the baby and everything. We can deal with that. Together.'

He burst out laughing. 'There's no need. Nikki came to see me. There is no baby. I was right all along. It was a lie to get me back.'

'*What*? I can't believe she'd do that!'

'I still can't quite believe it myself.'

'That's sick.'

'No, I think she's sick. I think she needs therapy, I don't know. But that's not something I can help her with.'

'I'm surprised you'd even think about helping her after what she's done to you.'

'I was more upset about losing you. I thought you didn't trust me. I couldn't bear it if you didn't.'

'It's more complicated than that. I didn't want to get in the way of you and a baby. Nikki would have never let you go if there had been a child.'

He nodded. 'You could be right about that, but I would have made it work. I was trying to do the right thing, but deep down, the only person I want a child with now is you.'

* * *

Liz gasped at his words. 'That's the other thing.' She forced herself to continue, knowing that she had to tell him the truth now. All of it. 'I might not be able to have children.'

He took hold of her arms and looked deep into her eyes. 'Why not?'

'Because of the anorexia.'

'I see.' She thought for a moment he was going to push her away, that he wouldn't want her now, but instead he pulled her to him and whispered into her hair, 'It doesn't matter, it's you I want.'

She pulled back from him. 'But I know you're still grieving for the baby you lost.'

'And I probably always will be. But life without you is unthinkable. Whatever happens or doesn't happen in the future, we can deal with it together, like you said.'

'Oh yes,' she whispered. She wrapped her arms around him and kissed him, long and passionately, not caring if she ran out of breath.

When they eventually came up for air he said, 'Liz, these last weeks without you have been unbearable. And last night, when Nikki told me there was no baby, I should have been euphoric. Instead, all I could think about was the fact that it was over between us . . .'

'But I was wrong—'

'I know, and I realise that you pushed me away to give me the chance to be a father.'

'I couldn't see any other way.'

'The fact that you were willing to make that sacrifice makes me love you all the more. But you've just lost your dad . . . you must be feeling very vulnerable now.'

'I've never been able to think more clearly,' she contra-dicted him.

'All the same, you need to understand that I want to spend the rest of my life with you, but now is not the right time for you to make that commitment.'

'But, Alex—!'

He hushed her quickly with a kiss. 'I'm not going to propose when I'm hungover and still wearing yesterday's clothes — and you're still grieving. Let's take things slowly for now, and then when the time's right . . .'

He trailed off and she smiled. 'Just so you know, if you'd asked me, my answer would have been "yes". But let's do it your way. As long as we're together, that's all that matters."

EPILOGUE

Six Months Later

Liz was preparing for the biggest function of her life. Her wedding to Alex. Everyone said she was completely mad organising her own wedding breakfast, but she couldn't think of a more natural thing to do. As she told everyone jokingly, it made perfect sense to have the best function caterer in London for the most important event of her life. Not that she was going to be doing any work tomorrow — a fleet of chefs would do that. The wedding breakfast was being held at Diva's, Alex and Tia's new restaurant, which was being shut in their honour for the day. Since opening, the restaurant had gone from strength to strength, as had the function side of the business. Now its best rival was La Emporium; a fact that made Roberto extremely proud — almost as proud as he was to be a father to a healthy baby boy. Tia and Alex were so happy with the profits, they were looking at investing in a city hotel.

Liz's own business had also gone from strength to strength since Jay had joined her. She loved having someone to share her work life with, which was made even better because she had someone to share her personal life with too.

As Alex had wanted, they had taken things slowly at first, dating and getting to know each other properly. His proposal had come on a warm September evening, and was just as romantic as he had implied it would be. He'd hired a boat to take them down the Thames, and just as the sun was setting in front of Tower Bridge, he had gone down on one knee and asked her to marry him.

'Are you still here?' Mel demanded as she strode into the kitchen, breaking her out of the memories of that proposal. 'I've just dispatched your husband-to-be to a hotel and the coast is clear. There's bubbly in the fridge and a slap-up meal at your apartment. Come on! Jay can sort it out in the morning.'

'No need,' Liz said, placing the final tray in the fridge. 'I've finished now.' She was quite happy to put her feet up tonight. She was looking forward to spending an evening with her sister. In the last six months, Mel's life had changed too. Thanks to an inheritance in their father's will, Mel and Simon hadn't ended up losing the house, and Mel had worked hard to turn the business round. She was a different person now that she had something other than the children to focus on, and she admitted she'd wished she'd done it years ago. She'd also made steps to repair the relationship with their mother. At Liz's suggestion, they'd had a heart-to-heart after the funeral where Mel had told their mother how hurt she'd been. Mel said it had been a difficult conversation, but was glad that Liz had pushed her to do it. Slowly, they were building up a trust with each other. Diane was still living with Ruth, the two of them firm friends, but she'd started work in a pub kitchen — as she'd said previously, cooking was the only thing she'd ever been any good at.

Mel and Liz clinked glasses, and the dry champagne fizzed over Liz's tongue.

'So, are you looking forward to tomorrow?' Mel asked.

Liz smiled. 'Oh, definitely.' She hesitated. 'I just wish Dad was here to walk me down the aisle. I still can't quite believe he's gone.'

'There's a saying, isn't there? I can't remember it exactly, but it's something like "people don't die, they live on in the hearts of those who loved them". Here.' Mel reached into her handbag and pulled out a box. 'I have something for you.'

Liz opened the box, her fingers trembling. Inside was a gold locket, and when she opened it up, she found a photograph of their father inside. She let out a sob of joy.

'This way he can be close to you as you're walking down the aisle.'

'Oh Mel, thank you!' Liz reached out to hug her sister. 'That's so thoughtful of you.'

'Anything for you, sis. Tomorrow is going to be one of the happiest days of your life, and there's no one I can think of who deserves it more.'

'I'll drink to happy days,' she said, taking another sip of champagne. 'For us all.'

Liz reflected again on how lucky she was. Since that night at Tia's when she had bumped into Alex, her life had changed immeasurably. Not only was she about to marry the man she had dreamed of being with since her teenage years, she had healed the rift with her family, and her career was going from strength to strength — and it had all come about because she had learned not to bottle things up inside. The mistakes she had made in the past had been caused by her not being able to speak about her feelings. Never again would she be hampered by the things she couldn't say. It was a lesson she wouldn't forget.

THE END

THANK YOU

I would like to thank you for choosing to read my book. I hope you enjoyed Liz and Alex's story. I had so much fun writing this one.

If you enjoyed *Things They Never Said* then please do leave a review on the website where you bought the book. Every review really does help a new author like me.

You can find me on Twitter and Facebook (details on the 'About the Author' page next).

Please do get in touch for all the latest news. I look forward to chatting with you.

Much love,
Linda x

THE CHOC LIT STORY

Established in 2009, Choc Lit is an independent, award-winning publisher dedicated to creating a delicious selection of quality women's fiction.

We have won 18 awards, including Publisher of the Year and the Romantic Novel of the Year, and have been shortlisted for countless others.

All our novels are selected by genuine readers. We are proud to publish talented first-time authors, as well as established writers whose books we love introducing to a new generation of readers.

In 2023, we became a Joffe Books company. Best known for publishing a wide range of commercial fiction, Joffe Books has its roots in women's fiction. Today it is one of the largest independent publishers in the UK.

We love to hear from you, so please email us about absolutely anything bookish at

choc-lit@joffebooks.com

If you want to hear about all our bargain new releases, join our mailing list here.

www.choc-lit.com